Discover Britain's best kept secret
"one of the very best writers about crime"*
MARGARET YORKE
and her latest masterwork

Criminal Damage

"YORKE TURNS A PHRASE WITH THE
BEST . . . and if you enjoy tidy, mannered British
mysteries . . . there is much to recommend in
Criminal Damage."
—*Cleveland Plain Dealer*

"A PSYCHOLOGICAL THRILLER THAT
BUILDS SUSPENSE . . . the underlying theme is
not so much a 'whodunit' as a 'whydunit' as it
probes the dark minds and motives of the various
characters . . . a fine example of why Margaret
Yorke has been favorably compared with such
bestselling authors as P. D. James."
—*The News* (Southbridge, MA)

"VINTAGE YORKE. . . . If you are not yet a fan
of Margaret Yorke you are in for a treat with the
latest teacup mayhem in *Criminal Damage*, an
entertaining whydunit which establishes her as the
third lady in crime, if not the first."
—*Evening Standard* (London)

*Books magazine

MARGARET YORKE

YORKE

A

CRIMINAL

DAMAGE

THE MYSTERIOUS PRESS

Published by Warner Books

A Time Warner Company

1

The first thing he was aware of was the cold on his face. It seemed that he had always known it: the aching cheeks, the watering eyes, his nose perpetually streaming. His feet were icy, too; he wriggled his toes in his nylon mix socks and they were numb.

Too young to reason, too young to remember clearly, it seemed that his existence had always been thus: the chill and the menace, the advancing army of objects which threatened to engulf him. He would cry and shrink back from the forest of legs, the phalanx of huge shopping bags, as he was propelled relentlessly forwards, his mother using his flimsy chariot to cleave a passage through the hordes on the pavement. She bumped it up steps and down, and slung loaded carriers from its handles so that it became unbalanced, swerving under her determined direction.

She grew angry when he yelled. He'd been so docile at first, sleeping in a cocoon of blankets. When he was a few months old and could be propped up, you'd have thought he'd enjoy looking at what went on around him, but all he did was whine and grizzle.

She never considered that the child was in a perpetual state of bewildered terror, clamped into his pushchair to be whisked among the pedestrians and in and out of shops, isolated, never communicating with She who Pushed until at last he was released and set down, dazed and often crying.

As time passed he grew accustomed to his mode of transport and merely huddled against the backrest, chin on chest, fists clenched, enduring.

His elder brother had reacted differently. He had leaned out aggressively towards everything that approached, scowling, not afraid, just as later he flung himself with enthusiasm into life both in and out of school, well able to take care of himself and often his timid brother too. When their sister was born, the middle child was now a toddler who dragged his feet and scuffed his shoes, clinging to the side of the pushchair in which the baby travelled, waving her pink-mittened hands in the air while Neil's were bare, raw red with cold, the nails nibbled.

Their mother was not unkind, merely impatient and too busy. Theirs was not a deprived home; their father was a builder in steady employment and they lived in one of the old spacious council houses with a good-sized garden large enough to play in.

The little girl was much pampered by her father, who doted on her, and was taken to ballet classes by her mother who worked several evenings in a pub to pay for the lessons. At that time Mavis Smith had social aspirations for her family, but such aims withered as her marriage deteriorated. Her husband started having affairs and in the end he went off with another woman. Mavis was left with two adolescent boys and their sister, managing as best she could.

She did not sit back, existing solely on social security. For a while her husband sent irregular payments but after a time they ceased, and she took on more bar work, reinforced by cleaning jobs during the daytime. The boys had to babysit their sister but Kevin soon started going off with his friends, leaving Neil in charge.

Neil didn't mind. He liked it when the house was quiet. It

was nice when Kevin was out and he had their bedroom to himself. There he made models, saving all his pocket money for the kits. Cars were his interest; when he could afford it, he bought magazines about them and he dreamed of owning one as soon as possible. After he left school he started work at a garage, hoping to become a mechanic, but all he did at first was to sweep up the yard and take the money for the petrol—it was a self-service place. He learned to drive, however. Kevin by now was employed at a factory near Reading and he had passed his test and bought an old banger in which to go to work. He let Neil drive it on a farm track. Neil managed to save up for some proper lessons but he failed his test.

The lessons were expensive. He took more, but he had begun to steal to find the money for them. He went walking round the streets of Wintlebury on Saturdays and Sundays, looking for houses where there was no one at home. He took only cash, getting in through windows or doors left open, often finding money in drawers or tins in kitchens.

He passed his test but he went on stealing, because now he wanted a car. Meanwhile, he bought a scooter. One day he entered a house which he thought was empty, and an old woman appeared in the room where he was going through a cupboard. He had found fifteen pounds in notes and coins.

"What are you doing?" the old woman cried, and, instinctively, Neil raised his hand towards her, pushing her away.

He had not hit her, simply acting out of fear to make her move so that he could reach the door, but she lost her balance and fell, pulling over a lamp at which she clutched to save herself. It struck her on the head.

Neil fled, but someone who saw him mount his scooter identified him later. It was alleged that he had beaten the old woman about the face, which he denied, but he confessed to his other thefts and was sentenced to four years in custody. He was sent to a young offenders' prison and there, ironically, for the first time in his life he had a room to himself.

He loved the privacy. He could stand the noisy days, the

shouts, the discipline, the enforced activities, for at night he was alone. The place was run on the lines of a tough boarding school and Neil intended to be one of its successes. He was horrified at what he had done. Photographs of the old woman's injuries were shown in court, and though he knew he had not, as alleged, struck her, he was responsible and he realised that she might have died. He had to pay the price for this and even wrote her an apology. He managed, most of the time, to keep out of trouble while he served his sentence but he became unwillingly involved in several fights and in one acquired a small permanent scar above one eye. He lost remission for his part in that. Meanwhile he played football and attended joinery classes, emerging as quite a useful carpenter.

2

Mrs Newton enjoyed moving and made a habit of doing it every three or four years. Entering a new neighbourhood was a challenge, and renovating each house as she took it over was a further test of her abilities. She was good at discovering local workmen and getting the best out of them, giving them only one cup of tea during the morning and a second in the afternoon, not the constant supply with which other employers allowed their labours to be punctuated; and she rarely left them unsupervised. She liked choosing carpets, and fabrics for curtains which she made up herself—never the most expensive, for she would not be staying long, but always in quiet good taste. These were left for the next purchaser, at an advantageous price, while she moved on. She never walked on other people's carpeting in any home she owned; Mrs Newton was an extremely fastidious woman.

She made superficial acquaintances, never friends, in each new area, people whom it was no wrench to leave when going on to the next district. She bought fairly modern houses, those which needed no major renovation or structural repair apart from fitting out the kitchen, which was often necessary; she liked a new kitchen for herself. Sometimes she had to change a bathroom suite, either because there was an immovable stain or because she could not live with the existing colour. Plain white was best, in her opinion. The houses, whilst never large, were always spacious and well planned, with three or four bedrooms and sometimes with a study. There was a room for Jennifer, her daughter, although she had not lived at home for years, and space for her two granddaughters, her son Geoffrey's children, to come and visit. It was a sorrow to her that, so far, they had never done so.

For nearly three years Jennifer had been living in London in an elegant house which she had bought with Daniel Ferguson. Mrs Newton had understood that this meant they benefited from tax concessions, each receiving mortgage relief— a piece of bureaucratic munificence now ended. She was not sure how long the two had been, as one might describe it, a pair: very occasionally they came to see her, but it was only for a day. She had never been faced with the fact of them as an unmarried couple sharing a bedroom, a situation she found easier to accept in the abstract than if confronted with it. In some ways, Mrs Newton thought, times had not changed for the better.

"It makes economic sense," Jennifer had said, about the house. Until then she had been living in a one-roomed flat which was, in Mrs Newton's view, a grand name for a bedsitting-room, though it had its own bathroom, which was something. Mrs Newton had never cared for other people's hairs blocking up the basin, their tide mark left upon the bath, their smells and scents. She sometimes had nightmares about living in such conditions herself.

Like their friends, Mrs Newton expected that one day Jennifer and Daniel would marry. Before him there had been other men, mentioned occasionally by Jennifer, even produced from time to time. Some of these relationships had lasted for a year, but never more. Daniel, it seemed, was different, and he was easy to like, Mrs Newton found. After they met Jennifer had seemed to bloom. This, her mother thought, could be Mr Right, or Mr Nearly Right, or even Mr Will Do, which was good enough; Mr Newton had fallen into this last category and theirs had been a contented, successful marriage until his sudden death from a heart attack. At the time, Geoffrey was eleven and Jennifer only seven years old.

Before she came to Yew Cottage in Middle Bardolph, Mrs Newton had lived in Woodbridge for some years. She had liked the place, and even thought of staying on; the air was bracing, and you could reach London easily by train. She liked to be within reach of Selfridges and the theatre; occasionally, when funds permitted, she allowed herself small jaunts to town. However, she had received a good offer for her house and had found Yew Cottage, which had been built in the thirties and pretended to be older than it was. It was long and low, painted white, with a tiled roof. There was a big mock-old beam above the sitting-room fireplace; smaller ones adorned some ceilings. Mrs Newton thought they added character and had decorated the house in a more cottagey style than any of her former homes. There were sprigged curtains in the bedrooms, yellow and gold striped ones in the sitting-room, and blue covers on the chairs and the small sofa which had accompanied the family on all their moves. It had once been in Frederick Newton's study in Bournemouth.

A venerable yew tree occupied a central spot in the back lawn at Yew Cottage. At first Mrs Newton had found the tree ominous, forbidding, and she had planned to cut it down, then realised that the village preservation society, of whose existence she had been unaware before she bought the house, would protest and might prosecute her. Now she had grown used to it, even found it a comfort, for it had been there longer than the cottage to which it gave its name. Birds nested in it; on sunny days it gave shade to the garden and it would outlive her occupancy.

Middle Bardolph was a cluster of haphazard buildings from many periods which had grown piecemeal until there was little space between it and Upper Bardolph, a mile to the north. Lower Bardolph had disappeared and now was marked only by a pub at the crossroads on the way to Wintlebury, The Prince Hal. Daniel had shown interest in this and wanted to know details of its history but the landlord had been unaware of any link with Elizabethan players or John of Gaunt. Mrs Newton had enjoyed his theories but Jennifer had said there he was, romancing away as usual.

Small groups of new houses had been built in large gardens in the village, but expansion had stopped before Mrs Newton arrived. Prices had fallen; property was difficult to sell and Mrs Newton was caught. She had overstayed her time in Middle Bardolph and could not move without financial loss. Meanwhile the house next door to her had been sold and extensive renovations were in progress. Her days were disturbed: radios blared; a cement mixer churned incessantly; several vans occupied the driveway and the lane, and mud was transferred from where the men were working to the surrounding area. She was weary of it.

Now she had fresh cause to worry, for she had just heard from Geoffrey, her son, that Daniel was getting married, but not to Jennifer. The pair had spent their summer holiday in Italy, staying in a Tuscan villa with a group of friends, the sort of thing they had done several times before. Mrs Newton had received a postcard of Siena from her daughter. According to Geoffrey, soon after their return Daniel had moved out of their shared house and declared that he planned to marry a much younger woman, Stephanie Dunn, whose father was a retired army officer who lived near Salisbury. They would have a May wedding with a marquee on the lawn and a honeymoon in Venice, Geoffrey had said, but Mrs Newton was uncertain if he was sure of these details or had made them up. The main facts, however, were correct: Daniel and Jennifer had parted, and he was involved with someone else.

She waited for Jennifer to tell her the news and ten days went past before, on a postcard of the Tower of London, Jennifer simply said that he had moved out.

Mrs Newton telephoned that night, concentrating on the practical, asking about the house: what would happen? Would they sell? Would she, if they could not get their price, have to buy Daniel out? Had they, perhaps, some agreement at the outset which would cover this situation? She knew that Geoffrey had warned Jennifer of the need for such a precaution but Jennifer had ignored his prudent advice. She and Daniel were together and they trusted each other; that was what mattered.

It was not what mattered now, thought Mrs Newton grimly. She had real sympathy for Jennifer's state of mind, apart from her finances, but she did not say so on the telephone. Emotions were so hard to handle; better to ignore them.

Jennifer could not believe that she had lost Daniel. In Tuscany, everything had seemed perfect: on a hot afternoon when the rest of their group were in San Gimignano, they had made love on their sagging double bed with the sound of cicadas outside, then swum in the small pool. She had asked him if he was pleased that they had not gone, as had first been planned, with the others, and he had kissed her and said, "Of course." Then they had made love again. During their weeks away they had drunk red wine and eaten pasta in various guises in local *trattorie*, usually the whole group together but sometimes one or another couple would peel off independently. All had been friends for some time; none were married. All earned good salaries and were buying houses or flats together. On their return, one couple had married, a cheery ceremony swiftly arranged because of an unplanned pregnancy happily accepted and parents who thought the conventions important: so did the couple; events had simply speeded up their plans.

Daniel had met Stephanie at Victoria station, which showed that all things were possible. As they stepped off the underground, an elderly woman in front of them tripped and fell. They had both stopped to help her, Stephanie checking her physical state while Daniel collected her dropped possessions. She was shaken, slightly bruised, but not really hurt, and they had seen her to the surface and into a taxi, then parted. The next day, on their morning train, they recognised each other and discovered that they must have travelled at the same time over many months. So it began, weeks before the Tuscan holiday, and gathered force inexorably.

Stephanie was young, she was fresh, she was sweet-tempered. Daniel had, at first, enjoyed the fireworks in his relationship with Jennifer and he had liked being seen with her, for she was attractive and was always well turned out, but she was unpredictable, and that could be uncomfortable. Because he was calm and equable, she needled him to provoke response. She borrowed one of his most expensive shirts and hacked the tails off to make it fit better but all he did was shrug and remark that replacing it meant plonk to drink for the next few weeks instead of the good wine they both enjoyed. She spent time devising other minor torments, but the most he ever said was, "Oh, Jen, must you?"

She could twist a conversation round so that if he said he was playing squash with a friend, as he did regularly twice a week, she would interpret this as a signal that he found her boring company.

"Don't be silly, Jen. You know I need exercise," he would say, and pat his taut stomach. "I don't whinge when you go off with the girls."

But she didn't, much. Her life, apart from her work, was centred on him and she needed constant assurance of his love.

When she first went to London, Jennifer had been a secretary with an insurance company; she had been there seven years, then moved to a firm of investment advisers where she was soon promoted. Hers was a good position; she became more confident, and with the advent of Daniel in her life she lost what diffidence had remained when they met, and which he had found endearing. She grew more assertive, more challenging, more dominant.

Their friends recognised this.

"He cut and ran," said one. "He didn't feel so good with her any more. She didn't need him like Stephanie does."

"You're wrong," said his wife. "He was her core. She'll

collapse now. And Stephanie's no damsel in distress. She's her own woman. She'll be an equal partner for him.''

"It's tough on Jen," said the husband.

"Watch it," said his wife. "Don't you go round there offering sympathy and a shoulder. Or anything else. We'll ask her to dinner and see if we can find some man to invite for her."

"Good idea," agreed her husband. He did not need her warning. He had seen Jennifer make a scene when Daniel broke a cut-glass bowl she had paid a lot for only two weeks previously. It was an accident and Daniel had cut his hand, but Jennifer had flipped.

She might flip again now, unless pride held her together.

3

Mrs Newton was going to London to see her daughter. During Jennifer's years with Daniel they had rarely met in this way, though until then, on Mrs Newton's excursions to shop or to a matinée, they had sometimes had lunch together. Jennifer's and Daniel's weekends were often spent visiting friends with country cottages and they had shared a busy social life. Now, for Jennifer, everything had changed.

After her husband's death—he was only fifty, twelve years older than his wife—Mrs Newton had been left reasonably well provided for. Geoffrey, at the time, was away at the same preparatory school his father had attended, and later followed on to a minor public school, but Jennifer was at a local day school. Mrs Newton's first removal bore in mind her needs and each subsequent one was timed to coincide with stages in her education which did not affect examinations. She passed her eleven-plus and went to a grammar school which saw her through her O levels. During that time, their one move was less than forty miles, to the further side of the town where the school was. She went to a new school for A levels; then did a top-level secretarial course. After that the plan had been for a year abroad to learn French or Italian, but Jennifer did not want to go into the unknown. Instead, she began work in a local office, remaining in the area when her mother moved. Just before the Woodbridge period, Jennifer went to London.

It had been hard for her, losing her father at such an early age, Mrs Newton reflected in the train. The window had jammed open and a crisp breeze ventilated the stuffy diesel with its worn fabric seats and brown scuffed floor. It had left fifteen minutes late; luckily she had plenty of time. She was meeting Jennifer at the Strand Palace Hotel which was a short bus ride from Jennifer's office, had a convenient, agreeable ladies' cloakroom and was near Charing Cross, whence Mrs Newton could catch a tube back to Marylebone.

One of the escalators was out of action at Marylebone. Mrs Newton plodded down the central dark stone steps, watching her footing carefully, visually impeded by her bifocal spectacles, a small, neat woman with fawn-rinsed hair, dressed in a camel coat over a beige wool dress.

She looked like a tiny camel, Jennifer thought in a moment of hysteria as she entered the hotel and saw her mother, sitting in the foyer, rise to greet her, but she had no dowager's hump, not even a slight stoop. Her mother's cheeks were pale; some blusher would help defeat the overall neutral impression, but Jennifer would never presume to suggest that she should use one.

"Mother," she said, in greeting. Neither kissed. Jennifer sometimes wondered if her mother ever touched another being. Once she had had a dog, but it had died and Mrs Newton had professed herself glad to be rid of moulting hairs about the place.

"Well, dear, how are you?" Mrs Newton was not only curious, but anxious.

"Oh, fine," said Jennifer, and as they moved to their table she burst into a lively account of a recent shake-up at the office where someone had almost been sacked because of letters getting into the wrong envelopes and so disclosing confidential information. Then she asked her mother about Middle Bardolph, enquiring about the work on the house next door, which she knew was irritating Mrs Newton because of the noise and the mess. It would soon be finished, Mrs Newton said.

Once each house move was over, Mrs Newton enrolled for further education classes, usually about art or history. She had tried learning Spanish, but found it very difficult, and, besides, she had no plans to travel anywhere outside Britain. She never went abroad, but had been away on several special interest weekends, always alone. She had learned to play bridge and this gave her an introduction to a circle of acquaintances in each new area, but she played rarely, not wanting to become obsessed with the game as people sometimes did. Despairingly, Jennifer admired her self-sufficiency. She had been a widow since she was thirty-eight; Jennifer herself was thirty-seven now, and she, too, had been bereaved, but not by death.

"I'm going out to dinner this evening," Jennifer said, to account for choosing a light meal now. Mrs Newton was tucking into steak; whatever she ate, she stayed slim, and so did Jennifer, who recently had lost weight and was now extremely thin.

"Oh?" Mrs Newton knew better than to ask a direct question about where Jennifer was going, or with whom.

But Jennifer wanted to tell her.

"The friends we—I—went to Italy with," she said. "They've got some man coming—they want to square the table." She laughed, a sound devoid of humour. "It's odd, being unattached."

"Yes." Mrs Newton could remember the sympathy which surrounded her after her husband's death: so young to be a widow, oh dear, how sad: then, after a few weeks, it had ceased. Suddenly, unexpectedly, she wanted to find out how her daughter really felt; if she was heart-broken or was full of anger, but she could not do it. Suppose Jennifer confessed to desolation: what then? Mrs Newton had never encouraged the display of strong emotion.

For her part, Jennifer felt an impulse to tell her mother that she could barely get through each day, so great was her hurt and misery, but it was impossible for her to make such a confession.

"Just as well we weren't married," she said brightly.

"I suppose so." Mrs Newton was not sure. In her day, it was important not to be passed over, and marriage meant security. You achieved, too, the position in life attained already by your husband, and Frederick, an architect, conferred status upon her. He had very nearly succeeded in making her forget the past, and she was grateful.

Jennifer, occasionally, had wondered about her mother. Had she ever had a lover? She could remember few male visitors to their various houses; there had never been the least sign of a suitor. She would have resented a stepfather; no one could have replaced the father she adored.

Now her main concern was to get through this lunch as soon as possible and escape back to the safety of the office, where the figures with which she worked swirled before her eyes and made no sense. Her whole being was consumed with hatred towards her supplanter, Stephanie, fair haired and always faintly smiling.

Jennifer had once had a small smile, too, and because it held a tinge of apprehension, it had drawn Daniel to her; he had wanted to drive away whatever it was that made her fearful and had succeeded, but now she never smiled.

She told her mother that she was putting it about that a half share in the house was for sale.

"But you can't let a perfect stranger move in with you!" Mrs Newton was dismayed.

"A female, mother," said Jennifer. "That's what I'm looking for. Someone in a good job who can take on half the mortgage." Daniel had given her three months in which to make some plan.

"Couldn't you rent a room? Then you could get rid of her if you didn't like one another," said Mrs Newton.

"That wouldn't pay enough."

"Daniel ought to buy himself out." Mrs Newton had dared to speak his name and waited for some consequence, but Jennifer's reply was uttered in an even tone.

"Yes," she agreed. "But where's he going to find the money? He wants to set up with Stephanie. Any cash he's got will go on that." Though maybe Stephanie's father would buy them a little pad in Islington with roses round the door, thought Jennifer bitterly.

Mrs Newton allowed the possibility of advancing some money to Jennifer to cross her mind, but her own finances were not designed to cope with something in the region of twenty thousand pounds or more—she did not know how much Daniel had put up—and why should he be let off so easily? She dismissed the notion. Jennifer must learn from this experience.

They parted briskly, and Mrs Newton took herself to a matinée, obtaining an excellent seat at reduced rates, a pleasant perquisite available to her as she had reached pensionable age.

She enjoyed the play.

Jennifer had found out quite a lot about Stephanie, who worked in an office near Victoria and shared a flat in Putney with two other girls. Daddy had helped, of course, thought Jennifer sourly. That evening, on the way to the dinner party which she must attend in order to show how well she was standing up to Daniel's defection, she walked past the big old house which sheltered her successor.

It was a windless night, with dampness in the air, a night to meet frogs and toads, thought Jennifer, almost expecting one to hop across her path as she went along the road towards her destination. It was a long time since she had been out alone like this; Daniel had always collected her for such engagements, or they had met at a central point. Now she must enter their friends' house, survive their scrutiny as to how she was coping—an assessment which might subsequently be revealed to Daniel—contribute to the conversation, even feign interest in her dinner partner, and then go home alone. She gripped her small folding umbrella, stepping from the bus stop. Now, things that had made her nervous years ago scared her again: shadows were menacing: footsteps behind her might be those of some prowling maniac. She should go to self-defence classes, she thought vaguely, buy an alarm.

Would this pain ever cease? There was, literally, a physical ache in her chest, where she supposed her heart, that poor broken vessel, lay. The only cure would be, she had concluded, to win Daniel back. Why should Stephanie have him?

This was her house. Jennifer paused in a pool of darkness outside it and stared at its Edwardian elevation behind a low wall and tiny frontage. There were lights on in several windows. Stephanie must be in there now, getting dressed up to go out with Daniel. Why not ring the doorbell, demand to speak to her? Better still, why not hit her, strangle her, at the very least scream at her, let out her hatred for the world to hear?

Jennifer glanced down at the gutter near her feet and saw an empty milk bottle lying against the kerb. She did not rationalise any further than looking up and down the street to see if what she did could be observed, but there was no one in sight. She simply picked up the milk bottle, crossed the road till she stood by the steps leading to Stephanie's door and hurled the bottle through the front window, walking on quickly as the glass shattered, hurrying, taking the next turning so that she left the scene as fast as possible.

She had picked the wrong flat. Stephanie lived upstairs on the second floor. The incident, reported by the downstairs tenants to the police, was thought to be the work of vandals.

Jennifer arrived at the party flushed, and with shining eyes.

Afterwards, people said she was taking it all very well and gave her marks for courage. The man she had been invited to meet thought her brittle but attractive; he invited her to dinner in a few days' time, and when she declined, was surprisingly relieved.

and the interest on the mortgage they already had had soared. He saw no way of gratifying Lynn unless he could persuade his mother to join with him, contribute the proceeds from selling Yew Cottage and occupy a granny flat in the house, or, better still, a maisonette in a stable block.

"It makes sense. You're getting no younger, Mama," he said.

Mrs Newton hated this form of address, which he had used since the age of sixteen when someone had told him it was what the Queen was called by her children. True or not, Mrs Newton saw no reason to adopt the practice.

Geoffrey had gone on to say how much they would enjoy having her near them and that the girls would love it. As they had never been allowed to visit her, Mrs Newton thought this unlikely, but she could see that Lynn had her marked down as a constant unpaid babysitter. She had had a hard enough time bringing up Geoffrey and Jennifer and saw no reason why she should have to take on the next generation. She was not particularly fond of children but had accepted her own as natural results of marriage, though once they had arrived she was astonished to discover how much she loved them. Lynn was a brisk, smart young woman whom Geoffrey had met at a business seminar; she was ambitious and thought he was, only to discover her mistake after they were married, since when she had been prodding him to seek advancement. She had gone back to work herself but the children's school holidays presented problems and she took temporary jobs; with a mother-in-law on the spot, she could pick up her own career.

Every so often Geoffrey came to see his mother in an effort to persuade her to this plan. Now was the time to buy the big country house, while the market was depressed. Mrs Newton pointed out that it was not the moment to sell his existing house, or hers, and refused to change her mind. She found his pressure distressing. Luckily she was not so old that she must worry about her physical well-being; she did all her own housework, to a high standard, and most of the garden, though occasionally paid help was needed to trim trees or do other heavy tasks. She had felt confident that if she had an illness or an accident, Jennifer or Geoffrey would support her through it, and the advent of Daniel had reinforced that view; his kindly nature was apparent. Now, however, he was gone, Jennifer was at a crossroads, and Geoffrey was a puppet manipulated by his wife. Mrs Newton had no comfortable feeling of reliable backing, and resolved to hold on to her autonomy and direct her own fate.

One is always alone in the end, she reflected, sitting in the train wedged between a stout man with a briefcase on his knee and a thin woman with two large Marks and Spencer's carriers which she clutched instead of putting them on the rack. Mrs Newton had barely room to hold her own handbag and her library book, which was about China. Though brave in many respects, Mrs Newton was not bold enough to travel overseas and did her voyaging vicariously, with the aid of writers such as Colin Thubron and by means of television. She had only just caught the train herself, after the matinée; how stuffy it was, she thought: all those germs being breathed in and out by the various travellers packed in with her. She did not like to think of her own lungs absorbing air which had circulated through those of, for instance, the stout man who, as if reading her thoughts, now coughed rather unpleasantly. Mrs Newton managed to extract her handkerchief from her bag and put it to her nose. Vitamin C would be necessary, she decided, shifting slightly towards the thin woman. There were times when Mrs Newton felt distinctly unfriendly towards the human race.

The congestion thinned as the journey progressed, and the stout man eventually got off. Mrs Newton and the thin woman eased gently apart, but did not speak. Darkness fell, and the train clattered on towards Wintlebury Halt, where Mrs Newton had left her small Vauxhall in the station car park.

She held her car keys in her hand as she approached her car, looking around her to make sure that no ne'er do well was lurking about, for you never knew; cars had been broken into on several occasions at this station, and there was menace in shadows. But all was well as she took her seat and, fumbling beneath it, found the flat pumps in which she drove, slipping off her smart tan low-heeled court shoes. You soon wrecked good shoes if you drove in them. Mrs Newton had small, narrow feet, and though she never wore high heels, was still vain about them; there were times when quality counted, and buying good shoes was an investment. Mrs Newton had always been careful about her appearance, and had tried to teach Jennifer to copy her example but with limited success, for Jennifer followed what she thought was fashion and her present frizz of hair was not, in her mother's opinion, a becoming style.

She reversed out of her parking slot and drove through the car park entrance. As she did so, it began to rain, a sudden sharp fusillade of large wet drops thudding against her windscreen. She turned left towards the town of Wintlebury which she must skirt before taking the road to Middle Bardolph, and as she changed into third gear her headlights picked up a trudging figure in a dark coat, barely visible against the black road and the leafless hedges by the verge. Mrs Newton pulled out to pass the lone person and saw green Marks and Spencer's bags in either hand. It was the thin woman who had been her neighbour in the train.

She must be walking into town. Mrs Newton, who rarely went out of her way for others, hesitated for only an instant before braking and reversing to offer her a lift.

"You really shouldn't walk along here alone in the dark," she admonished, after her grateful passenger was installed, already damp, her parcels in the back.

"I know, but my car broke down this morning and as I'd arranged to meet a friend in London I carried on and took a taxi in," said the woman. "I wasn't sure which train I'd catch back, so I hadn't arranged to be met, and then I couldn't telephone because you need a phone card and I haven't got one. And I couldn't reverse the charge to the taxi firm."

Mrs Newton, peering ahead through the driving rain, frowned. She always carried a card for emergencies, but younger people were less prudent. She wondered if the woman would have accepted a lift if a male driver had stopped for her. It could have been difficult to refuse.

"Perhaps you should get a card," she suggested.

"I will," promised the woman. "It was good of you to stop. Those parcels would have got heavy if I'd walked all the way home, and I'd have been soaked."

"An anticlimax to your day," was Mrs Newton's dry comment.

"Yes, and it had been such fun," said the woman. "Expensive, though."

But her packages came from Marks and Spencer's, not Harrods: still, you could tot up quite an amount if you moved from counter to counter in the popular store, thought Mrs Newton, who held shares in the company.

The woman lived in a close leading up to Wintlebury church, and her house was once the vicarage, but now the vicar lived in a modern brick box built in part of the former vicarage's garden. Mrs Newton said she would take her to her door, and as they drove on Lucy Moffat told her her name and said that her husband was luckily out at a meeting, or he would be cross about her landing herself in this scrape at the station.

And quite right too, thought Mrs Newton. Even in a rural area like this, dreadful things could happen and one had a responsibility not to court disaster. She stopped at the gates of The Old Vicarage and Lucy said there was space to turn outside the house.

"Won't you come in and have a drink, or a cup of coffee?" she added.

Mrs Newton declined the invitation as she drove the car between tall stone gateposts and up a short gravelled drive between patches of lawn. Her headlights picked up a square house built of stone, its windows dark.

"I should like to make you promise never to attempt such a walk alone again at night," Mrs Newton told her. "But I have no right to do so."

"I'll promise to keep a phone card in my bag," said Lucy, who had extracted exactly the same undertaking from her own daughter not a year before. "Will that do?"

She extricated herself from the car, uttering profound and genuine thanks as she collected her parcels. Mrs Newton waited, letting her benefit from the headlights to find her key in her bag, then, as she opened the front door and a light came on, Mrs Newton swung the car round and drove away. She wondered about her passenger all the way home, and even while she drank her first sherry of the evening. On long days out, such as today, she allowed herself two glasses, though one was her normal ration; on Fridays she abstained, to prove that she could, and on Sundays she had one at lunch time as well.

Next day she went to Wintlebury and drove past the close leading to the church, glancing up the quiet road. You could not see the grey house from the end. She was curious about the woman. What did her husband, who had been at a meeting that night, do? Were there children? Were Lucy Moffat's parents still living and if so, where? She was surprised at her own curiosity; it was a long time since she had felt more than passing interest in anyone apart from her own family. In the library, exchanging Colin Thubron for Jonathan Raban, she felt a reluctance to hurry home. That morning, work on the house next door had been very noisy; tarmac was being laid in the drive, and someone was using a drill that made an excruciating noise. She decided to have lunch at the Jacaranda Tree, a café popular with shoppers. Then she might stroll round the churchyard, look inside the church to see if the planned abolition of pews and reseating arrangements, which had caused an outcry in the correspondence columns of the local press, had been carried out. Mrs Newton herself went occasionally to St James's in Middle Bardolph. Sometimes she found the services soothing, but there were other days when children raced up and down the aisles and the hymns sounded like jazz. To go from time to time, however, set an example, though she could not have said whom she hoped to influence by attending in this uncommitted way.

If she looked at Wintlebury church, she would have a legitimate excuse for walking past The Old Vicarage. Since the road was a cul-de-sac, it could be done no other way.

Mrs Newton had a mushroom omelette and a cup of coffee at the Jacaranda Tree. Then she walked past the market square, along to the war memorial and down the short road to the church. The day was grey, but it was not raining; it had been misty earlier, and drops of moisture clung to the trees and the hedges behind fences. Mrs Newton approached her goal and saw that her first impression of the house had been accurate; it was well proportioned, saved from an austere aspect by the shrubs around it and the plants which climbed up its façade. From the gate she could not tell what they were: roses, she thought, and clematis, most likely. Fearing to be observed, Mrs Newton walked on and entered the churchyard, strolling about among the graves, noticing that there had been several recent funerals, and finally she tried the church door. It was locked.

Well, really! She knew that St James's was often locked during the day because of vandals but surely this did not apply in a town like Wintlebury? Surely here there was more demand for sanctuary and a bigger pool of custodians to guard the church if they were needed?

But old rules did not apply. Sanctuary could no longer be guaranteed.

As she passed The Old Vicarage for the second time someone came out, almost knocking her over with the pushchair which she was propelling. It contained a very young infant, its body clad in a bright red ski-suit, lashed to the structure like an ambulance patient to a stretcher. Two naked fists, blue with cold, waved feebly in the autumn air. A wail emerged from the tiny face.

Mrs Newton darted nimbly out of the way.

"Sorry, love," said the pusher, swinging her charge round on two wheels to head towards town.

She was not Mrs Newton's passenger of the previous evening, and she looked a little old to be the mother of the child. She was striding off, ignoring Mrs Newton, the baby now yelling loudly, and no wonder, Mrs Newton thought; it must be frozen through. It could be only a few months old but it had no protection from the weather apart from its padded suit, not even one of those transparent plastic envelopes in which children were imprisoned without air. What could it see? There was only the grey sky, or, if it could focus, the faces of approaching strangers.

Jennifer and Geoffrey had had a big deep solid pram in which they slept in the Bournemouth garden. You never saw them now; people had no space in which to keep them and were always bustling infants into cars or on to buses. There was never anyone to leave them with, at home, and tranquillity was denied them in those early years.

She was still thinking about this as she drove home. She had managed to forget Jennifer's troubles for several hours.

Jennifer could not stop thinking about Daniel. She was sleeping badly; the bed felt cold and empty. She was used to his occasional faint snore and the smell of him; she missed him and she ached for him. All purpose had left her life, and she felt as if she was a million years old. How could he do this to her? How was such a thing possible? Why, they were as much a pair as any married couple; she had not felt the need for any ceremony to make their bond more permanent.

The money problem worried her, but just as her mind whirled with confusion over what was best done about that, she was overtaken by misery because Daniel had rejected and betrayed her, and the blame for this lay with Stephanie: if they had never met, this would not have happened. Stephanie was the enemy: eliminate her, and all would be restored. She lay in bed at night tormenting herself by imagining them together; then she wove dreams in which Stephanie was run over as she crossed the road, or fell victim to a fatal illness. In either script, Daniel came flying back to Jennifer at once, proclaiming that he could not understand why he had ever left her. In the morning, after very little real rest, she would get up, sweating, and shower away her exhaustion before dragging herself to the office, where she wore an undaunted expression in a brave attempt, recognised by her colleagues, to pretend that all was well. To the few who dared make some sympathetic comment—the news had leaked through a mutual connection—she simply said that he would realise his mistake and come back.

In her bleaker, most defeated moments she decided she would like to run away—to Australia, or Malaya, or the Argentine; somewhere very distant, out of reach, where she could find a big empty space—a desert, perhaps—and scream aloud until either the pain left her or she died. But to go, even if it were possible, meant abandoning all hope of winning him back and she had not done that, not utterly. Even though he had removed all his personal possessions from the house, his presence haunted it, and some of the furniture was his, brought from the flat where he had lived before. Each evening she still expected to hear his key in the lock, his footsteps in the hall, and she was so used to seeing him there that she would sometimes forget and speak to him.

This must be what being widowed was like. Had her mother felt like this when her father died? But Daniel wasn't dead. If he had never met Stephanie, this would not have happened. Her thoughts, travelling in a circle, always returned to this point. She would not let herself admit that the seeds of their separation might already have been there, and that it could have happened at any time. If she allowed that thought to take root, she could not blame the break-up on Stephanie.

The sheer physical ache she felt made her wonder if anyone would do to appease it, but when, after a party, a man she met there took her home and tried his luck, she felt only disgust. She had let him come into the house and made him coffee. On the sofa, her dress dishevelled, she was nauseated and had difficulty breaking free.

She was fortunate. He left with only a few crude remarks

about come-ons and teases, adding that if you had to fight for it, it wasn't worth the struggle. She knew he might have raped her, and the episode frightened her. She and Daniel had been a pair for so long that she had forgotten about the jungle, and she wasn't in the mood to learn.

She began to refuse invitations, and she started following Stephanie, morbidly curious about her.

She was so young. Daniel would soon find her boring but he could control her. Was this the secret? Someone her age must still be finding her way, be soft at the edges. Maybe she made Daniel feel powerful. Jennifer had met her on a dreadful evening at a restaurant.

"I want you two to get acquainted," Daniel had said. Even he knew that expecting them to be friends was going too far.

Stephanie had smiled and held out a hand.

"Dan's talked a lot about you," she said.

Jennifer ignored the proffered hand.

"I've heard very little about you," she answered sourly.

Stephanie believed in meeting things head on.

"Dan said your—er—partnership—" here, having found what seemed to her a useful euphemism, Stephanie swallowed hard and plodded on—"had run out of steam. I think you were brave to face it," she said. "And then I came along."

So that was what he had told her! Implied that Jennifer had dropped him! She did not see this as an attempt to spare her the humiliation of an open rejection, understanding only that he had falsely trawled for sympathy.

"So you were just in time to bind his wounds," she said, trying not to snarl. "How lucky for him."

"I hope you'll be happy too," said Stephanie.

"How kind of you," said Jennifer icily. "Thanks for the drink. I won't stay for dinner." As she had no hemlock with her, eating with them would be intolerable.

I hate her, she fumed, walking away from the restaurant. At least he hadn't chosen one where they had been together. I hate her simpering smile. I hate her peaches skin. Jennifer, like her father, was dark and sallow.

Now she spent time plotting what she would like to do to Stephanie, apart from cutting her in pieces and feeding her to vultures. She wrote her several letters, all unsigned, but tore them up. Then she wrote some to Daniel and she tore those up, too. Her pride asserted itself. She would not let him see what he had done to her.

But it grew no easier.

She knew where Stephanie worked and telephoned her there, then hung up as soon as she heard the light, breathy voice. Those were the tones which had seduced Daniel and whispered in his ear at night. She tortured herself with visions of them locked together. Did Daniel ever think of her then and remember how it used to be?

By day, she carried on, apparently normal, a little thinner, a little paler, a lot more tense. She began leaving the office early, hurrying to catch Stephanie leaving hers. She would watch her from a doorway opposite. Once she saw Daniel waiting for her on the pavement; when they kissed on meeting, her own throat filled with vomit.

She threw no more bottles at the flat but she took to prowling past at night. She wore special clothes for this, a black cloak with a hood, a muffler and boots. When she felt cold she walked round the block to restore her circulation; then she would take up her post again. Often Daniel's car was parked outside.

One night she let his tyres down. Another time, she snapped his wiper blades. Two days later she brought a knife with her and scraped a line all along one side of the paintwork. That showed on his Audi.

Vandals were blamed.

5

On her way home from Wintlebury Mrs Newton called at a garage on the edge of the town to put her car through the automatic car wash, something she did, instead of washing it herself, when it was extremely dirty after a spell of bad weather. Lately, because of the mud churned up and deposited by the builders' vehicles in the road outside Yew Cottage, this had become necessary more often. She parked away from the pumps and the entrance to the wash area, and went into the shop to buy her token. As she approached the counter a thickset young man in a leather bomber jacket and pale crumpled trousers pushed past her demanding one.

"Excuse me. I was here first," said Mrs Newton in her precise, clipped tone.

The man turned towards her. He did not meet her eye but, glaring past her, spoke.

"Get out of my way," he said, and held his hand out to the assistant who put the car wash token into it.

Involuntarily, Mrs Newton took a step backwards as the man moved away from the counter, his body still confronting her.

"You stupid cow," he said, and if she had not retreated another few steps, he would, by his sheer bulk, have knocked her over.

Mrs Newton took a deep breath and mustered her composure.

"Well!" she said, in a gasp.

"Sorry, love," said the assistant, a young girl with stringy brown hair which needed washing. "It's no good arguing with them sort."

Mrs Newton was shaking as she paid for her token. She returned to her car and drove it carefully through the narrow passage between the garage workshop and the shop towards the car wash. The man, in an old beige Mercedes, was waiting while a red Escort was processed. Mrs Newton drew up behind him, leaving a wide gap. She was still trembling, but not from fear; the emotion she felt was rage. Such aggression: such impertinence: such a lack of respect: such absence of good manners: get a few similar men together and you had the nucleus of a mob with a potential for violence. She would not put it past him to get out of his car and subject her to further verbal abuse, and she pressed the lock switch so that she was physically protected. However, the Escort's programme had finished and it drove off; the Mercedes moved up into position.

Something made Mrs Newton note down its number in her pocket diary, under the day's date. She would know that man if she met him again, she thought.

She was still angry as she drove home, her car sparkling clean, droplets of water flicking from it as she went past Wintlebury's small industrial estate and up the hill to the crossroads where The Prince Hal inn stood. One road led to Upper Bardolph, and she turned right for Middle Bardolph, driving carefully; cyclists could appear here, and sometimes there were people on horses from the local riding stables. A drain was being repaired near the post office, which was also the village shop. She had to wait for a man with a Stop/Go sign to notice her presence and permit her passage. Past here was the primary school; it was too early for the mothers to be lined up outside waiting for their children. From soon after three o'clock the pavement was crowded with them, some with other children in pushchairs, and there were cars parked all along the kerbside. Children came here from Upper Bardolph and Little Nym.

In the Bardolphs, life without a car would be extremely difficult. Though the villages had been spared mass expansion, small clutches of new houses had been built in large gardens and in some cases on the sites of larger houses which had been pulled down. Mrs Newton had been fearful, when the Blaneys sold their house next to Yew Cottage and work began there, that this was what the buyers had in mind, and was relieved when she found it was not so. Because the school survived, there was a good age mix in the population, but many of the original village families were being divided as the younger members were forced to seek cheaper housing in the towns. Until now, Mrs Newton had never stayed long enough in any one place to become more than minimally aware of the social implications of rural development. She realised that if the time came when she could no longer drive, she would have to move, but that, she hoped, must be at least ten years hence. Then, perhaps, a house designed for someone of retirement age would have to be her choice, she feared; she dreaded the possible involvement with other older people in similar surrounding houses, but it might be the only way to maintain her independence. She was determined to keep control of her capital so that she could decide her own future without the interference of her children, but she dreaded being forced into intimacy with neighbours. Guarding her own privacy was essential to her.

Over the years she had made steady gains on all her house deals, reinvesting her profits under the guidance of Mr Booth, the third generation of Booths in the firm of solicitors who had advised her since her husband's death. Such operations had meant that her original pension had been subsidised considerably and she was able to live in comfort. She never liked to sit wholly idle, and, no knitter, had for years done tapestry work, making handbags and cushion covers, fire screens, and anything that she could later sell to a few outlets which she had discovered when she began to do the work. Her profits were not great, but they existed, and she enjoyed the quiet occupation if she were not reading. While she sewed, she listened to the radio and had begun to borrow recorded books from the library.

As a younger woman she had suffered from frequent severe migraine headaches which had handicapped her seriously. When she was widowed no immediate financial need forced her to work. An insurance scheme took care of Geoffrey's school fees and Jennifer's less heavy educational expenses. The children were her priority and the fact that she was regularly forced to go to bed in a darkened room, in agony and vomiting, for several days, made her aware of her limitations as an employee and led to her refusing other commitments; what use would she be if people were depending on her and she let them down? Over the years she developed a self-protecting carapace which kept her away from activities with which other women her age filled their lives. The educational classes she attended and the small amount of bridge she played gave her the little social contact that she knew she must sustain if she were not to become a total recluse, but she was, she acknowledged, living a selfish life. However, it was free from hurt, both to herself or others.

Today's brush with the boor at the car wash had disturbed her more than was permissible, and she was not pleased to find, when she reached Yew Cottage, that the entrance was blocked by a builder's van.

She parked behind it, stepped out of the car and advanced towards the site of operations. Recent work on the drive had reduced the muddy area and she did not have to pick her way through many obstacles, but a cement mixer was noisily rotating. A man stood beside it, and Mrs Newton had to tap his arm to get his attention. She indicated her problem and he nodded.

"Sorry about that. I'll get it shifted," he said.

Leaving the machinery on, he stepped across what had once been Mr Blaney's bed of prize Michaelmas daisies shouting for Neil, and Mrs Newton returned to her car.

Soon a thin young man appeared: Neil, presumably. He got into the van, started it up and drove it along the road, parking it on the grass verge outside the Clarksons' thatched cottage. The Clarksons were both out all day at work, so they would not object; the builders would be gone by the time they came home, thought Mrs Newton, turning in at her own gate. She opened the big black double doors of the garage and put the car away, and as she walked towards the house she felt a stab of pain above her right eye.

She was sitting down with a cup of tea and two Anadin tablets when the doorbell rang.

Lucy Moffat, safely delivered to her door the previous evening, was grateful to her rescuer. She had been very stupid and had done just the sort of foolish thing against which she and Simon had warned their daughter. She had kept quiet about her adventure when Simon came home, and as he parked his own car outside the house he did not see that hers was absent; while she was out the garage had collected it. She rang them in the morning, learned that it had been repaired, and said she would come and fetch it shortly. She was walking up the street when, long-sighted, she saw her good Samaritan leaving the bank. Lucy had not learned her name the night before.

Now she hurried into the bank where she was well acquainted with the personal adviser who had a desk near the door.

"Who was that who just left?" she asked. "The elderly woman in the camel coat?" and added, in case it was against bank practice to reveal their customers' names to one another, "I've met her, but I can't remember her name."

"You must mean Mrs Newton," said the adviser. "She lives in Middle Bardolph. Comes in regularly once a week."

"Oh, of course," said Lucy, as if she had known this all the time. She asked about the adviser's little girl, picked up a leaflet about raising loans, then left.

Two doors further down the street there was a florist's, and, ever a creature of impulse, Lucy went in and bought a pink chrysanthemum in a pot. Then she walked on to the garage. When she reached home, she consulted the telephone directory to discover Mrs Newton's exact address and saw that the only Newton in Middle Bardolph, E., lived at Yew Cottage.

Lucy could not go there at once. She had promised herself the morning in her workshop, where she made jewellery. In London she had sold some pieces to a boutique in Covent Garden whose owner had said he would consider more if they sold quickly.

In London, she had met Tim for lunch. Nothing untoward had happened; it was only lunch; but she had felt excited at the thought of seeing him again. They had met on her initiative; she had telephoned him at his office and he had suggested it immediately. Afterwards she had done her shopping, wondering if she would go up, as he had suggested, for another meeting. The temptation and the secrecy were exciting. She had not made her mind up yet.

She set out for Middle Bardolph in the afternoon, rather regretting, now, her impulse. In the post office she asked where Yew Cottage was, and, while in there, bought a phone card. Then she took the road to which she had been directed, watching out for builders' operations which, it seemed, were in progress near her goal.

She found the house and rang the doorbell, standing there with her plant in its wrapping paper. At first there was no answer, and she was on the point of deciding that Mrs Newton must still be out, in which case she could leave the plant and a note on the doorstep and be spared more effort, when there was a sound from inside the house and the door was opened.

A tired, crumpled face was turned up to her. Mrs Newton wore glasses with gingery frames, through which now peered weary, anxious grey-blue eyes. She wore a beige checked pleated skirt and a fawn cardigan over a cream blouse and looked, thought Lucy, tastefully assembled.

"It was so kind of you to rescue me last night," said Lucy, smiling at her. "I brought you this," and she held out the plant.

A faint colour came into Mrs Newton's cheeks. She had not immediately recognised Lucy, now wearing jeans and a shabby waxed jacket.

"Oh—how very kind of you," said Mrs Newton. "Won't you come in?" Then she added, in a rush of words, "I've just made some tea. Perhaps you'd like a cup?"

"Why not?" said Lucy, whose whole expedition was the result of a whim and who had yet to plan what she and Simon were to eat that night. But she had forgotten to have any lunch, and the thought of tea was pleasant. "Thank you," she accepted.

Mrs Newton regretted her invitation as soon as it was uttered, but the unexpectedness of the visit when she was already flustered by her experience at the car wash made her relax her normal reserve.

"I'll fetch another cup and saucer," she said. "The tea's only just made." She indicated the sitting-room door, to the left of the hall. "Do go in."

Still clutching the plant, Lucy obeyed, and entered a bright, pleasant room with a french window overlooking the garden to the rear. There was an open fireplace, but the chimney was closed up and an electric fire with simulated coals stood in the hearth. On the low table in front of it was a tray with a pretty china teapot, matching milk jug and cup and saucer. Wow, thought Lucy, to whom tea meant a teabag in a mug in the kitchen while she did several things at once like washing up, or peeling vegetables and looking at designs for something she had planned to make. The room was very tidy, but Jonathan Raban's book lay on the sofa, a leather marker lying across its jacket, since Mrs Newton had not yet had the chance to start it.

Mrs Newton soon returned with a second tray on which were another cup and saucer, a hot water jug, a sugar bowl and a plate of Hob Nob biscuits.

Lucy did not take sugar.

"I love these biscuits, though," she said, eagerly taking one.

"So do I," said Mrs Newton, almost smiling. "I'm afraid there's no cake. I seldom bake these days."

In a quick glance round the room, Lucy had seen no photographs. Was there a Mr Newton? Somehow it seemed unlikely. The room was very feminine, yet impersonal, the furnishings pleasing but indefinite; there were a few china figures on shelves in an alcove beside the fireplace, and some unremarkable paintings, all landscapes, several in oils but two in watercolours, on the walls. One showed a windmill.

"That's nice," said Lucy, looking at it. "Sorry, how rude of me, but I'm inquisitive."

"It's in Suffolk. I lived there for a while," said Mrs Newton. "I always buy a painting from a local artist wherever I happen to be living."

"Oh?"

"I move a lot, you see," Mrs Newton explained. "But I've been here four years now."

"It's not your house, then? You rent it?" Lucy asked. It seemed the only explanation.

"No—it is mine," said Mrs Newton. "But I find it better not to settle," and she primmed her mouth.

Better than what, wondered Lucy, but said aloud, "Sorry. I'm being nosy again." Then she laughed, and went on, "May I have another biscuit?"

"Of course. Forgive me," said Mrs Newton, offering the plate.

Both of them kept apologising, Lucy thought, but she had cause, and Mrs Newton hadn't.

"I forgot to have any lunch," she said. "But I've got my phone card," and a gleam of triumph lit up her face, making her look quite pretty. She wore no make-up and had a few pale freckles on her nose. Her strongly marked eyebrows were crescent shaped, giving her a startled look when, as now, she was animated. She must be much the same age as Jennifer; perhaps a little older, Mrs Newton thought.

"I went to Wintlebury today," she said. "On the way back something nasty happened," and she found herself telling Lucy about the encounter at the car wash.

"How rude," said Lucy. "What louts some people are. I shouldn't waste good thinking time on him, if I were you."

The sympathy was welcome, and the advice good. By now the tea and the tablets she had taken were easing the sharp nag above Mrs Newton's right eye and she thought her threatened headache might retreat; prompt action was the secret.

"He had a big car," she said. "He looked clean."

"Villains wear many disguises," said Lucy lightly.

"Oh, I'm not saying he was a villain. Just a selfish—" Mrs Newton sought for the appropriate word and found it. "Yob," she pronounced, with satisfaction. Then she could not resist adding, "If I hadn't taken you home last night, someone like him might have come along and offered you a lift. What would you have done then?"

"Said I preferred to walk, I hope," said Lucy, but she wasn't sure.

"I think you'd have taken a chance," said Mrs Newton. "And it would have been difficult to refuse if he insisted."

"Well, you said he was no villain. Simply mannerless," said Lucy.

"The circumstances would be different," Mrs Newton said, primming her lips again, but less repressively this time.

"Yes—well, I take your point. Anyway, it was beastly for you," Lucy said. "I'd have told him off, if he'd done it to me."

"I don't think he'd have tried it," Mrs Newton said. "You're tall, and you're young." And confident, she thought, secure in some solid, inner way.

"I'm not so young," said Lucy. "But thanks." She decided to change the subject. "Are you planning to leave here?'' she asked. "You said you often move. This is such a nice house. I'd hate to leave it, in your place, though I suppose the building work next door is rather irritating.''

"It is, but it will stop,'' said Mrs Newton. Then she would have new neighbours, and what would they be like? "I'm waiting for the market to pick up,'' she added.

She was looking much brighter than when Lucy had arrived. Perhaps she had enjoyed the visit, Lucy thought, and glanced at her watch.

"I must go,'' she said.

"And I must find a nice pot for your plant,'' said Mrs Newton, who had pulled the paper open to admire it.

She showed Lucy to the door, and as they parted, the cement mixer ceased its whirring.

"What a relief,'' said Mrs Newton. "They'll be stopping altogether now. Their day ends early. Is your car all right?''

"Yes. It was nothing much,'' said Lucy. "The alternator, whatever that is. Goodbye. Thanks for the tea.''

Long-legged, in her very clean jeans, Lucy climbed into a small yellow car whose make Mrs Newton was unable to identify, gave a final wave, then drove off.

I might see her again, thought Mrs Newton, unwrapping the plant. It was in a plastic pot; florists' and nursery plants always were, these days. Mrs Newton rarely bought flowers herself but Jennifer and Geoffrey occasionally gave them to her; it was years since she had received anything in a proper flower pot. She supposed these were cheaper, and they retained the moisture longer than terracotta, which absorbed it, but they bobbed about in the sink when you attempted to stand them in water. She had plenty of old pots stacked under a bench in the garage. She would repot it before putting it in a pretty container. Then she would put it on the table in the hall, near the telephone, where she would see it every time she passed through or used the stairs. It would remind her of Lucy, its donor. She had suggested that someone nice might move into the renovated house, reaching out as she spoke for another biscuit, her nails short, unvarnished, a plaster on one

6

N eil enjoyed driving the van. He was allowed to take it home and he parked it off the road in the drive of the council house where he lived with his mother. He knew he had been lucky to get the job with Len Harding, the builder. Years ago, Len and Neil's father had worked together, but that was long before the trouble. While Neil was inside, Len had said he would give him a chance, after his release, and Neil was determined to justify this trust. He guarded the van tenderly, washed it at weekends, and was saving up to buy a car of his own.

He shared the back bedroom with his brother, as he had done all his life, but he longed for privacy. Kevin was noisy; he went on drinking benders with his friends and had been known to bring girls in, shutting Neil out while they were occupied. Those nights Neil spent on the sofa in the sitting-room and, to be fair, if their mother found out what had happened, Kevin received an unsparing ticking-off. The third bedroom was occupied by their sister and her four-month-old baby, Jason. Roseanne had been ditched by Jason's father when she became pregnant; the family had rallied round her then, persuaded her not to move out though the council would have been obliged to find her, as a single mother, somewhere to live. Kevin and Neil brought in two wage packets and Roseanne worked as a chambermaid at The Bell, sometimes doing extra waitress duty. Mavis, their mother, did several evening shifts in the bar and looked after Jason when Roseanne was out. She had three cleaning jobs, too, taking Jason with her when Roseanne was working. Usually he was quiet while she undertook her chores.

Kevin changed jobs from time to time, but was seldom out of work for more than a week or two. At present he had a job in an electrical assembly plant on an industrial estate some ten miles from Wintlebury. He was rarely at home except to sleep; this suited Neil, though when Kevin returned from a night out drinking with his friends, his subsequent snores and other anti-social conduct made Neil long to have the bedroom to himself. Roseanne had acquired a boyfriend, a sales representative who stayed regularly at The Bell; if they married, she would leave home and Neil could have her room. But he would miss Jason; he liked the little kid.

Sometimes Neil noticed, in the boot of Kevin's big old Mercedes, boxes and packages which Kevin, when asked, always said were stuff he was moving for a friend. Some of the boxes found their way, for short periods, to the bedroom cupboard in the room the brothers shared. Neil was suspicious about their contents but thought it best to accept what he was told, though his doubts were reinforced by Kevin's periodic bursts of spending, when he would take the whole family out for lunch at a Berni Inn or a Trust House hotel. Once, soon after Jason was born, he took Roseanne and Mavis and the baby to Tenerife for a week. Neil could have gone too, but he would not take the time off work; instead, he had a blissful week of solitude at home and, in the evenings, redecorated his mother's bedroom.

Mavis liked having them all at home. Her whole adult life had been centered on the family, especially since her husband had departed. Things had been very difficult then, with money short, as she struggled to keep them all together and retain the house. Roseanne had been the one worst affected by her father's defection; they had been very close, or so it seemed, and she had felt betrayed. Now another man had let her down. Mavis hoped the sales representative, whose name was Mike, would prove more reliable; she longed for Roseanne to be conventionally married and installed in her own home. She feared, though, that Mike might be already married and had once asked Roseanne, who brushed aside the question.

Neil was often left babysitting in the evenings when Roseanne was out and Mavis was either at The Bell or playing Bingo, but he did not mind. The child was born soon after he came out of prison and his new life seemed to mark the start of Neil's.

Len Harding found Neil a good worker; he learned quickly, and was always willing to do anything that came along, though he seemed happiest when sent off with the van to collect timber or other supplies. He had been working constantly on the house in Middle Bardolph where he had fitted doors and windows and installed kitchen units, helping out with painting when required.

Neil had noticed Mrs Newton going in and out of Yew Cottage and working in the garden, though in the long hot summer he had not seen her sitting outside, as one might expect. He had watched her mow and trim the edges—not often, for the drought had meant the grass did not grow and a ban on hosepipes prevented the use of a sprinkler, if she had one. Apart from some rose bushes, the garden was mostly grass and shrubs, with that big gloomy old tree on the lawn. It was a large place for one old woman on her own; there she was, with all that space, while he had to share a bedroom with his brother. It seemed unfair when you thought about it. Sometimes he imagined moving in with her as her lodger, telling himself she could do with a man about the place, someone who'd keep an eye on things, chop firewood, wash the car, be a deterrent to villains. There were plenty of them about, even in villages like Middle Bardolph: kids who vandalised the public telephone and scrawled graffiti in the bus

shelter. Given the opportunity, many lads would nick anything they saw lying about just asking to be taken; that was
how he had started on the road to trouble.

The old woman had thanked him quite nicely for moving
the van. He decided that she was all right, not stuck up,
though she looked it. He'd seen the yellow Fiat drawn up
outside, but not the driver; it was rare for her to have a visitor.
The car had gone when he packed up to go home, and lights
were on in Yew Cottage. Before going back to the van, he
walked up the path and rang the bell.

Mrs Newton, opening the door, recognised the overalled
youth with the denim jacket whose name was Neil. He had a
spot on his chin and greasy hair.

"Just came to say sorry I blocked your entrance," said
Neil, and he smiled diffidently. "I wasn't thinking."

"No—well, never mind. I'm sure you won't do it again,"
said Mrs Newton.

He was quite tall, very thin, and his shoulders were
hunched as if he was nervous. What did he want?

Neil had hoped she might offer him a cup of tea, ask him
in, show him round, but this did not happen.

"Nice place you've got here," he said. "A big garden,
too. I could give you a hand in it, summer evenings, if you
like."

"Thank you for offering, but I don't need any help,"
said Mrs Newton firmly. "I appreciate your apology. Good
night."

She began closing the door and Neil had to leave. Never
mind. This was enough for a first meeting. Why should she
employ him straight off like that? He'd go round again if it
snowed, or there was a hurricane like they'd had before, offer
to clear up any damage. The chance would come. In the end,
she'd need him, and he would soon make himself indispens-
able.

Weaving this dream, he drove cheerfully home, stopping
at the video shop to pick up a film. It was one of his mother's

Bingo evenings and he and Jason would be on their own. His meal was ready, sausage and mash with beans, and custard tart to follow. He ate every bit, then washed up his things; he always did that; it was only right; his mother worked hard enough as it was. Neil was rather afraid of his mother, but he loved her, and he knew he was lucky compared with some inmates he had met in prison, who had no family support.

Jason began yelling just as Neil had settled down to his film. He brought the child downstairs, propped him up on the sofa so that he could enjoy it too, and gave him his dummy to keep him quiet. By and by he fell asleep, and Neil had him back in bed, as good as gold, by the time Mavis came home.

Roseanne and Kevin were still out when he went to bed.

Mrs Newton would be thankful when the building work next door came to an end. She had been sorry when the Blaneys left; they had moved to Cornwall to be near their daughter. Apart from holidays, Mrs Newton had not tried the West Country in her peregrinations, but property was, on the whole, cheaper there. She might think about that, when the market picked up. Very occasionally, she and the Blaneys had visited each other for sherry on Sunday mornings after church. The trio grew more friendly as the time came closer for the Blaney's move, safe, by then, from risk of real involvement. Mr Blaney, a retired civil engineer, had always come round after any storm or power cut or other disruption to make sure things were all right at Yew Cottage, and when both the Blaneys were laid low with flu Mrs Newton had shopped for them and taken them a fish pie, made especially, and a cold lemon soufflé.

"What a good cook you are. You hide your talents," they had said.

When they were better, they had taken her with them to a matinée at Stratford-upon-Avon, where they often went; they both enjoyed the theatre and feared they would miss it in Cornwall. They spoke of Mrs Newton going to stay, but all of them knew this would not happen. Christmas cards would be exchanged for a year or two; then the fragile acquaintance would wither away.

Mrs Newton had envied them the excitement of the move: the detailed plans; the necessary lists; the steps taken to avoid confusion; the prospect of discovering, in a tea chest, some object half-forgotten, not noticed in the packing. There were the ways of the new house to be learned: its internal sounds; the quirks of its equipment; the particular roar of the boiler; the speed at which the bath water ran and the efficiency of the waste flow; then the feel of the area. However well researched that might be, moving brought surprises: a persistently barking dog, a donkey braying in the night, bird scarers. In Cornwall there would be the caw of the seagulls, perhaps even the sound of the sea for they were near the coast.

She had been rather curt with that young man, Neil, she reflected. It was thoughtful of him to apologise, and his offer of help was, no doubt, well meant, but she knew nothing about him apart from the fact that he worked for the builder on the site. She'd look out for him, though, in future; be pleasant, say "Good morning." She had not meant to administer a snub.

Mrs Newton put him out of her mind and allowed herself a moment's anxiety about her prospective neighbours who would move in when the builders left. The Blaneys had said they were a couple in their forties with two teenage children and a dog. Loud radios, thought Mrs Newton; also barking. It had been so quiet before. Nothing ever stayed the same.

Meanwhile, her own garden was ready for the winter. She had put in more daffodils to add to those which already flowered in the rough grass at the end of the lawn. She had grown to like gardening, taking it seriously, freeing her mind from other thoughts, wearing neat slacks and a poplin jacket kept for the purpose, and gloves; one should take care of one's hands.

She gave the pot chrysanthemum a drink. Strange how some florists failed to water stock, she thought. It was kind of Lucy Moffat to think of saying thank you in this way; Mrs Newton wondered how she knew who she was for she had not told her, during their journey. Perhaps she had noticed, in the rear window of Mrs Newton's car, the trade label from the garage who had sold it to her and somehow traced her that way; probably it was the same firm who had repaired Lucy's car. Yes, that was doubtless how it had been done. Mrs Newton had always known that, however difficult it might seem at first, almost everyone could be located, even after many years and after many moves.

It was a pity Jennifer was not more like Lucy instead of being such a creature of moods; in a way, Mrs Newton could understand Daniel's change of heart. Perhaps he had found someone calmer, less touchy. Jennifer's father had been so calm, so benign; she had not inherited those genes, it seemed. Such thoughts filled her with guilt, and that evening she telephoned her daughter.

Jennifer was out. That was good. It meant she was getting on with her life, ceasing to brood. Mrs Newton had not encouraged confidences about the break-up; some things were best kept private, though the vogue now was for counselling at every least setback in life. What had happened to good old-fashioned courage and reticence, she wondered; where was pride?

Jennifer must get about, make new friends. She would find someone else, must indeed know other men; she worked among them, after all. Marriage was, in Mrs Newton's view, the best role in life for a woman as long as she did not expect too much from it and if she could find someone unexcitingly reliable and not too young, in a job with prospects. Daniel, who was in advertising, had seemed to fill all these requirements and perhaps if they had married when they set up house, they would have stayed together.

But people didn't, these days. Nothing lasted for ever. She, of all people, had learned that lesson.

7

When her mother telephoned, Jennifer was standing in the road outside Stephanie's flat. She had followed Stephanie from work, caught the same tube, walked along the road behind her, seen her enter a small shop and waited while she was inside. Stephanie soon emerged with a bulging plastic carrier bag and set off homewards.

Jennifer maintained her pursuit. She had no plan but was drawn as if by a magnet, as though by haunting the younger woman she maintained a place in Daniel's life. Whilst obsessively curious, she continued to nourish a bitter hatred for Stephanie who had ruined her whole future. Jennifer had expected a secure and lasting partnership; she had made a total commitment to Daniel and had imagined that this was mutual.

Diagonally across the road from the house where Stephanie lived there was a big tree, bare of leaves now but still offering cover and concealment. Jennifer stood beneath it and saw Daniel arrive after parking his car further down the road.

The street was always full of cars and finding space was difficult; Jennifer had passed several vigils there before realising that his Audi might be some distance away. She saw him

48

cross the road, hurry up the short path to the front step and peal the bell. The door opened almost instantly and he was silhouetted for an instant against the light inside; then he vanished. She did not see the girl.

That night she let down one of his tyres again. There was no time to do a second as she heard someone coming along the street. She did not wait.

Stephanie had seen her near the office and on the tube, or thought she had, then persuaded herself that she had imagined it, although part of Jennifer's journey home lay in the same direction as her own; had it been otherwise, she and Daniel would not have met. Jennifer was not very tall, with dark hair worn in a frizz; plenty of women looked much the same and Stephanie decided she was becoming obsessed, thinking everyone she saw remotely like her was Jennifer. It must be awful for her, having to live without Daniel, but he had implied that their partnership had run its course and that both of them had known it. Stephanie knew that he meant his promise of fidelity to her and she would see that he kept it; she had youth and determination on her side, and she would bind him to her as they grew together with the children she meant to have at once, or pretty soon.

This haunting, though, was worrying. After a time Stephanie was convinced that Jennifer was, indeed, following her deliberately. One night she thought she saw her outside the shop where she stopped on the way home to buy the supper. That evening, as Daniel told her later, one of his car tyres had been let down, and that had happened before. The Audi had been scratched, too. She thought he should report these incidents to the police but he said it was par for the course these days and he'd been lucky not to lose the whole car, its radio, or the wheels. Jennifer couldn't be responsible for the damage, could she? Stephanie had banished the idea and did not mention it to Daniel, but now she consciously took notice of who was near her when she travelled. Often she definitely recognised Jennifer, but the other woman, usually dressed all in black, never met her gaze.

After a while Stephanie changed her mind and told Daniel. "I get the feeling she's following me," she said.

"But she gets off first. She doesn't have to come out here," said Daniel.

He had not moved in with Stephanie. It wasn't that sort of flat, though he stayed the night if the other two girls were away. At the moment he had a base in Wimbledon where he slept on a sofa in the sitting-room and kept his possessions in the downstairs cloakroom. He had moved around from friend to friend, accepting hospitality where he could find it; it was most unsatisfactory and could not continue. He and Stephanie had priced flats to buy, and it was likely that he would have to get another mortgage even before he had extracted himself from the first. He must grasp the nettle and bring things to a head with Jennifer, force her to make some arrangement to release him.

Stephanie's remarks about seeing Jennifer worried him; she wasn't fanciful. She could be right. Could it be Jennifer who was damaging his car? She was capable of it; she had turned on him once, fighting like a cat, and he had gripped her hands and held her tightly till she calmed down. Then they had kissed and made up and it was over till the next time.

He should have broken with her long ago, should never have embarked on their joint household, in fact, but it had been an easy thing to do and meant they benefited from their double mortgage relief. It had seemed a safe enough investment at the time, and they had undertaken it when her changes of mood and lapses into sudden helplessness were still beguiling. He remembered some tricks which subsequently she had played on him: she had put salt instead of sugar in his coffee, locked him out of the flat one night after a quarrel and refused to let him in. He had slept in the car. She hid his mail for two days when he was expecting an important letter from his father, who lived in Canada near his married sister; Daniel's mother had died some years before he met Jennifer. Some of her actions had been, to say the least, unkind, and pointless in an adult. She had a very cruel streak, he recognized.

He decided that the time had come to go and speak to her. Burdened with guilt, he dreaded such a meeting.

The next morning, early, Daniel rang her and asked her to meet him for a drink that evening.

Jennifer told him to come round to the house. Otherwise, she said, she was not interested in seeing him. He was forced to accept this and so, feeling rather sheepish and even apprehensive, he arrived at the appointed time and rang the bell.

"You've still got your key," she said, confronting him in the doorway. "Why not just come in?"

He was shocked at her appearance. She had always been thin, but she had lost at least half a stone, and her eyes seemed very bright and staring in her haggard face. Conventional words of greeting faded on his tongue.

"You're tired," he said, genuinely concerned.

She went into attack straight away.

"You mean I look a hag? Yes, and whose fault is that?"

Daniel was seeing her as a familiar stranger, and at the same time wondering how he could have found her attractive in the first place. He had, he knew, recognised her vulnerability and wanted to protect her. Her sudden changes of mood had not disturbed him then because he thought that he could calm her down, but this had been a false assumption. Now it seemed to him incredible that for so long a time they had been close.

"You didn't own me," he said, and immediately wished the words unsaid because she had succeeded in provoking him and had therefore scored a point. "People break up all the time," he added feebly.

During the day, Jennifer had woven a fantasy in which his reason for seeing her was to seek a reconciliation but this hope had died the moment she saw him. His round face wore an anxious expression, the sort of look he had when, on holiday, he was shocked by begging children in Italian streets. People in London, sleeping in cardboard boxes, evoked the same reaction, while Jennifer was inclined to blame their plight on innate fecklessness. Once she had snapped, "Do something about it, then, if you mind so much," and he had simply shrugged.

Instead of seeing ardour in his eyes, she recognised a wary look, and, uncontrollably, she began to tremble.

"This is us, not people," she said and, hoping the movement would hide her involuntary shaking, she started to walk up the steep flight of stairs leading to the sitting-room, where she sat down on the sofa. Would he come and sit beside her?

He did not. He took a chair and perched on the edge of it, leaning forward earnestly, his blue eyes bright. Irrelevantly, she noticed that his thick brown hair was shorter than he used to wear it; that would be to impress Stephanie's military father with his manliness, she thought.

"Have you come to arrange about taking your furniture?" she asked.

"No. I was going to ask you to put the place up for sale. I need my capital. You know that," he said.

"We'll both lose, with the market as it is at present. We've discussed all this," she said.

"I think we should cut our losses. Get what we can. I mean, you take out your original stake and I'll have what's left when the building society's had their loan back."

"At present prices, that won't be much," said Jennifer. Anger made her add, "I'll buy you out for fifteen thousand. I'm owed something for the years I've given you."

"Where will you get it?" he asked. How could she raise a sum like that, if he accepted such a loss himself?

"That's my business."

He had seen that she was trembling. She was in a terrible state, blowing away the conviction about her resilience with which he had deluded himself. Perhaps fixing the money side of things would enable her to cut loose, pick up her life again. But how would she do it?

Jennifer, having made her proud gesture, had worked none of this out. In fact she had no wish to release Daniel from his obligations: as long as he had money in the house, she had a lien on him. He would come back if she was patient.

Daniel, however, knew that being free of the financial shackles tying him to Jennifer would, indeed, be liberation and he could not wait to tell Stephanie the good news. Now they could make firm plans. He stepped lightly down the road and Jennifer, watching from the window, recognised his jaunty stride. Bile rose in her throat. She went to the bathroom where she was literally sick.

Daniel, walking back to his car which was parked some way down the road, realised that he had not tackled the question of Jennifer trailing Stephanie. The whole idea now seemed fantastic. Jennifer was unhappy and mixed-up—yes, he admitted that—but she had always been volatile and he had once enjoyed calming her; it made him feel a sense of power; only as time went on he had come to dread her sudden rages and her depressed moods. With Stephanie he had found tranquillity sparked with joy, and the potential for something deeply fulfilling; time would nourish their commitment to each other; time, and, eventually, a family.

He'd never contemplated that with Jennifer. They had never even talked about it. He could not picture her with a baby: it would be too demanding, too difficult, would make her too uncomfortable, and she'd hate the mess. He'd been too easy, though: too casual. He'd drifted into the shared house because of the attraction of the tax relief, not looking far ahead. He told himself that Jennifer, if she had wanted to, would have walked away from him. When things didn't work out, that was what you did: split up, and limited the ensuing damage. She'd get over it; maybe she'd soon meet someone else.

Never one to brood, he had talked himself into a cheerful frame of mind by the time he met Stephanie. It was Friday night and he was going to the flat; the other girls had both gone away for the weekend. He bought a bottle of champagne

on the way there and decided that he would take her out to
dinner. It would be a celebration; they'd forget money problems and other people's pain. Now they could begin to look
ahead.

Stephanie thought there had to be a catch in it.

"Where's she going to get fifteen thousand pounds?" she
asked.

"Don't ask me," said Daniel. "Maybe she's found someone else to pitch in with her. Some girl at the office. Or a
man," he added, most unrealistically.

"But they won't get joint tax relief any more," said Stephanie. "It won't work out like that. How can they fix it?"

"That's not our problem," Daniel said. "She'll do it. She
keeps her word."

"We'll go flat-hunting tomorrow," said Stephanie.

Jennifer rang her brother up, passing the barrier of speaking to Lynn who asked her how she was in what were
meant to be very caring tones but which Jennifer found
patronising.

"Could you lend me fifteen thousand pounds?" she asked
Geoffrey.

"You must be joking," Geoffrey said. "Where do you
think I'd get it from?"

"You're the rich one," said his sister. "Director of your
company and all that."

"I've got problems," Geoffrey said. "You'd better try
Mama."

"I'd rather ask you a favour than her," said Jennifer. "It
wouldn't be for long. Just till I straighten things out about
the house. Daniel wants his stake back. Couldn't you borrow
from the company?"

"Certainly not," said Geoffrey. "I should let Daniel whistle for it."

"I told him he could have it soon," said Jennifer. "He's
being totally unreasonable but I suppose he wants to settle in

a lovenest with that milk and water creature who's got hold of him.''

Paraphrased, this was probably the truth, thought Geoffrey. Surely Daniel had staked more than fifteen thousand pounds originally?

''Sell the place for what you can get and move into something you can afford yourself,'' he advised. ''A one-roomed flat.'' Sometimes Geoffrey felt that was what he would like, a bare-walled cell with no one to berate him for his shortcomings. ''Or go down to Middle Bardolph for a while while you save up. Mama would take you in, poor Orphan Annie, and charge you nothing. Even with commuting fares, you'd be quids in.''

Jennifer ignored this, to her, ludicrous suggestion.

''I wouldn't get a quick sale,'' she said. ''There are other places like ours that have had boards up for months.''

''They may be over-priced,'' he said. ''You cut your losses and wash Daniel out of your hair. Then go to Yew Cottage and work on Mama to sell it and split the takings between us. She's good for seven years.''

''Why seven years?''

''Inheritance tax, stupid. If she made the money over to us, we'd escape it.''

''But where would she go?''

''Why, we'd have her with us, of course,'' said Geoffrey. ''Lynn's set her heart on finding a nice place further from the works. Bit pricey, though, even with the falling market. It'd have space for a granny flat. She'd be snug there. No more worries.''

For you, no, Jennifer thought. She could imagine what Lynn had in mind: an impressive mansion set in several acres, manna for her social aspirations.

''It's an idea,'' she said, neutrally.

''It's a damn good one,'' said Geoffrey, who almost never swore. ''See if you can swing her round, Jen. It would help us both and make no difference to her. She'd have her pension for spending money, after all.''

Big deal, thought Jennifer.

"Perhaps you'd let her keep her car." Jennifer's tone was caustic. "So that she could buzz around?"

"Why not?" he answered, and added that their mother would enjoy seeing more of her granddaughters. Since she saw them only very rarely as it was, that had to be an improvement, Jennifer decided.

They prolonged this line of talk for further minutes, each producing reasons to support the plan, but Jennifer saw no prospect of her self-willed mother fulfilling the role prescribed, and why should she? She had made all her own decisions for a long time; why should she place herself under Lynn's jurisdiction—for that was what it would mean—unless compelled by circumstance? Had she always been so firmly in command? Jennifer's memories of childhood had become vague; she remembered her father as a kindly, quiet presence, always reassuring. He collected stamps and would sit at his desk poring over his trophies. Geoffrey had begun a collection, too, and had taken on his father's albums. Maybe they had all been sold by now, she thought; Lynn would have happily spent any money they might raise. Life had always been tranquil in the large comfortable house set among the pines, and with Geoffrey away at school, Jennifer had met little competition for attention. In those days she had liked drawing and painting, and often worked away in a corner of the study while her father was busy. Then they would play chess together. Had those years been happy for her mother? There had been no rows, no quarrels, and the house was smoothly run, with Mrs Davis coming every day to help. There had been summer holidays in Cornwall at a family hotel, swimming in a cove, surfing at a bigger beach; her father had preferred that to the sands at home, though at weekends they had sometimes gone down to the sea. He had seemed quite old: he was much older than the fathers of Jennifer's friends; he had been rather bald, and what hair remained was grey. He and her mother had lived contented lives, she thought in retrospect; they had not pulled against one another, as Geoffrey and Lynn seemed all the time to do. Jennifer did not care to examine the type of harness worn by herself and Daniel.

She went round to the building society, to see what would be involved if the mortgage switched entirely to her. It was a worrying discussion. How was she to find not only fifteen thousand pounds but the big payments that would now be solely her responsibility? But she must keep the house: Daniel would return one day, and it would be there, waiting for him, just as she would.

Each night, now, while sleep eluded her, Jennifer played scenes of their reunion on the screen of her imagination. She'd be difficult at first. He'd had his chance and she wouldn't give in easily next time; she'd have him cringing at her feet, imploring her forgiveness, which she would deny him until she had made him suffer as much as she was suffering now. Then, at last, magnanimously, she'd give in and they would come together rapturously.

During a quiet moment at the office, she wrote a letter to her mother asking for the fifteen thousand pounds. Her mother owned Yew Cottage outright and could easily take out a loan. Geoffrey, too, sat down with pen and paper to repeat his proposals for the evening of her years.

The postman called early at Yew Cottage. When Mrs Newton came downstairs next morning, the two envelopes were on the mat.

Her children rarely wrote to her; what could they want now, and in unison? It was not her birthday, when they would, meticulously, both send her cards. Lynn organised Interflora to deal with the problem of a gift; Jennifer sent toilet water or bath essence or some other such present, for her mother loved those little luxuries, a trait so out of keeping with her austere nature that Jennifer found it endearing. The coincidence of their both writing at the same time had to be deliberate. She was half prepared before she read their texts. Mrs Newton was already familiar with Geoffrey's thesis; here it was set out again—the advantage for the girls of the large house and garden, and the benefit to his mother who would be among her family when she grew old, and possibly frail.

I may grow frail, thought Mrs Newton angrily, but not yet: not for a long time, if I'm lucky. She was only sixty-nine; Winston Churchill, at much her age, embarked upon his finest hour. Dismissing older people, with their life experience, simply because they had passed a certain birthday was humiliating. Once, age had commanded respect; now it was deemed nothing but a liability.

Both her children had used their firms' writing paper. That was hidden theft, she thought, but perhaps they saw it as a perquisite. Jennifer's letter, which was typed, stated frankly what she wanted. Buying Daniel out seemed to her to be the only solution to a difficult situation. She felt sure he would, before long, realise his mistake and come back to her and then the loan—that was what she asked for, not, like Geoffrey, a gift—could be repaid. If her mother found the interest on a bank loan hard to meet, Jennifer would do her best to pay it. Meanwhile she would seek a lodger, a non-smoking professional woman, not too young, and that would help the cost.

Jennifer, at least, was honest, and to whom else should she appeal but to her mother? There was sense in what she said, and no spurious sentimental undertone. Mrs Newton decided that she would think the matter over and would telephone Mr Booth in Bournemouth for advice.

Was Jennifer justified in thinking this was just a fleeting fancy on Daniel's part? Or could she not bring herself to confront the truth?

Sex, thought Mrs Newton wearily. She never uttered the word aloud and seldom let it enter her thoughts. It had so much to answer for, not least responsibility for every individual's existence. It had drawn Daniel and Jennifer together in the first place and, no doubt, it was what had now caused their separation. Sex had similarly brought about Lynn and Geoffrey's marriage, though ambition on Lynn's part had contributed to her selection of him as a husband; she had seen that he was malleable. Mrs Newton had never warmed to her, though the girl was pretty enough and certainly extremely capable. What if they moved and then she tired of Geoffrey? Would her increased status satisfy her? There was no such guarantee.

Mrs Newton had spent the previous Christmas in their house. The year before, she had contrived a diplomatic cold at the last minute and stayed at home, free to accept the Blaneys' invitation to share their small turkey. Lynn had persuaded her to stay in bed for breakfast for the three days of her visit, and she had known this meant her presence was not required until midday. She had taken her portable radio and *Great Expectations*, a book she re-read frequently. There had been a drinks party one day, and she had seen Lynn radiating charm. Standing in a corner, where she could watch unnoticed, Mrs Newton had begun to recognise that much of this charm was directed at one of the male guests, a big dark man with a bushy moustache. Who he was or what he did was not revealed to Mrs Newton, but beside him Geoffrey looked a poor, pale wraith. A break-up there was not impossible.

Geoffrey's plea would receive a dusty answer, but Jennifer might receive some short-term help if it could be given without in any way endangering Mrs Newton's own autonomy.

8

Mavis Smith enjoyed looking after her grandson. It reminded her of earlier years when her own children were small and all their problems were to scale. Mrs Moffat made no objections to her bringing him with her when she came to clean at The Old Vicarage, though her other employers said that this would be less satisfactory when he became mobile. Mavis had decided to face that difficulty when the time came.

Lucy Moffat spent most of the three hours of Mavis's presence in the house upstairs in the room where she made jewellery. Mavis never cleaned in there but she liked looking at the equipment Lucy used, and the results. There was a workbench with a semicircular space scooped out in front and a piece of canvas underneath which caught filings and anything else dropped during construction. She had various tools: files and a tiny saw, and pliers, as well as a small soldering torch worked by blowing down it. Some of the things she did were very complicated; Mavis wondered how she had the patience. She made silver articles, and big metal brooches, dangly earrings, belt buckles, bracelets, necklaces. They were expensive, though; Mavis had asked her the price of a pair of gold earrings shaped like leaves; she'd have liked to give them to Roseanne for her birthday, but they were too dear.

It had been a blow when Jason's father dumped Roseanne, but better then than later had been Mavis's reaction, and there had never been any question of not having the baby or of giving him up for adoption; this was a time for the family to stick together and after all, he was her grandson. He was no trouble. There was always someone to look after him. Luckily Neil never wanted to go out at night so she could do her evening shifts at The Bell and go to Bingo, and Roseanne had steady work at The Bell where the fact that she could often do an extra spell if someone was ill was useful. Mavis had been able to get her the job there in the first place, and hoped she would better herself, rising in the hierarchy; she was capable enough, but perhaps a poor judge of men, a common enough failing if you looked about you, but then men were sometimes losers too. Apart from this hope for Roseanne's future, Mavis did not look far ahead; the next weekend was about as much as she could anticipate or plan for.

Pushing Jason around town to her jobs, or shopping on the way home, she remembered how she had taken her own children out in the same way. Kevin had been bold and confident, but Neil was always timid. He was saved from bullying at school by Kevin, and had bad patches when Kevin moved on and he had to fend for himself. But he grew tall, and that helped. She wished he would find a girl friend; that would bring him out of his shell; but he didn't seem interested. Kevin, however, had a new girl every few weeks; she seldom met them and if he brought them home it was not to meet the family. He spent most of his evenings in pubs, she knew, playing pool and drinking and that worried her; it had been the undoing of his father—that, and women.

Sometimes Mavis felt exhausted. It seemed to her that she had been struggling all her life. She wished just one of her children would marry well and wisely so that some security could be introduced into the family but at the moment it seemed unlikely, unless Roseanne managed it. People spoke of children following the examples of their parents, happy marriages providing good role models, broken ones leading to more. Mavis had read these theories in magazines Roseanne brought home from The Bell when they had been discarded as too tattered for the guests. They depressed her. She no longer believed in romance; a good provider was the best that a woman could hope for, and an absence of hassle. She had not always felt that way; when she walked up the aisle of St Swithun's church in Wintlebury twenty-four years ago, she was only eighteen. She had had one wonderful day of glamour when she looked like a princess in her white dress; all her friends expected that; what followed was pregnancy, sleepless nights, and metamorphosis from a slim pretty girl into a plump, coarse-featured woman struggling to hold things together. She was younger than Lucy Moffat, but no observer would have thought so.

The first years hadn't been all bad, though Ron had had no money sense and spent too much on drink, so that they were constantly in debt. When she challenged him about seeing other women he grew violent. In a way it was a relief when he went off; then she knew what her problems were, and that she had no one to depend on but herself. She wanted better for Jason, though; she wanted Roseanne to become a receptionist so that she could more easily meet the business men who came to conferences at The Bell.

Working in other people's houses brought surprises. With help hard to find, Mavis could pick and choose and went to nice places, but you could not tell, from outside, what lay within. She had been confronted with three days' washing-up piled in and around a filthy sink; she had met rooms that had not been cleaned for months, heaps of dirty clothes left lying about, lavatories that stank. She got satisfaction from sorting out dirt and chaos, but three times, after achieving a total spring clean in such houses, had been told she was no longer wanted. Now she was cautious, and if any job came to an end, never took on a new one without a prior inspection.

She liked Lucy Moffat, and the doctor was a lamb, almost restoring Mavis's shaky confidence in the male sex. He grew vegetables and often gave her some, a great help with the budget. He was a scientific doctor of some sort, working in a laboratory in Crimpford. Mavis seldom saw the son and daughter, who were both at university. She felt no envy of Lucy's easier life; she appreciated being part of it and enjoyed the chats they had over coffee in the mornings. Sometimes she had the feeling that Lucy was rather lonely, spending so much time in her workroom on her own, with the children both away and the doctor often working late or at meetings, even conferences abroad. Mavis liked having people round her, and almost never was alone.

Lucy felt very secure in her solid old house with its draughty corners, its Aga cooker, its quiet position in the road which ended at the church, and she knew that she was lucky to be living there. Beyond were water-meadows, flooded in the winter, with willows bending over the brook which flowed through them. Bell-ringing practice at St Swithun's was the one thing that disturbed her; she liked the peal of the eight bells marking a wedding or a normal service; she respected the tolling of the passing bell at funerals; what she did not enjoy, being so close to it, was the three hours or more of a campanological occasion, when complicated and sometimes discordant changes were rung. The noise literally hurt her ears and she had to stay indoors with the windows closed, playing music. Simon could not understand the fuss she made; he liked the clangour. It was just as well, thought Lucy, since he was the chief gardener.

After her visit to Mrs Newton, Lucy had spent a short time thinking about her, but when she reached home she put the old woman from her mind. The flowers had been an inspiration; adequate thanks had now been rendered and the incident could be forgotten.

Mrs Newton, on the other hand, often thought of Lucy, whom she had found so pleasant and stimulating. She was very different from Jennifer, with her quick, prickly temper. What if she had had a daughter more like Lucy? Mrs Newton, shocked at this disloyalty, sighed. Mr Booth had not been pleased at the prospect of Mrs Newton financing such a large loan for her daughter. She had so little capital and was dependent upon it and her pension for her standard of living; suppose an emergency arose when she might need the money herself? He was concerned that Mrs Newton's later years should be passed in comfort. Yet again, Mrs Newton wished that Jennifer had followed a more conventional path, married a rising man and anchored herself to safety with some children. Although marriages often broke up these days, the law protected mothers and children and they did not starve.

Meanwhile, work continued on the house next door and she became more aware of the young man, Neil. He had taken to waving to her when he saw her. She began waving back, a stiff acknowledgement not unlike the gracious salute of royalty. Hitherto, she had not picked out the individual workmen on the site, but now she saw that there was an older man, thickset with greying hair, and two others, probably in their early thirties, one of them blond, already going bald, the other with a mop of thick brown hair. The older man was not always there; he must be the boss, she thought, L. Harding, whose name was painted on the vans.

Then came a night of strong gales which caused a lot of damage in the area. This was not a hurricane like those which had devastated part of the country not so long ago, but the winds were strong enough to bring down boughs from several trees in the district, and part of the fencing separating Mrs Newton from what had been the Blaneys' garden collapsed. In the morning, Mrs Newton could look beyond her lilac and her flowering cherry to the trampled patch that had once been Mr Blaney's pride. Why had the men made such a mess of it? They'd dragged equipment over it and stored materials there and in the garage. Four men tramping round for several months meant quite a lot of traffic.

She put on a coat and went out to inspect the damage. Three fencing panels had been torn away from their posts. Two leaned, partly supported by the neighbouring syringa and the spreading Nevada rose; the third lay flat, prone on the spot where lilies of the valley bloomed each May. Mrs Newton frowned. This had never happened before, even in worse gales.

As she stood there, someone approached. It was Neil.

"The wind must have come gusting round where we pulled that old shed down to make the new kitchen," he said. "It doesn't half whistle down this drive. Makes a lot of dust."

Mrs Newton was aware that the fence was her responsibility. It was hardly likely that L. Harding would decide to put it up again simply because he happened to be working on its other side. Besides, she could see that two at least of the hurdles would have to be replaced, and probably the posts; it wasn't just a simple repair job, and until it was done she was exposed to any passing prying eyes—true, at the moment only those of the workmen, but she did not like the feeling.

"I'll fix it for you," offered Neil. "It's Friday today. I could do it tomorrow—get the new fencing and that. You'll need two panels. That third one looks all right." He rocked the posts. "There's your trouble," he diagnosed. "They've gone rotten at the base. That means four new posts and they'd better be sunk in concrete."

"Wait a minute, Neil," said Mrs Newton. He was rushing her. "I'm not sure—" she hesitated, thinking hard. Who should she get to do this for her? The builder she had employed when she moved in? A fencing contractor found in the Yellow Pages? Here was a youth working for what seemed to be a reputable firm offering to do it for her almost at once.

"I'll get the posts and everything," said Neil, and added, "I'll get proper receipts for all the materials and you can repay me, and I'll charge forty pounds a day, and in proportion if I have to finish off on Sunday.''

Mrs Newton felt ashamed of her suspicious doubts. After all, if Neil cheated her in any way or did bad work, she knew where to get hold of him, and L. Harding would help her deal with him. He was no itinerant cowboy; indeed, rather the reverse.

"Very well," she said. "I'll expect to see you in the morning."

"I'll get the posts and panels on the way," said Neil, beaming. "I'll match them to what you've got. Will that be all right?"

"Yes," she said, and, cautiously, she smiled too, but Neil, intent on his future task, did not notice.

"Bye, then," he said. "I've got to get back now," and he left.

Mrs Newton returned to the house. She supposed he could do the work alone; he was probably stronger than he looked. It was enterprising of him to have volunteered so promptly but then he had already expressed a wish to work for her.

Neil was delighted with his deal. He doubted if he would complete the job in a single day, but he would do it properly, and she would pay in cash, which would help his car fund. He'd see inside her house as well, with luck. She was the sort who would offer a cup of tea. He longed to experience for just a few minutes the comforts of a home so unlike his own. He'd told Kevin about her; one old woman living in a place three or four times the size of theirs. At this stage, Neil was only curious; Kevin, however, was already interested.

9

I'll give you a hand if you like," offered Kevin, hearing about Neil's arrangement with Mrs Newton.

Neil had got up early that Saturday morning. Most weekends, with nothing special to do, he and Kevin slept in, Neil for an extra hour, Kevin sometimes for longer. Roseanne went to work on some weekends but whatever her schedule, Mavis would pluck Jason from his cot, dress him, give him his breakfast, load up the washing machine which went on every day. Then she would put him in the pushchair and set off with him to do the weekend shopping.

Kevin had woken when he heard Neil moving around, and grunted complainingly about the noise.

"You'll not manage on your own," he said now. "Them hurdles is awkward."

"I know," said Neil, his own doubts reinforced, but he was tall, his reach was wide, and he was determined to succeed. "But she's only expecting me," he added. "I only quoted one man's pay."

"Oh, that's all right," said Kevin. "You can do me a good turn another time. Come and pick me up after you've got the stuff. Then I can get my head down for another hour."

He settled back under his black and purple duvet cover, bought by mail order, while Neil got dressed and shaved. He didn't always shave at weekends, but he sensed that Mrs Newton knew nothing about designer stubble and would not approve.

Kevin was ready when he returned from the timber yard with the new hurdles and posts in his van. He had bought cement and sand, and nails, and before leaving work the night before had borrowed a few tools from the site.

Mrs Newton was surprised when Neil arrived with a larger, older man who he said was his brother, but she was also relieved. Kevin looked more capable than Neil, and he had a confident, almost brash manner: too confident, too brash, she decided. He looked vaguely familiar; she felt that they had met before.

Kevin took scant notice of her. She was old; she did not interest him, but her house might contain items that friends of his would like to hear about.

"Let's have a look at it, then, kid," he said to Neil, striding off down the garden with Neil padding along behind. Kevin walked right across a rose bed, making a footprint in the soil.

"Please keep to the path," said Mrs Newton. She had on her gardening slacks and padded poplin jacket; a tweed hat was pulled over her pale hair and she wore heavy gardening gloves.

Kevin took no notice. He surveyed the damage and, single-handed, as if it were no heavier than a sheet of cardboard, he lifted up one of the damaged hurdles and laid it on Mrs Newton's lawn.

"We'll soon have this done for you, dear," he told her.

Mrs Newton frowned.

"My name is Mrs Newton," she said sternly. Time was when a workman would have addressed her as "madam." She did not expect that now, but she resented Kevin's familiarity.

"Sorry, I'm sure," said Kevin, but he scowled as he walked back to the van with Neil to unload their cargo.

"Stuck up, isn't she?" he said.

"Not really," said Neil. "Thinks you're cheeky, that's all, and she's right."

"Bet she's got some nice bits and pieces in the house," said Kevin. "We might get a look at them later when she asks us in for coffee."

"She won't do that," said Neil, who thought Kevin had now ditched their chances of receiving such an invitation.

"What d'you bet?" asked Kevin.

But Neil was no gambler, which was a pity, as he would have won this time. After they had been working for an hour or more, Mrs Newton brought them a tray with two large mugs of coffee, well sweetened, and some digestive biscuits on a plate.

"We'll soon be done, Mrs Newton," said Kevin, stressing her name in the tone which Neil recognised as the one used when trying to provoke a quarrel with Roseanne, which was one of his amusements.

"Good," was her curt reply.

While they worked, she kept an eye on them, at the same time sweeping up leaves blown down in the gale that had damaged the fence. The wind had died down now and she had a small, well-controlled bonfire burning at the further end of the garden. Kevin seized his chance, when her back was turned to the house and Neil was busy mixing his cement, to walk past the french window as if returning to the van. He gazed in and saw pictures on the pale walls and china ornaments in a recess. Those things weren't in his line but there was always someone who would handle them. There was sure to be a television and a radio, maybe a microwave, and jewellery. Two weeks ago, Kevin had lost his latest job and until he found another one, his sideline had become important, especially as he did not want his mother to discover he was out of work. He had made a nice corner in stealing things from the works and passing them on to a man who had an outlet for electrical goods. Now he must obtain his contraband elsewhere.

The old lady posed no threat. She was small. He'd be masked, if she did happen to see him.

Mrs Newton, indeed! She was bloody lucky to have the pair of them here, doing this job for her for peanuts. Neil could have taken her for twice as much; she'd have known no different. Old biddies like her weren't worth a second thought.

They finished the job that afternoon, and without comment she paid them each thirty pounds in cash. That showed that she kept money in the house, which was worth knowing. She wrote Neil a cheque for the materials. Kevin had made some alterations to the receipt before Neil handed it over, changing a three to an eight, a one to a nine, and a few other minor adjustments, taking time to add it up so that it tallied with the new total. She was just the sort of old witch to check up.

She was; she did; but she thought the scribbly figures simply those of your typical modern sales assistant.

Neil was shocked by this deception, but on reflection, and after discussion, decided it was just for, after all, she should really have paid them eighty pounds: two men for a day, even though they put in only five hours each, which included an hour's break for lunch at The Prince Hal along the road. Kevin's help had made a lot of difference to the job; he was so strong.

"I always look out for you, kid, don't I?" Kevin said.

So far in their lives, that had been true, thought Neil, meekly handing over the profits on the materials, which Kevin seemed to expect as well as his thirty pounds.

He paid the cheque into his Savings Bank account.

Jennifer was impatient to hear from her mother about the loan. She had expected an instant telephone call in response to her letter, or at least a reply by return of post, but so far there was silence, and she felt slightly ashamed of her request. After all, her mother had not had an easy life, bringing the two of them up on her own. Sometimes Jennifer blamed her mother for her father's early death; if she had taken better care of him, the heart condition which had killed him might not have developed.

This was unfair, and at bottom, Jennifer knew it. Her father had been a calm man; just to be with him had made her feel safe. He had not been stressed at home, whatever things may have been like at the office; he seldom returned late, and if he brought work back with him, did not treat it as urgent. Their diet was, she had to acknowledge, healthy enough even by modern standards, and he took regular exercise, rarely missing his weekend golf. In fact he had died in a bunker at the seventeenth hole, after hitting a spectacular extricating shot.

Her mother had laughed hysterically on hearing this. It was the only time in her life that Jennifer had ever seen her lose control, and even then, it had swiftly been regained. Jennifer could not see what was funny about it to this day, and she could not understand her mother's reaction. She had never yet, in her life, seen her mother shed a tear. Perhaps she had no feelings. Perhaps that was what had killed her father: the want of love.

Jennifer thought that her own life would have been very different if her father had lived. For one thing, they would have remained in the Bournemouth house instead of doing all this moving around, and he would have been there when she needed him. She knew that he had loved her. Perhaps no one else had ever done so; perhaps no one ever would. Such thoughts were terrifying. There were doomed people and maybe she was one of them. Ill luck had brought Stephanie into Daniel's life and taken him from hers. She refused to remember the quarrels they had had, the arguments which Daniel would never allow to develop into real rows. He walked away from them, wishing them over; it was like trying to fight with a blancmange. But they had always ended in rapturous reconciliations. Jennifer thought that love between the sexes had to be like this, a roller-coaster of emotion; she had no conception of the tender passion which Daniel now enjoyed with Stephanie, his sense of having come into a calm harbour.

Mrs Newton had written to Geoffrey. She said that she had not changed her mind since they had last discussed his idea. She spelled out her reasons clearly, expecting the letter to be shown to Lynn, mentioning that she intended to maintain her independence until or unless it became physically impossible for her to do so, which, because she was fortunate enough to enjoy good health, was unlikely to be for some considerable time. When that day arrived, she wished to have enough funds at her disposal to keep her in comfortable retirement accommodation where she would have the privacy which had been important to her all her life. She felt sure his career would prosper once the present recession ended, and then he would be able to move without recourse to her, though she could not see what was wrong with the agreeable and spacious house where he had lived for the past twelve years.

Lynn would not be pleased with this response. Who could have foreseen Lynn's greed, her grasping ambition, in the fair, pretty girl Geoffrey had brought to meet her so many years ago? Behind that fragile appearance there lurked a selfish will of steel, soon revealed; yet without that force behind him, would Geoffrey have done as well as he had?

Maybe not, his mother thought, but he might have been a happier and more pleasant person. He had become so pompous, even boring, and he was at least a stone overweight. To escape from this depressing reflection, Mrs Newton cast her mind back to her children's infancy, their days spent sleeping peacefully in the big pram under a shady tree in the garden. She recalled the walks they took, how she had enjoyed watching them as she pushed the pram, seeing their early smiles, their interests develop beyond the confines of their immediate world. She had blossomed, then, herself, able to put behind her all past anguish, almost forget the horrors which still returned to her in dreams. In those days, Geoffrey, sitting in his pram, would laugh and gurgle; she had photographs to prove it. Later, when he was a toddler, she had taken him out in a folding pram with a drop end while Jennifer slept in the garden under the eye of Mrs Davis, who came every day. There had been communication, then, between her and the children.

Geoffrey and Jennifer had had happy early years. There was security, there was kindness, and there was space, all often absent nowadays, yet neither of them was happy now. Mrs Newton knew that you could recover from a terrible catastrophe, could later live contentedly, as she had done; but she had been very lucky, for she had met Frederick at a crucial period in her life. She had recently moved to Bournemouth because it was a long way from everyone she knew; she had gone to work in his office as a temporary secretary and, in an effort to make some sort of social life for herself, had joined the local tennis club. He was a member, too. When he seemed to like her, she had withdrawn and had changed her job, but he had gently pursued her and, in the end, had persuaded her to marry him. Their partnership had worked, and would have gone on working, had it not been so suddenly cut short. She had felt real grief then, and panic, though she had tried to hide both from the children. In those days people kept their feelings to themselves; now they were encouraged to parade them publicly.

After adding a few remarks in her letter to Geoffrey, telling him that strong winds had blown down her fence but that it had already been repaired, she signed off, *Your affectionate Mother*, as her own mother, until her death in an air raid during the war, had done to her.

Then she settled down to answer Jennifer.

She did not immediately dismiss the possibility of providing the money, but Mr Booth's advice had been that Jennifer should sell the house for what she could get and cut her losses. She earned a good salary and should be able, with what was rescued, to house herself again quite adequately, though more

modestly and in a less expensive area. She invited Jennifer
to come for a weekend as soon as she could, to talk things
over.

How did Jennifer spend her weekends now? Was she using
them constructively or brooding about her situation? Her apparent composure when they met for lunch could have been
spurious. Pride enabled one to act defiantly. Mrs Newton, if
invited, would have liked to spend a weekend in London
while Jennifer still had the house and with it space for her to
stay. They could dine out, go to the theatre together in the
evening; it would be a treat, a return to the times before
Daniel when Mrs Newton would sometimes stay in a hotel,
since Jennifer's flatlet was too small for her to put up there,
and meet her daughter for an evening out.

Of course your children drifted away from you; it was only
right; yet you could be friends. Mrs Newton was not sure if
she was friends with either of hers. Did they even like her,
or she them? Liking was not synonymous with love, though,
and anyway how did one analyse that difficult word? Love
could mean possession, obsession, sacrifice. Sometimes Mrs
Newton thought it was a myth, dependent on conditioning.

She ended her letter and went up the road to post it. Coming
back, she saw Neil on a ladder doing something to a window
on the Blaneys' house, as she still thought of it. Soon the
builders would be gone. Things would change.

Jennifer was still trailing Stephanie, who, wherever she went
seemed to see the other woman, her dark frizzed hair confined
under a knitted cap, dressed always in black, often in a cape
but sometimes with a reefer jacket on over black slacks.

I'm getting paranoiac, thought Stephanie, after she thought
she saw Jennifer enter the tube station ahead of her and then
hang back, so that she stood above her on the escalator.
Descending, Stephanie glanced over her shoulder and saw
Jennifer walking down beside the stationary passengers towards her, glaring at her, hatred in her face.

She was coming for her. She was going to push her, cause

a domino collapse of people on the staircase. Stephanie summoned her paralysed limbs together and began walking down too, going as fast as she dared, hurrying on towards her platform, where she stood well back before the train arrived, then huddled in a mass of people, refusing to look up in case she saw the proof of what she feared: Jennifer waiting to push her on the line.

I'm being ridiculous, she thought, but even so she began to note in her pocket diary the dates on which she thought she saw Jennifer, and where. Sometimes she was outside the office when Stephanie emerged; sometimes she left the tube behind her and walked down the long dark street towards the flat in silent pursuit. Her presence on the tube at the start of the journey could be expected, but she should get off first. There was no rational explanation for the haunting in the street. What was in Jennifer's mind?

Stephanie did not speak of it again to Daniel. She must deal with it on her own. Perhaps it all boiled down to money: Daniel was pressing Jennifer to release his capital; take away that pressure and the harassment might cease. The next time that she was certain Jennifer was following her home, Stephanie turned, choosing her moment when she had just passed a street light, then spinning round and walking back towards the other woman. Jennifer stopped abruptly, then continued on towards Stephanie, who had a small can of hair spray in her pocket, defence against muggers and admissible in law because it was for personal use and not a weapon. She reminded herself that she was bigger and heavier than Jennifer, at least ten years younger, and probably as fit, if not fitter.

"Why are you following me, Jennifer?" she demanded. Her hand closed round the tin, its smooth coolness helping her remain calm.

Jennifer's immediate impulse had been to flee; she had not realised that Stephanie had noticed her. She decided, however, to stand her ground. This was a public thoroughfare and she had as much right as Stephanie to be there.

She said so.

"But you don't live here. What are you doing? You've been following me for days," said Stephanie.

"You flatter yourself," said Jennifer. "But then you would, wouldn't you?" Suddenly what little self-control she had slipped, and her words tumbled out. "Daddy's little pet—always getting what you want. But he'll come back to me, you'll see. He'll get sick of you. You're just a child. He needs a real woman, someone mature. He'll dump you just as he thinks he's dumped me. He needs me, and he knows it."

Stephanie clutched her tin, her finger over the button. Jennifer was staring at her, her face white under the knitted border of her woollen hat which was pulled down to meet her strong dark brows. Big black hollows pitted her face under her eyes. She looked ghastly. Stephanie took a deep breath as pity for her replaced fear. She released the tin and took her hand from her pocket.

"We can't argue in the street," she said. "Won't you come in and have a proper talk?"

"I'm not arguing," said Jennifer. "I'm telling you what will happen. And I don't want to see your filthy love-nest."

"It isn't—" Stephanie began, then stopped. If Jennifer had made up her mind that she and Daniel were living together in the flat, nothing would dissuade her unless her flatmates were at home, and tonight they were not; one, who played the flute in an orchestra, would be on her way to a concert and the other, who worked for a publisher, was away at a sales conference. And tonight Daniel was playing squash; they had no plan to meet. "Please leave me alone," she said. "Can't you let Daniel be happy even if you can't be happy yourself?"

"Who says I'm not happy?" demanded Jennifer.

"Look at you," said Stephanie. "Anyone can see you're miserable. Haven't you got anyone to help you? Friends? Your mother?" There was a mother, somewhere in the country; Daniel had mentioned her.

"Mind your own business," Jennifer cried, almost shouting.

"If it's the money, forget it," said Stephanie in desperation. "We'll manage."

"Hah! Will you? Will you keep him, then?" Jennifer uttered a wild laugh which made Stephanie's flesh creep. "Perhaps your Daddy will help you. No, he'll come crawling back to me, you'll see. Just you wait," and she waved a black-gloved hand in the air. For a moment Stephanie thought that Jennifer would strike her; the suppressed violence emanating from her was almost tangible and so raw that it was terrifying.

Stephanie could bear it no longer.

"I pity you," she said, and trying not to break into a run, turned and walked away towards her flat as fast as she could go. Her key was in her pocket, with the tin of spray, and her hand shook as she took it out and tried to fit it in the lock. At last she succeeded in opening the door and almost fell into the safety of the hallway where she stood, gasping and trembling, for some seconds before she was able to go upstairs to the flat.

Jennifer, across the road, saw the upstairs light come on.

So it was the top flat, was it?

Next time it would be a stone, and she would take careful aim.

10

When she received her mother's letter, Jennifer was angry. Surely you should be able to depend on your own mother to help you? It wasn't as though her mother was hard up, and she had good security against which to raise a loan. Of course, probably not all Daddy's investments—there hadn't been a lot, she knew—had prospered and the widow's pension from his insurance might not be much, but she had her state pension, surely? It wasn't as if Jennifer had asked for an outright gift; she had only wanted to borrow the money; and in any case, what difference did that make? In the end, handing it over now could save death duties.

Jennifer had been churning all this over during the day before her meeting with Stephanie. Afterwards she alternated between bitter moods of hatred for the other girl and rage against her mother, whom by now she blamed not only for her father's untimely death but for all her own mistakes, and her brother's. Anyone could see that his marriage was a disaster. Jennifer had stayed, with her mother, at Geoffrey and Lynn's house for Christmas several times but for the past three years she had gone skiing with Daniel; it had been a way to evade the annual charade of family peace and accord. What would happen this year?

She pushed the thought from her mind. Daniel would be back by then.

Unable to sleep, unable to concentrate on her work, she planned to go down to Yew Cottage and force her mother to provide the money, make her sit up all night if necessary while she persuaded her. She mentally ran over all the items in the house that could be of value: there was the big desk that had been her father's; if it were sold it might raise the greater part of what she needed. None of the paintings was likely to be worth a lot but some of the china figures could be special; Jennifer did not know much about ceramics but her mother did and might have had a reason for collecting them. She'd bought them in the brief years of her marriage, Jennifer had understood, and had not added to them since that time. There was silver, too, and there were a few pieces of jewellery. Her mother would be moving as soon as the market picked up; she'd have to sort things out then. If she were to move north this time, even to Scotland, where property was cheaper, she could release capital and hand it over. It would be her last move before she was ready for some sort of twilight home and if that was a long way away, so much the better; then Jennifer could not visit her too frequently.

Her thoughts ran riot, uncontrollable, devising plans and theories, appointing blame for all the disappointments of her life and Geoffrey's; her moods ranged from rage to utter despair. Her work was already suffering, for with exhaustion she had lost the power to switch her mind away from her obsession. Small errors had begun to appear in accounts she handled; then she debited one client for a deal conducted for another, and put through a sale of stock in thousands where it should have been only hundreds. Because her record hitherto was good, she was forgiven; the errors were due to carelessness, not anything dishonest, and could be put right without too many complications. It was suggested that she was tired and might like a few days off. Jennifer refused: without the framework of hours spent in the office, she felt her life would disintegrate.

It was all Stephanie's fault. She was to blame for everything.

Rest was impossible. Food was forgotten. She paced the flat, turned the television on, then off again. At last she sat down long enough to write a letter to her mother, mentioning that *Daddy would have helped me. You've no need to live as you do*, she went on. *You could have a much smaller house in a cheaper area*, and more in that vein. She addressed and stamped the letter and, because she was still far too upset to sleep, decided to go out and post it.

There was a letter box two hundred yards down the road. Jennifer dropped the envelope into it and then, instead of turning back, walked on, scarcely aware of her route, going southwards across London down streets that were deserted, crossing the river, striding on in her black tracksuit under her jacket, her hair uncovered, damp in the cold night and frizzing out around her head. Walking past a building where construction work was being done, she saw a skip, with old bricks and stones stacked high amid the rubble filling it. She reached in and took out a brick. It was heavy—too heavy to throw very far. She put it back and tested several stones, choosing one about the weight of a cricket ball. It had a pleasantly jagged edge, and she hugged it to her, holding it against her body almost in a caress.

By no rational process, she arrived again at Stephanie's flat. It was very late and the house was in darkness. Jennifer rang both the doorbells, pealing them, hearing their shrill sound inside the house. She had passed beyond all caution now. Words she had never used before flowed from her as she cursed Stephanie. Then, as lights came on in the house, she stepped backwards far enough to take aim and throw the stone at Stephanie's window. There was a satisfactory shattering crash as it hit its target and went through. She thought she heard a scream.

She ran off then, up the road, and out of luck. Her dark fleeing figure, crossing the street to take a side turning, raced in front of a cruising police car. Since she was acting in a suspicious manner the officers in the car turned round and went after her. At once, she turned back the way she had come and one of the policemen leaped out of the car to pursue her.

He was bigger and stronger, and he caught her.

By this time she was crying and unable to explain what had been happening, and at first the two policemen thought she was the victim of an attack. They were sitting with her in their car, trying to calm her down, when a radio message came through reporting that a stone had been thrown through a window in the next road.

Stephanie was sure she knew who the culprit was and had not wanted to call the police, but Julian from the flat below insisted, while David, his flatmate, who had looked out of the window when Jennifer began cursing, pulled on some clothes and went after the fleeing figure, though he was not quick enough to catch her.

He identified her by her clothes and the frizz of her hair when the police car drew up at the flat. She was insisting that she knew nothing about the incident and had been out jogging.

The stone was found in Stephanie's room. Jennifer wore no gloves, but the surface would not yield prints; it was, however, carefully placed in a polythene bag for it was evidence.

Stephanie, in a pink woollen dressing gown, stared at Jennifer as she stood between the two policemen, having been cautioned.

"I don't want to press charges," she said.

She would have a pink dressing gown, thought Jennifer; she probably had a teddy bear as well.

"Well, now, Miss—" began one of the policemen. They did not yet know Jennifer's name.

"She's ill. It's not her fault," insisted Stephanie.

"So you know each other, do you?" asked the second policeman.

"Slightly," said Stephanie, cautious now.

"Well, I'm sorry, but this isn't your decision," said the officer. "Throwing stones at windows is a police matter."

"What will she be charged with?" Stephanie asked.

"If she's charged, it will be criminal damage," said the officer.

So there was a chance that she would be let off. Stephanie watched as Jennifer was taken away by a policewoman who arrived in a second car, with a male officer at the wheel, while the first two policemen took statements from her and from Julian and David. Again Stephanie insisted that Jennifer should not be charged, that she was under strain and needed medical attention, but Julian and David took a more robust stance. They had heard some of her curses: she might be off her head, as Stephanie implied, but she was dangerous and might do something worse next time. Julian told the police that she had used lurid language, and David supplied the words. That, said one of the officers, amounted to an offence in itself.

Stephanie asked where Jennifer had been taken, and as soon as the police had gone she rang up Daniel and told him what had happened.

"You must go and help her, Daniel," she said. "I explained that she isn't well and I didn't want her arrested but it made no difference. They'll be locking her in a cell."

"Oh God!" said Daniel. It was half-past two in the morning and he had been deeply asleep when Stephanie rang. His host had been none too pleased at being woken up and having to crawl out of bed to go downstairs and tell Daniel that the call was for him.

"Your Stephanie," he had said. "She's desperate," and he made a lewd remark.

Daniel said he would come round to Stephanie's flat at

once to hear full details of what had happened. "Then we'll see what can be done," he said.

He arrived less than fifteen minutes later to find Stephanie downstairs with Julian and David, who both worked in television on the production side; she was drinking Horlicks laced with brandy. They had lit their coal-effect gas fire and were all toasting themselves in front of it. Stephanie seemed outwardly calm but her face was pale.

The two men said that she could not sleep in the room with the shattered window, and had offered her their sofa for the night, but Stephanie said she would use one of the other girls' rooms. The musician had not come home after her concert and it could be assumed that she was staying with her boyfriend, who played in the same orchestra; the other girl would definitely be away until the weekend.

"The police will prosecute your pal," Julian told her. "She's a menace. Hell hath no fury, and all that."

Stephanie saw that she must tell Daniel the whole story.

"You know I thought that she was following me," she said. "I was right. Earlier tonight I tackled her about it—she'd followed me all the way home from the office." There was no need to repeat what Jennifer had said. "She's very upset about your breaking up," she added. "I thought you said she took it well."

"I thought she had, apart from the financial side of things," said Daniel.

"I suppose she's got her pride," said Stephanie. "She didn't want you to see how upset she was." How could he have been so dense, when he had known Jennifer for so long? It was obvious that she was, at the very least, extremely overwrought. "She needs a doctor, Dan. You must go to the police station and see what you can do to help her."

"Yes. At least I can find her a lawyer," said Daniel. His present host was one. "Steph, you might have been hurt. That stone—if it had hit you—" Or if Jennifer had been directly violent, he thought. He knew she had the potential;

he remembered her feverish passion, her scratching nails, her
bites, her screams. At first he had found that exciting, and
there were long intervals when she was meek and fearful,
needing reassurance: those were the good moments when he
had the power to calm her. As time went on, they had occurred
less often; the termagant—now, in his thoughts, for the first
time he used that word regarding her—had been the person
he was living with, and he had grown weary of her, understanding what a trap he was in only when he met Stephanie.
"I'll come back," he promised. "Try to get some sleep,
though. I might be some time."

He saw her into Annabel's bed, tucking her up with a hot-
water bottle supplied by Julian, then left.

When he reached the police station, Daniel was not allowed
to see Jennifer, nor was he assured that a message telling her
he was there would reach her. He began to fear that she would
be put in a cell for the rest of the night—maybe for much
longer. Unclear about what the law permitted, he had visions
of her being incarcerated indefinitely. One thing he was,
however, certain about was that she was entitled to a solicitor
to guard her interests.

He rang William, whose house he had left some time earlier.

William was distinctly disgruntled at being disturbed yet
again; when taking Daniel in, he had not expected to take on
all his troubles, too. He had not acted for Daniel over his
house purchase and was intent on keeping out of any squab-
bles over its division. He saw no reason, now, why Jennifer
should not stay where she was until the morning.

"She did it, didn't she?" he asked.

"I think so," answered Daniel cautiously. He was using
the telephone in the police station and did not want Jennifer
convicted on hearsay.

"Hm," said William. "*Crime passionel*, eh?" He felt a
flicker of interest. Some of his clients were credit defaulters,

even shoplifters, but most of his work was simple conveyancing, wills, and trusts.

"It's no joke," said Daniel crossly. "Stephanie could have been badly hurt."

"I'll come over," William decided, since now he was sure sheer curiosity, not to mention disturbed metabolism, would come between him and sleep if he returned to bed. "We can try to get her bail."

Daniel had to sit on a hard chair in the front hall of the police station until William arrived. He had plenty of time to imagine Jennifer chained and manacled, though that seemed unlikely. In fact she was in an interview room with a woman officer who was coaxing her to drink some tea and explain her actions.

William exchanged only a few words with Daniel before disappearing into the back regions of the police station. A long time seemed to pass before he reappeared, accompanied by a Jennifer who looked, not sheepish and ashamed, as might be expected, but defiant. Her face lit up when she saw him.

"Oh Dan," she said. "You came." She seemed about to throw herself into his arms but he drew back. The pity that had filled him, and the guilt, vanished as he recognised her elation. She had always dipped and peaked; now she was on a real high.

"Naturally," he said, but coolly. "Someone had to."

William was making frowning faces at him, implying that he should be discreet in what he said. There were formalities, he explained, adding that Daniel would stand bail for her.

"It's very good of him, Jennifer," he told her sternly.

Her conduct had amazed him. He had liked her well enough; the chemistry must have worked between her and Daniel. He had long ago given up hoping to understand what drew couples together; most people, in the end, settled for some sort of compromise with their expectations. Daniel had not indicated that she had found it difficult to accept their break-up; now it was obvious that she had been blown apart.

Daniel, though reluctant to stand surety for her, could see no option; he could not telephone her brother, and certainly not her mother, in the middle of the night and pass the buck to one of them. It was, after all, merely a formality; she wouldn't abscond, and it seemed that she must appear before the magistrates the following morning. That was only a few hours away.

At last they were free to leave, and Jennifer immediately linked her arm through Daniel's. Much as he wished to detach himself, he could not bring himself to do so under the gaze of the police officer dealing with them. The three of them walked out into the darkness.

"What now?" asked Daniel.

"Jennifer goes home, and you take her there," said William firmly, determined to return to his own bed for at least a warm snuggle against the plump body of his pregnant wife.

"Well, all right," said Daniel, with poor grace. Someone had to, obviously, and as two cars were parked outside, his and William's, both must be removed so they couldn't all three go together. As he opened the door of the Audi for Jennifer, he reflected that at least no one had let down its tyres while he was in the police station.

Jennifer had done that, he knew now with sickening certainty. She had scratched it, too, and broken the wiper blades; all the small recent acts of vandalism were hers. He did not want to understand the message this implied.

He drove her home in silence. She sat beside him, belted into the passenger seat, and he could hear her breathing; she was almost panting, as if, he thought in horror, she was in a sexually excited state. Perhaps she was: perhaps what she had done had aroused her.

With the streets deserted, the journey did not take them long, and as he stopped the car he realised that he could not simply leave her on the doorstep. In common humanity, he had to see her in.

If she had wept, been apologetic, shown any remorse, he might have felt more pity but her manner did not change.

"A drink?" she said, in the sitting-room, smiling at him brightly.

To him, it was a terrible, frightening smile, like the glare of a wild animal. Her excellent teeth gleamed in her pale face and, to him, they appeared sharp and predatory. As he knew they were.

"No," he said curtly, and added, just as he had directed Stephanie, "Try to get some sleep."

"I don't want sleep," said Jennifer. "I want you," and she moved towards him, softening now. "You came," she said.

Daniel, appalled, backed away.

"Someone had to help you," he said, and added, weakly, but in an attempt to rescue the situation, "We could have stayed friends, Jennifer, but you've gone too far this time. Stephanie might have been hurt. I know you were only trying to scare her, but it could have been serious."

"Pity it wasn't," said Jennifer.

"You don't mean that."

"I do. If it hadn't been for that milksop bitch we'd be together still," said Jennifer.

Was she right? Daniel did not want to think so.

"We'd have split up eventually," he said firmly, not totally convinced. For want of an alternative, or from inertia, he might have stayed within their partnership, might even, in the end, have drifted into the marriage which was always, as he realised now, in her mind. "You're not well," he said, more gently. "You should see a doctor."

"I need you," was Jennifer's answer. "You're my medicine."

They were both standing, and as she moved towards him again, so he backed off and they began circling the room, he in retreat, she pursuing in the parody of a dance.

"Sit down, Jennifer," he barked at her at last, and her

eyes gleamed. She was getting a reaction. She slumped backwards on the sofa, arms apart, legs spread, in invitation.

"I'll make you a hot drink," he said, turning to leave the room.

"I don't want one. I want you," said Jennifer, stretching towards him.

"You're tired. You're under strain," he said. "Forget the money." He'd let it go, if it bought her off.

"That's only incidental," Jennifer replied. "I'll forgive you, Daniel. You'll soon forget that milksop."

"Jennifer, can't you get it into your head that I love Stephanie? I'm sorry if I've hurt you, but you'll get over it and you'll meet someone else who you'll be much happier with than you were with me."

"Who says I wasn't happy?" Jennifer answered. "I was, and so were you."

There was truth in what she said. He had been content enough at first, partnered, out of the hunt; then he'd settled for avoiding quarrels, keeping the peace at almost any price. When he came home from work the last thing he wanted was a big argument, a battle. Meeting Stephanie had been the miracle, and he did not intend to lose her now.

He decided to forget about the hot drink. Let her get her own.

"I'm leaving," he said. "I'll see you in court tomorrow. Don't be late."

He'd telephone her brother. Directory Enquiries would provide the number; he knew where Geoffrey lived, had been there several times, finding Geoffrey dull but pleasant, with a restless, rather pretty wife.

He hurried from the room, closing the door behind him in case she came after him, scurrying down the stairs and out of the house as fast as he could go. He leaped into the car and drove off without a backward glance; he did not want to see her standing on the pavement if she followed him.

He went back to Stephanie's flat, letting himself in with

the key that she had given him. She was asleep and did not stir when he looked at her. He left her undisturbed in Annabel's room, and lay down in her bed in the room with the shattered window, where he began worrying that Jennifer might be slitting her wrists, swallowing pills, throwing herself out of an upstairs window. In his imagination he attended her inquest and was asked by the coroner if he had thought it prudent to abandon her when she was clearly in no fit state to be left alone.

He decided, in a mood of unusual robustness, that he must be prepared to take the consequences and the subsequent reproof and at last he dozed, fitfully, and not for long.

He rang Geoffrey at seven o'clock. While he was speaking, Stephanie came into the hallway where the telephone was. She put her arms round him from behind, leaning against him, warm and soft, so unlike hard, thin Jennifer, and held Daniel while he gave Geoffrey the bare facts and suggested that he should come to London to the magistrates' court.

"She did it. She admitted it to me, even if she didn't to the police," said Daniel. "She's been following Stephanie around, haunting her, you could say. She needs to get her act together, Geoffrey. I've told her I can wait for the money, or even do without it." He did not want to say too much in front of Stephanie about Jennifer's mental state, which last night had alarmed him.

There followed some financial discussion and the conversation ended.

"I don't think he'll come down," said Daniel. "He said he had an important meeting."

"Perhaps that's true," said Stephanie.

"Hm, well, maybe. But it's not every day your sister's up before the beak on a criminal charge," said Daniel.

"They'll let her off," said Stephanie, and thought, and then she'll do it again, or something else, till she hurts me. Kills me, even.

She shivered.

"You're cold. Why don't you go and have a bath and I'll make some coffee," Daniel said.

"All right." Stephanie kissed him lightly and went off, wondering if she should move out of the flat, for safety; but if she did, Daniel would know that Jennifer had frightened her, and that might alarm him. "Are you going to the court?" she asked.

"No," said Daniel, but he had told Jennifer that he would see her there. "No," he repeated, less certainly. "William will be there. He can see to things."

He had not told Stephanie that he had stood bail for Jennifer and with any luck she need never know.

11

But Daniel did attend the hearing, though he did not tell Stephanie that he had changed his mind.

He took her to her office, then telephoned his own, saying he would be delayed. A police matter had arisen, he said truthfully, telling himself that if he had fallen ill or had an accident, they would have to do without him. There were complaints and grumbles from the other end but it was decided that an appointment could be rearranged and various other matters deferred. After arranging all this, he went round to collect Jennifer, not trusting her to turn up on her own.

She was in the bath when he arrived. She had not yet decided whether or not to go to court. If she did not, there would be more trouble, but also notoriety, and Daniel vouching for her publicly would seem like a declaration. Stephanie would be routed. She felt dazed, as if she was in a dream where nothing was quite real, and was half dozing in the warm water when there was a knock on the bathroom door and Daniel's voice called out to her.

"Are you in there, Jennifer? Hurry up. You're due in court in an hour."

He'd kept his latchkey. That showed that he meant to

return. She looked down at her narrow, shiny body and smiled.

"Come in," she said. "The door's not locked."

Daniel opened the door an inch and as steam wafted towards him, addressed her through the gap.

"I'm not coming in, and you're coming out," he said. "That is, if you want me to go with you to court. I'm waiting ten minutes and if you're not out of there and fully dressed by then, I'm leaving, and they can send some coppers to arrest you for contempt of court."

Was it, if you didn't turn up? It must be some sort of crime, anyway.

Jennifer stayed unmoving for a full two minutes, pouting, calling his name once. Then, slowly, stiffly, like an old woman, she got out of the water and, dripping, opened the door. Daniel was not to be seen. She thought about pursuing him through the flat, naked as she was, but she had begun to shiver—from shock, though she did not realise that—and decided to wrap a towel around her first. She tracked him to the kitchen, where he had put coffee on; there was a machine which they had bought together in Italy and it made excellent coffee.

"I don't suppose you've had breakfast," he said brusquely. "Get a move on, Jennifer. You haven't got all day."

He turned away from her, unexpectedly moved by the sight of her familiar face, flushed from the bath water, her eyes bright, expectant, as he had so often seen her before. Her hair was pinned to the top of her head and the large yellow towel had slipped to reveal one thin, bare shoulder. A few months ago the sight of her like this would have automatically aroused him, but now he recognised that that was what it would have been: an automatic response. She was his partner; that meant sex together: lust which could be loveless. Now what he felt was pity and regret, and an increasing sense of irritation. Other people split up without all this fuss; why couldn't they?

"Daniel, how can you be so cruel?" She spoke in a whimper and went up to him, laying her head on his upper arm, leaning against him in a way which once would have evoked an instant response. Now he felt a spasm of disgust.

He shook her off, then dabbed at the damp patch she had made on his jacket.

"Don't do that," he said angrily. "You'll make my suit wet. Go and get dressed at once."

She was getting her reaction, though not the one that she had wanted; even so, scoring a dent in his mild temper was some sort of achievement. All the same, his anger was evident and she did not like his hostile tone; it frightened her.

She turned away and padded from the room. He heard a sob and decided it was faked. Crossly, he made toast, buttered it and added marmalade. He ate a slice himself and drank a cup of very strong black coffee. By the time he had done that she reappeared, wearing a full black skirt, her black jacket, black tights and ankle boots. Her hair was pinned back and tied with a black bow. Her face was white and matt.

"Drink your coffee," he ordered. "Eat some toast."

In silence, she obeyed, and when he stood back to let her leave the room before him, she went meekly.

He opened the door of his car for her, as he had done last night and countless times before. She got in, and did up her seat belt. He did not speak as he drove towards the court, where he had to drop her while he found somewhere to park.

"What do you think will happen to me?" she asked submissively, as he stopped the car, the only words uttered on the journey.

"I expect you'll get off," he said. "William seemed to think you would, if you don't blow it."

He almost wished the law would take her off his hands, lock up her malevolence, teach her a lesson. But that wouldn't happen. Like the albatross, she was still about his neck.

The hearing was a formality. Jennifer was remanded on bail for a further week to enable full enquiries to be made as to the circumstances of the incident. It was implicit that this would also permit a defence to be prepared.

At this point, Daniel realised that Stephanie might be called as a witness. She could not refuse to attend, if required to do so, but she need not mention Jennifer's other acts of harassment. Had she already told the police about them? Oh, what a coil! The repercussions of a simple change of heart—for that was what he'd had—seemed to be unending.

William was insisting that Jennifer should see a psychiatrist.

"Why didn't she just plead guilty this morning and get the whole thing over?" Daniel demanded. "She doesn't deny doing it."

"She'd be wise to deny being responsible," said William. "Due to stress and strain, and so on. Otherwise she might be given a short sharp sentence inside."

"For a first offence?"

"It's possible. To warn others. If a teenage lout had thrown that stone, wouldn't you have thought he should be properly punished?"

"I suppose so."

"Well, then. Why should Jennifer escape just because she's a middle-class woman in a well-paid job?"

"Put like that, I see your point," said Daniel.

"The prosecution may decide to put it just like that," said William. "What if she does it again? Will she?"

"How do I know? Stephanie says she's been following her around for weeks. Haunting her."

"Hm," said William. "Well, you get her to a shrink, and fast. I'll see if I can find out who's the best for this sort of thing."

"What if she won't go?"

"If you can't persuade her, how about her family? She's got one, hasn't she?"

"I rang her brother this morning. He didn't show much concern. Said he had a meeting."

"Probably he did. People do."

"Um. There's a mother. I've met her."

"Effective?"

"Remote. But not ga-ga, not all that old. Late sixties, I should say," said Daniel. "Spry. Dry. Harmless." Humourless, too, he thought, as was Jennifer; Stephanie, though, laughed a lot, and made him laugh, too; that mattered, to be merry together.

"Will Jennifer have told her what she's done?" asked William.

"Most unlikely. They're not particularly close. She lives in the country, in a place called Middle Bardolph."

"Oh." To William, as long as the mother did not live in the Outer Hebrides, her exact location was not important. "I'd rope the old girl in. Send Jennifer down there for a rest. They won't want her in the office, with this business pending."

"Need they know about it?"

"They'll learn," said William. "It could be in the papers. There were some reporters in court. Nice little yuppie scandal, wouldn't you say?"

"Oh God!" Daniel thought about Stephanie's parents, the brigadier and his lady, down in Wiltshire. They wouldn't care for any of this.

"Well—be ready," William advised. "Get her away if you can."

"Offload the responsibility, you mean."

"Exactly."

It was sound advice. Unless someone else took it on, Daniel could be burdened with it, *faute de mieux*. Could he ask Mrs Newton to replace him as the bail guarantor? He asked William, who said it might be possible but at this juncture could be tactless. Anyway, for all her foibles, Jennifer wouldn't simply not turn up, would she?

Daniel thought that could be prevented, forcibly, if necessary.

"Thanks, William," he said. "You've been great."

"Only in the line of duty," William said. "You'll be paying. Or someone will. My time doesn't come cheap, you know."

''Well, thanks anyway,'' said Daniel, who had not yet thought about the situation in terms of cash. ''Will you help me persuade Jennifer to go down to Middle Bardolph?''

''If I must,'' said William. ''But surely she'll do anything for you? Isn't that the trouble?''

''She extracts a price,'' said Daniel, deciding not to tell William about the scene when he took Jennifer home after her arrest, or the kitchen interlude this morning.

''A woman scorned, you know,'' said William lightly. ''I've seen this sort of thing before.''

''But what should I have done? Stuck with her? We weren't married,'' Daniel said.

''Some marriages are like your relationship with Jennifer,'' said William. ''Couples get locked into a love-hate thing where one or both of them can't function on their own. The hate's as necessary as the love.''

''Well, it isn't to me,'' said Daniel. ''And she'll find someone else.''

''Not while she's like this, she won't,'' said William. ''Besides, she won't be looking. It's you she wants, I can't think why.'' He grinned and slapped Daniel on the back. ''The shrink's your answer,'' he said. ''She might do a transference and become his problem.''

Mrs Newton had heard the news from Geoffrey, who, reluctant to let Lynn know what had happened, had rung her as soon as he reached the office. He played the situation down; there was no point in alarming their mother.

''There was some minor argument,'' he said, omitting the detail about the stone and implying that unladylike behaviour was the extent of Jennifer's offence.

''I'd better go up there,'' said Mrs Newton, but Geoffrey told her that there wasn't time before the hearing. ''I'll get back to you later,'' he said, explaining that he could not go himself.

Could not, or would not? Mrs Newton knew the answer.
Daniel was involved somehow, Geoffrey had said. It was

he who had been in touch. Perhaps Jennifer had been drunk. Daniel had found her a lawyer and was handling everything.

Mrs Newton dialled Jennifer's number, but heard only the engaged signal. Jennifer had taken the telephone off the hook when she went to have her bath. It took Mrs Newton some time to realise that the number was unobtainable, not simply engaged, and then she rang Jennifer's office. She was not there, but they had had no message from her and thought she was probably on her way in, delayed by some hold-up on the tube, no doubt. Mrs Newton did not mention what had happened: best if the office never learned about it.

She would not try to get in touch with Daniel. That was something better left, as well. She could do no more.

That morning she had an emergency dental appointment, needed because a wisdom tooth had worked loose and become painful. Since she could not help Jennifer at present but might be needed later, she decided to keep the appointment; at least that problem could be dealt with. It was an unpleasant ordeal and afterwards she felt quite shaky, so that she decided to have a cup of coffee and some painkillers before going home, but as she left the surgery she almost bumped into Lucy Moffat who was passing in a hurry, hair adrift, jacket open to reveal a fluffy sweater in mixed shades of mauve and blue.

"Oh, good morning," Mrs Newton said. She had been thinking about Lucy constantly since their meeting, but not this morning, with her own and Jennifer's troubles to preoccupy her.

"Oh, hullo!" Lucy took a moment to recognise her. "Have you been to see Mr Carey?" Such was the dentist's apt name.

"Yes. I had a tooth out," said Mrs Newton. "I was just going to have some coffee, as a matter of fact." Suddenly the thought of having company, especially that of Lucy Moffat, for a short time was more essential than the coffee. "Won't you join me?" she suggested.

Lucy was hurrying home because she was expecting a telephone call from her daughter Jane about her weekend plans, but looking more closely now at Mrs Newton, she saw that beneath the matt make-up she was very pale, and wasn't one side of her face a little swollen?

On an impulse she said, "I've got to get home, but why don't you come with me? Let me give you some coffee."

Mrs Newton was delighted to accept and she lost count of time, sitting in Lucy's kitchen where it was warm and comfortably cluttered. She forgot about everything, Jennifer included, so happy was she to be inside this pleasant rambling house and learning about the Moffat family and their activities.

She met Mavis Smith, too, recognising her as the sturdy woman who had nearly bumped into her with the pushchair, and she saw that again, parked in the hall, the infant in it fast asleep. In the end, Mrs Newton spent nearly two hours with Lucy, who even showed her the workroom where she made her jewellery. Mrs Newton was intrigued. She wouldn't have cared to wear any of Lucy's creations herself because her tastes were conventional, but there was a big silver brooch which she felt sure Jennifer would like, and she contemplated asking Lucy what it would cost to make one for her. Presents for her were always such a problem. The expected telephone call from Jane came while she was there; she would not after all be bringing her boyfriend for the weekend.

Lucy hoped they'd had no quarrel, but she did not ask.

"I like the chap," she said. "He's rather solemn and very polite. The good manners are a plus, but I wish he laughed. I wouldn't like to see Jane tie herself down to a no-fun person. Not that I think this is likely to become permanent, but then how does one know? I met Simon when I was twenty."

Laughter was a strange thing to consider so important, Mrs Newton thought. How long was it since she had laughed herself? As you grew older, you didn't find things quite so humorous as in youth. Then she remembered the Blaneys; they were always laughing, and not at foolish jokes. They were happy people, and one felt happy with them. The same was true of Lucy Moffat; in her company, Mrs Newton was content.

Lucy asked her what hobbies she had; her visitor must have

some interests, surely? Maybe she would liven up and forget her aching jaw if she talked about them. But the reply was discouraging.

"Oh—I have no particular passion," she said. "I enjoy my garden—it's shrubs and roses mainly, as you saw. And lately I've been going to art exhibitions. My husband was fond of paintings." She had not mentioned him for years, though she thought of him from time to time.

"Have you been a widow long?"

"Yes," said Mrs Newton flatly. "Over thirty years."

"I'm sorry. Things must have been hard for you."

"He was quite a lot older than I was," said Mrs Newton, and compressed her lips. "Even so, it was very sudden. Quite a shock."

She had mentioned passion. It was difficult for Lucy to imagine her experiencing it, but there were other passions people enjoyed apart from the obvious one of sex. Even growing vegetables, as Simon did, could become obsessive.

She showed her guest round the garden, and Mrs Newton admired Simon's orderly rows of sprouts and leeks and celery, and the well-dug soil waiting to be sown with next year's crop of peas and beans and all the other things he grew. Lucy spoke cheerfully about her children, sure that Jane would, among her many friends, make comparisons unless she felt she should shoulder the dull young man as a crusade, regard it as her task to wake him up. Martin, her son, was always changing girl friends, it appeared.

"That's best, I think, when you're very young. It's a pity to get too serious too soon," said Lucy.

It was what Jennifer had always done. She had gone from one intense relationship to the next; it was all or nothing for her. Before Daniel there had been Ian, a banker; that had ended suddenly, for a reason not explained to Mrs Newton. Before him there was Alan; before him, Nigel; Mrs Newton could remember several others, all presentable, all doing well; Jennifer had never favoured long hair or sandals. Yet none of these romances had endured.

Now she had been reminded of her daughter, and the trouble in which, for whatever reason, she had landed herself.

"I must go home," she said, to Lucy's relief, for she wanted to return to her own work and thought that courtesy would oblige her to offer Mrs Newton some sort of lunch if she stayed much longer. Lucy herself usually ate bread and cheese while doing odd jobs such as ironing, or sorting out old newspapers.

"Are you all right now?" she asked. "You're certainly looking better." Mrs Newton had more colour but she still seemed tense; perhaps she always was. Lucy supposed she was in a fit state to drive; it wasn't far.

"Yes, thank you," said Mrs Newton. "You have been kind. It was nice to see you again."

She looked round wistfully as Lucy took her to the door. Would she ever come here again, be counted as a minor friend? Would Jennifer ever live in a place like this, with satisfactory children and a capable cleaning lady like Mrs Smith?

"Where's your car?" asked Lucy, suddenly remembering it. They had walked together from the surgery, not three hundred yards away.

"It's round the corner," Mrs Newton said. "I sometimes park in your road." She had just acquired the habit.

"Ah," said Lucy. "That's all right, then," and she watched while the small figure in the camel coat walked down the drive to the gate and disappeared.

Driving home, Mrs Newton's thoughts returned to Jennifer, whose London house had, as its garden, a small paved yard ornamented with tubs containing geraniums and petunias in summer, and daffodils in spring. It was a very pleasant house but too expensive for a woman on her own in Jennifer's income bracket. How different was her life from Lucy's! Would Jennifer think Lucy's life a dull one? Would she scorn the shabby kitchen with the old, chipped Aga, the worn carpets on the floors, the faded curtains? Lucy's husband, though no doubt a brilliant man, would not earn the sort of salary that even Daniel received, she thought: scientists in Britain were not rewarded as they ought to be, according to the papers.

Children did not necessarily bring their parents the joy and fulfilment associated with the notion of family life. There was Mrs Smith, for instance, Lucy's domestic help, with that illegitimate grandchild to care for; nowadays it seemed to be fashionable to have babies outside marriage but in Mrs Newton's youth such an event meant ruin and disgrace. Little Jason would not always be the docile baby, petted by those who had time to give him some attention; he would become a mobile toddler, a schoolboy, a lad thrusting his way in the world. He might scrawl graffiti on walls, get into fights, turn to real crime. None of this was foreseen by those who hung dotingly over a crib, or who, indeed, pined for a family and took extraordinary steps to acquire one. A puppy is not for Christmas, it's for life, as the poster said, and so was a baby.

She had had a puppy once: Binky, a Sealyham. She was fond of him and took him everywhere. They went for walks together, and Binky lay across her feet in the evening while she sewed, or listened to the radio, or read. It had been difficult for her to go anywhere without him. He had grown into a sober, steady dog and she had loved him. He never yapped or barked continuously except at cats, which he loathed. If he saw one, his hackles rose and he would chase it, regardless of all else. One day he had dashed across the road in pursuit of a neighbour's tabby which he had already attacked several times, to be met with spits and snarls. This time a passing motorist hit Binky, leaving the cat the victor.

Mrs Newton never had another dog. To love an animal, or a person, was to be vulnerable; she had learned that long ago.

Jennifer had offered to replace Binky, a generous gesture. She had been a satisfactory child, doing well enough at school, though there had been occasional tantrums. Where had it all gone wrong?

I shouldn't have moved so much when she was growing

up, thought Mrs Newton now, when it was too late, whilst still acknowledging that she had had good reasons for doing so. Though Mrs Newton had moved within range of the area covered by the grammar school, the change had meant travelling to school with different girls; at first there were shared car runs, then Jennifer went by bus. Mrs Newton tried to remember those distant schoolgirls, Jennifer's friends. Different ones were brought to tea, none remaining constant; she thought of Marilyn and Sophie, both quick-witted, sometimes rather spiteful, Mrs Newton had thought, and had not been sorry when their time seemed to have passed. There were Joanna and Felicity, tough little girls who giggled together, but was Jennifer excluded from their private jokes? It seemed to Mrs Newton, looking back, that girls had come in twos, and Jennifer was the third; had that been significant? Had she failed in understanding Jennifer, all that time ago?

One can only do one's best, thought Mrs Newton, driving homewards through the grey November day. Leaves clung sparsely to the trees along the way, and the road was greasy after rain. The light was poor and cars had their headlamps on. Mrs Newton turned hers on and sent the wipers swishing over the spattered screen. Her jaw, the effect of the injection now worn off, was aching. A needle of pain above her right eye signalled the onset of a migraine attack, but she knew that it would vanish if she were to be called upon for some great effort to aid Jennifer. Past experience had shown her that a crisis could be tackled, lived through; then, in the aftermath, would come the torment in the head, the gut-wrenching nausea. This afternoon she would indulge herself in a rare manner by spending the afternoon in bed, with a hot-water bottle—she did not like electric blankets though she had them for the other beds at Yew Cottage so that they could easily be aired. She would draw the curtains and turn the radio on, its volume low; there might be an absorbing play which would distract and lull her. After an hour or two's repose, even sleep, she would get in touch with Jennifer, or Geoffrey, even try to trace Daniel if all else failed. By that time someone would know what had happened in court this morning.

Court this morning: what a phrase to use in connection with Jennifer!

She turned off at The Prince Hal, went past the school and the village shop and reached home, getting out to open the garage doors and put the car away. Work seemed to have stopped on the site next door; it was silent and no vans were to be seen. That was a relief; banging and churning would not disturb her siesta. She had no shopping to unload, and was soon inside the house.

In the kitchen, she reached out to put the kettle on; she always kept it filled. She had planned to have a bowl of instant soup and some toast before she went to bed.

The kettle was warm. It had recently been boiled and it was almost empty.

Someone had been here in her absence, in this room.

12

Mrs Newton took several deep breaths to calm herself, her hand to her thin chest which was clad, over her underwear, in a fine cream blouse and a pale beige cardigan. She still wore her camel coat.

She looked carefully round the kitchen. Nothing seemed out of place; no burglar had stripped it. Walking very quietly, she went on to the sitting-room which was just as she had left it, undisturbed. There were no signs of a break-in. In any case, did burglars brew up? Reason told her that someone who knew where the spare key was had come in, and that cut down the number of possibilities. Mrs Newton had once locked herself out of an earlier house and so now always kept a key in a place known only to very few people—her children, naturally, and in case of emergency the Blaneys had known where it was. No one else.

This left little choice.

"Jennifer? Is that you?" Mrs Newton called out, standing at the foot of the staircase. She spoke as if she had heard a noise, but nothing broke the silence. Slowly she went up the stairs, a hand on the banister rail, still in her coat.

Jennifer's bedroom door was closed, but then it was

always shut, like the other bedroom doors. Mrs Newton knocked.

"Jennifer?" she called out.

There was no answer.

Mrs Newton knocked once more and then tried the handle. Jennifer was quite capable of locking herself in, refusing to speak. What then? Could she have taken some foolish step, like swallowing pills?

Mrs Newton forbade her thoughts to take this direction without cause, but the door was locked.

"Jennifer, if you won't speak to me I shall have to get someone to climb a ladder and look in through the window— or do it myself," she threatened.

There was a mumbling sound in response to this. Mrs Newton could not distinguish the words.

"Jennifer?"

"I'm trying to sleep," said Jennifer.

Surely she must know that her mother had heard about her arrest? Mrs Newton stood on the landing, wondering if she did.

"Are you ill?" she tried.

"Just tired," came Jennifer's voice, more audibly. "Leave me alone."

Mrs Newton decided to do as she was asked. She took off her coat and hung it up, then went downstairs to carry out her own programme of consuming soup and toast, and retiring herself. After that she filled her red rubber hot-water bottle and left a note on the kitchen table.

I had a tooth out and am lying down. M., she wrote. A dose of her own medicine might be the best way of dealing with Jennifer. At least she hadn't been sent to prison. Mrs Newton hoped nervously that she had turned up in court, had not absconded, jumped bail, or in some other way made her predicament still worse. If she had, no doubt a policeman would come banging on the door before long.

Time enough to worry about that, she thought, and checked the small bottle of sleeping pills prescribed for her own occasional use, which she kept in the bathroom cupboard. It seemed untouched; at any rate, it had not been plundered and two or three capsules would do no lasting harm.

She took two painkillers herself and removed her outer clothes. Then, in her dark blue dressing gown, she slid under the duvet, one of the few modern customs she had adopted after a visit to Geoffrey and Lynn, who had equipped every bedroom with them.

She lay there with the curtains drawn, and at first she was trembling. Shock, she told herself, caused partly by toothache and partly by her daughter. What could Jennifer have been doing? Had she been taking part in some sort of demonstration? She had her faults but being negative was not among them; she might have espoused some popular campaign or other, and got into trouble for it. At least she was not, at this present moment, in any immediate danger either from herself or others, safely locked up in her bedroom. Mrs Newton must use the time herself to nurse her painful jaw and her aching head.

She clutched her hot-water bottle and tried to remember the Bournemouth days: the pram under the big beech tree; the swing; the very clean sandpit; the relaxing air; the safety all so suddenly ended when Frederick, the provider of it all, had died.

He had saved her first.

She never liked to think of that, so she turned on the radio, its volume low, and heard a woman talking about sexually transmitted diseases.

Mrs Newton snapped it off at once, and tried to think about Lucy Moffat, a happy and confident woman with a productive life and a satisfactory family. Those children had good role models before them, she thought; they would choose life partners wisely. Geoffrey and Jennifer must both remember their father, and the calm atmosphere at home; they must have hoped eventually to attain that for themselves, but as they grew older they had not witnessed the ups and downs in any marriage, the give and take, the dovetailing essential to success. Perhaps they believed in happy-ever-after, she thought, not understanding that immediate attraction was not enough on which to build a life. Concluding this, sad, she closed her eyes and dozed a little.

After the hearing, Jennifer had declared that she must go to the washroom. In fact she felt sick, and she looked very white, so neither William nor Daniel was surprised, and her absence gave them the chance to discuss her situation frankly. Intent on their confabulation, they did not see her slip out of the ladies' cloakroom and slink off down the passage to the court entrance.

She had no thought, no plan but to run away. Briefly, while she clung to the basin in the washroom wondering if she was going to be sick, she understood the enormity of her offence. She was no schoolboy vandal throwing stones—and that was bad enough; she was a member of the privileged classes who did not do such things. Hot shame swamped her. She had humiliated herself and Daniel, and she had not touched Stephanie, which was her aim. Flight was the only answer for the moment, until she had time to reorganise her thoughts and her strength. When she saw the two men conferring, any vague idea of trying again to make Daniel move towards her in some way vanished and she acted instinctively. She did not have to pass them in order to leave the building, and she ran off down the road as fast as she could until, by a lucky chance, she saw a cruising taxi.

She told the driver to take her to Marylebone. For once she wanted her mother.

In the train, she calmed down. She had had to wait forty minutes for the next one to Wintlebury Halt, and she kept fearing that Daniel would arrive before it left, for surely he would come after her when he saw that she had gone. He would try the house first; then, when he found that she was not there, he might begin to worry, and after a while he would think of Middle Bardolph and would come for her.

She liked this thought. Her brief lapse into remorse ended

as she embroidered and improved upon it. Now she was administering punishment. This mood lasted throughout her journey as she sat staring out of the window imagining the bliss of their eventual reconciliation.

At Wintlebury Halt she telephoned her mother. Jennifer always carried a phone card in case of emergencies though Daniel never did; he relied on her to be efficient in such things. There was no answer from Yew Cottage, and this brought Jennifer down to earth. What right had her mother to be out when she was needed? She fumed, and had no choice but to telephone for a taxi, and when she reached Middle Bardolph she had to pay the driver, since her mother was not there to do it for her.

Some workmen were busy on the building site next door. They seemed to be loading things into vans, but she paid them no real attention, walking past the garage and round the side of the house to where a large water butt stood beneath a gutter pipe. She reached behind the water butt. There, under a brick, was a spare front door key, tucked so far away that, reaching for it, she made her jacket dirty.

Neil, on a ladder polishing the final window of the finished house, saw her. He had not seen the taxi, and was not curious about who she was, but he watched her.

When Jennifer did not reappear from the washroom, William asked a passing female solicitor to find out if she was ill.

She returned to report that there was no one in the place—no one at all.

He and Daniel stared at one another and dismay filled them both. Now what had she done?

"She must be lost somewhere in the building," said Daniel.

"Nonsense. How could she get lost between the loo and here? It's a straight walk down the passage," said William. "We were talking. She's somehow given us the slip—dashed off. Probably couldn't bring herself to face you. She wouldn't mind me—I'm here on duty."

She had faced him well enough this morning, Daniel thought.

"She's in no state to be running around on her own," he said.

William was inclined to agree, but rather because he considered her a danger to others more than herself. She might run under the wheels of an oncoming car, not to commit suicide but from carelessness, and if she were hurt she would cause enormous trouble and grief to an innocent motorist. He gave silent thanks for his own kind wife and calm, if dull, home life.

They made a thorough search of the place, aided by a police officer and one of the clerks, and were finally satisfied that she was not in the building.

"Perhaps she's gone home," said Daniel. "I suppose I'd better go and see."

William frowned.

"I don't want to be alarmist," he said. "But if I were you, I'd check on Stephanie first and then, if she's all right and hasn't seen Jennifer today, I'd leave her—Jennifer, I mean—to get on with it. This is your friend speaking, not Jennifer's solicitor. You'll never get her off your back if you give her too much support now, and how will Stephanie feel if she hears you've been chasing round London after her?"

"How will I feel, if she's done something stupid?" said Daniel, but William had a point about Stephanie. "I'll ring Stephanie," he said. "And perhaps I'll go back to the office. After all, I do have one to go to, where I'm expected."

"Good thinking," said William.

"I could ring Jennifer's brother later. Or her mother. Let them know what happened in court." Would Jennifer tell them herself? He didn't know.

"You could," agreed William.

"I can't just walk away," said Daniel. "After all, in a sense I'm responsible."

"I don't see it like that," said William. "You don't want to take her on again, do you?"

"Certainly not."

"She needs the cold turkey treatment," said William. "She's got to get a grip on herself and let you go."

"She wasn't always like this," Daniel said. "She was just—" he hesitated, lost for the right description.

"Volatile?" suggested William.

"That's it," said Daniel.

William knew that Daniel was far from out of the wood with Jennifer. She might well go in search of Stephanie again and she might try actively to harm her, even attack her directly.

"I think Stephanie should take extra care for a while," he said. "Perhaps she could stay with a friend for a bit, till Jennifer calms down. If she sees a doctor, he may be able to treat her, but if not, she might repeat this sort of thing. Of course, Stephanie could take out an injunction against her, but that's heavy stuff among friends. But she probably didn't really mean to hurt Stephanie," he added. "She may have meant only to frighten her, or relieve her own feelings."

"That's a good idea about Stephanie moving," said Daniel. "I'll get her to fix something up. She certainly shouldn't be at the flat alone. The other two girls were away last night."

"What about the broken window?" asked William.

"Julian in the flat below was going to get someone to mend it today," said Daniel. "He's going to be in and he said he'd see to it."

"A good neighbour," William commented.

"The best," agreed Daniel.

"Well, I'll try telephoning Jennifer at the house," said William. "Of course, she may have gone to work."

Neither of them had thought of that. Bravado was part of Jennifer's repertoire in a difficult situation and she might employ it now.

They parted, agreeing to let one another know if Jennifer was traced. William had a sneaking anxiety in case she took some melodramatic action and he might be reproved for not exercising care, but he had no responsibility for her outside the court. He hurried off, anxious to stem the tide of mounting paper always rising on his desk, and Daniel found a telephone from which to ring up Stephanie, who was perfectly safe at the office and who had not seen any sinister figure dressed in black hanging about outside. She promised to find somewhere to stay that night, and to take a taxi home to pick up what she would need to take with her. Daniel said he would call her later to learn what she had arranged. They already had a plan to spend the weekend in Wiltshire, with Stephanie's parents.

When he returned to his office, Daniel, still uneasy, telephoned Geoffrey's office, to learn that he was out and would not be back until the late afternoon.

"Has he gone to London?" asked Daniel hopefully.

"No. He's gone to look at a house, with his wife," said Geoffrey's secretary.

So that was Geoffrey's meeting. Daniel had not heard about his plans for moving.

After that, he telephoned Mrs Newton, but there was no reply. At that moment she was sitting in Mr Carey's surgery while he inserted the needle into her gum before extracting the tooth which had been causing such discomfort.

Jennifer slept. When she woke, the light had gone outside; the day was over. She felt as though she was being dragged up from the depths of some comfortable warm cavern where she need strive no more and where all was repose, only to be forced into a burst of fevered activity against her will. She closed her eyes and drifted into oblivion once more, but when she woke from that, she was unable to retreat again. At first she could not think where she was; she had hardly ever slept in this room, though it was full of things that had accompanied her throughout various removals. Her childhood possessions were still displayed: china animals; some prints she had liked; patchwork cushions her mother had made her when she was fifteen. She had always been consulted about curtain fabrics and carpets at each move, even this last one.

Slow recollection of what had happened in the past twenty-four hours came to her: she blotted out the court scene, and her own subsequent loss of courage, concentrating on Daniel's presence, clear proof of his love. Stretching her limbs in the warm bed, she smiled. It would be all right. He would be frantic, wondering where she had gone. By now he could be on his way to fetch her and take her back with him to London. He and William between them would get her off the legal hook, even if it meant a fine. She pictured him chasing about, looking for her in every possible spot, then frowned. Surely by now he should have arrived at Middle Bardolph? Or at least he should have telephoned to see if she was there.

Perhaps he was already here, sitting downstairs with her mother, waiting for her to wake up. At the thought, energy filled Jennifer and she sprang out of bed and put on the dressing gown kept here for her. She padded down the stairs.

The sitting-room was empty, and it was chilly; though the heating was on, the electric fire which normally burned in there on a winter's day was off.

Where could her mother be?

Jennifer went into the kitchen and saw the note. The fact that her mother had surrendered to physical weakness dismayed her, as it had done throughout her childhood when the dreadful headaches had struck. Seeing her unable to function, green-faced, lying in a darkened room, a bowl nearby in case she could not reach the bathroom in time, sometimes even to hear the sound of retching, had terrified her, shattering her sense of security. What would happen if her mother did not recover? She did not remember the headaches occurring before her father's death, but Jennifer made no connection between cause and effect.

Geoffrey had become philosophical about the attacks, and practical. He would bring cool damp cloths, drinks of soda water, tidy up the bed, but Jennifer had to hide from such a scene of distress. It was easy for Geoffrey; he was away at school and seldom witnessed an attack whereas Jennifer saw them constantly. Surprisingly, her mother was never prevented from taking Geoffrey out on an exeat day, though she was often laid low afterwards. Jennifer, however, had often been fetched from school by other girls' mothers and returned to find the dark bedroom, the nearly helpless woman who would get up and crawl about putting together a meal for the schoolgirl before retreating again.

Now, however, Jennifer felt a fleeting benevolence. This, after all, was only toothache. She put the kettle on, made tea, found a pretty china cup and saucer, poured her mother out a cup and took it upstairs.

As she passed through the hall she glanced at the telephone sitting silently on the table by the window, a potted pink chrysanthemum in a china container beside it. The receiver was off the hook.

No wonder there had been no call from Daniel. Of course he would have rung, but would have thought the number engaged unless he concluded that it was out of order. Her mother must have realised that someone would want to get in touch with Jennifer; how could she be so selfish?

Her mood changed completely. She did not go as far as to throw away the cup of tea or smash the china, but she delivered it in a belligerent manner, striding noisily into her mother's room, snapping on the main light, crashing the cup and saucer down on the bedside table, slopping the tea in the saucer.

"You might have left the phone connected, Mother," she said angrily. "People will want to contact me."

Mrs Newton did not answer. The interruption had made her heart thump painfully. This was the daughter she did not want to recognise: the angry woman who apportioned blame to everyone but herself; the one who frightened her; who was, her mother feared, capable of violence.

She managed not to apologise, and she thanked Jennifer

13

"Seen that old biddy lately? The one we did the fence for?" Kevin asked Neil that evening.

"I see her most days," said Neil, exaggerating. Then he could not resist embroidering. "She's taken a shine to me. Often chats, if she's out in the garden and that. She feeds the birds," he romanced. Mrs Newton did not, in fact, ever do this because the Blaneys had had two cats which stalked anything in feathers and had killed the robin that used to perch on a twig watching Mrs Newton at work outside. She had felt a great sadness when that happened; she had liked the robin following her about, sometimes perching on the window-sill, cheekily regarding her with its bright eyes. It was a mistake to grow fond of anyone or anything; its loss subjected you to sorrow. Nor did Neil see her daily, for he was not always around if she went out, but he hailed her whenever he saw her. Once he had gone to Yew Cottage to see if she was satisfied with the fence, hoping to be invited in, but all she did was thank him and say that it seemed to be sound.

"Got some nice things, hasn't she?" said Kevin. "Wonder she doesn't have an alarm fitted. It'd be easy to get in there."

"So would most places," Neil said. "If you're determined, that is. Unless there's a rottweiler," he added, grinning. He never knew how seriously to take Kevin when he talked like this. There were those things he'd had in his car, for instance, and the boxes which at the moment were stacked in their bedroom cupboard. Neil wondered their mum hadn't noticed all Kevin's stuff, but she'd given up their room, making them clean it themselves. She left their neatly ironed washing on the landing outside, and sometimes the vacuum sweeper as a hint. Neil, a tidy individual made even neater while in prison, never minded doing the room out, and his own few belongings took up little space as he dusted round. Kevin had told him he'd make a nice little wife one of these days.

"Got some jewellery, I shouldn't wonder," Kevin went on.

Neil shrugged.

"I suppose," he said. Then he could not resist adding, "I know where she keeps a key."

"No!" Kevin tried not to show too much interest. "Where's that, then? Under the mat?"

"It's behind a water butt at the back. Under it somewhere," said Neil. He did not enlarge.

"Lives there alone, doesn't she?" said Kevin, just to make sure.

"Uh huh." This was certainly true, and she had very few visitors.

Kevin changed the subject.

Daniel had dialled Mrs Newton's number several times during the afternoon, always getting the engaged tone, and eventually he had asked the operator for help. No one was talking, he was told; it seemed to be out of order. He reported it, and abandoned the problem for the moment.

He had a lot of work to get through and it was after five before he tried Geoffrey again, this time to be told that he had already gone home.

It's well for some, thought Daniel, dialling Geoffrey's house.

An answering machine replied. That was something, at least. Daniel spoke carefully into it, hoping that his words would be heard by someone passing by who might take in their significance and lift the receiver. He gave his name and went on firmly to report that Jennifer had been charged in court that morning with criminal damage and had been remanded for a week on bail. He gave William's name and telephone number, saying that he was acting for Jennifer, but that she had disappeared after the hearing and had not been traced. Mrs Newton's telephone number was out of order so that he could not check if she had heard from Jennifer.

That was quite enough to put on the tape. It would make interesting listening for anyone who bothered to check. He wondered if Lynn Newton was preparing dinner, having a gin, helping the daughters with their homework.

He could do no more for Jennifer, and his desire and duty lay with Stephanie. She had found herself a refuge with a girl from her office who had her own flat in her parents' house in Highgate, in quite the opposite direction from the scene of Jennifer's activities during the night.

Daniel was relieved. He said he would take her there when she had packed her things. They'd have dinner together somewhere first, if she'd like that.

She would.

"Why did you take the telephone off the hook?" Jennifer demanded.

She was not going to let her mother get away with this without a scene. It was all very well lying in bed looking wan and not answering when Jennifer had taken the trouble to bring her a cup of tea; she must be made to repent, and, if possible, atone.

Mrs Newton had at last found the strength to rise, put on her skirt, her blouse and cardigan, and her neat tan shoes.

She had washed her face and repaired her make-up. Her head still throbbed, but dully; at least she did not feel sick. Left to herself, she would have spent the rest of the day in bed, but she must face her daughter, discover the extent of her predicament.

"I did not wish to be disturbed," she said coolly. "You saw my note. I was not feeling well." It was a statement, not a question.

"But you knew I was here," said Jennifer. "People will want to speak to me." She had not quite the nerve to say Daniel would be the caller.

"Then they will ring again," said Mrs Newton calmly.

She sat in her usual chair, waiting for Jennifer's attack, thinking how agreeable it would be if instead of firing a salvo she were to apologise for arriving without warning, even enquire if her mother was feeling better, but such were vain hopes.

"Daniel will be sick with worry," Jennifer dared to say.

"Why should he be?"

"He doesn't know where I am," said Jennifer.

"Then why don't you put him out of his misery by ringing him up and telling him?" Mrs Newton suggested.

For an instant Jennifer's defiant expression was replaced by a hunted look, but she soon thought of a barbed reply to this.

"Let him suffer," she said. "He's caused me enough grief. Now it's his turn."

Was this all Jennifer could manage? Spite towards Daniel instead of recriminations to her mother? Mrs Newton remembered long ago rages about suitable clothes for teenage parties and other occasions of dissent in the past. Was she going to escape further chiding?

"Geoffrey told me you were in some trouble," she tried. What would Jennifer disclose?

"It wasn't my fault," said Jennifer.

"Of course not, dear," said Mrs Newton. Nothing ever was.

"It was that mealy-mouthed Stephanie," said Jennifer. "The one who's got hold of Daniel. She's made a fool of him and he can't get out of it. He's so kind-hearted."

This last statement was certainly true. On his few visits to Middle Bardolph Daniel had washed Mrs Newton's car, repaired a broken window latch, and generally made himself useful as well as being pleasant and very well mannered. But how was Stephanie involved in Jennifer's brush with the law? Geoffrey had not mentioned her.

"Geoffrey said you had some sort of argument," she probed cautiously.

"It wasn't quite an argument," said Jennifer. "I was accused of causing damage."

"And did you?"

"It depends how you look at it," said Jennifer sulkily. "A window got broken."

What could have happened? Had Jennifer got into one of her rages?

"What did the court think?" she asked.

"I was remanded for a week," said Jennifer.

Remanded! What a dreadful word. But Jennifer was standing here, free.

"On bail?" Mrs Newton asked, as the shaft of pain above her right eye strengthened and spread right round the side of her head.

"Yes."

"Who stood bail? Geoffrey?"

"Daniel did," said Jennifer proudly, and she smiled. There was something terrifying about that smile; it was more a grin, and ghastly, thought Mrs Newton, who found herself beginning to shiver. She drew her cardigan around her, hoping Jennifer would not notice.

"Did you break the window?" she asked.

"Yes."

"Where?"

"In Stephanie's flat."

"Why do you dislike her so much?"

"Because she's a scheming little cat. A hussy," said Jennifer untruthfully. "She should have left Daniel alone but no, she had to flaunt herself in front of him."

"Aren't you blaming the wrong person? It's Daniel who's hurt you, not this girl," said Mrs Newton. "You and Daniel had some good years together, didn't you? Can't you just be thankful for that and let him go? Your anger is only hurting yourself."

"You don't know what you're talking about," said Jennifer harshly. "Married to Daddy all that time, so safe and peaceful. You don't know what the jungle's like."

"And do you?" asked Mrs Newton. "Are you sure it isn't your pride that's suffering?"

"I'm heart-broken," Jennifer declared. "I gave him everything—all my love, all my strength."

"Perhaps it was too much for him," said Mrs Newton. "Perhaps he wanted someone less intense. Gentler."

Jennifer gave a scornful snort.

"Everyone wants love," she said.

"Some people don't know how to give it," Mrs Newton said. "They demand too much in return. Anyway, it seems to me that Stephanie is innocent of any offence."

Jennifer was about to make a furious reply to this when the telephone rang. Without a word she flew from the room to answer it.

Mrs Newton, still shivering and with her heart pounding against her ribs, heard her high, excited voice say "Hullo?" and then the deflated tone as she said, "Oh, Geoffrey, it's you." After that she was silent while Geoffrey spoke. Mrs Newton listened to the one-sided conversation. She could hear all Jennifer's remarks.

"Oh, did he?" was uttered eagerly. Then, "Yes, well," and after a pause, "I suppose," and "Don't be stupid." Finally she said, "I'll get her," and called to her mother that Geoffrey wished to speak to her.

Geoffrey told her that Jennifer had run off after the hearing without a word to her solicitor or to Daniel. He had rung the solicitor who thought that Jennifer should see a doctor, preferably a psychiatrist, so that a report stating that she was in a nervous state and not responsible for what she had done could be given to the court at the renewed hearing. "Premenstrual tension. Something like that, he said," Geoffrey told his mother, sounding embarrassed even over the telephone. They had never discussed anything intimate. "She's furious because Daniel's chucked her, and I can't say I blame him. She's always had a violent temper." Then, before his mother could ask it of him, he said, "I can't come down just now. I've got some important deals on here. It sounds as if Daniel is rallying round and the solicitor seems to know what he's doing. Or do you think Mr Booth would be better?"

Mrs Newton was not sure how Mr Booth would take to being asked to represent Jennifer in a criminal case.

"I think we should leave everything in the hands of whoever Daniel has found," she said.

"I hope it doesn't get into the papers," said Geoffrey. "Lynn will flip her lid if there's a scandal in the family."

"That would, indeed, be dreadful," said Mrs Newton drily.

Her ironic tone was wasted on Geoffrey.

"I'm glad you understand that," he said. "We went to see a house today. She's set her heart on it."

"Shall you buy it for her?"

"You know I can't, without your help," he said.

"Then I'm afraid she will be disappointed," said Mrs Newton.

She asked after the children and sent them her love, wondering if he would pass on the message. "It's a long time since I saw them," she added. Several times a year she suggested they might like to visit. She could take them to Windsor, where there was so much to see, and to London, and all sorts of other interesting places. Lynn never allowed them to come. The girls were always too busy; there were parties and gymkhanas, and visits to the dentist, or tennis tournaments they could not miss.

"You'd see them every day if you came up here," was Geoffrey's parting remark. "Please give it some thought," and he rang off before she could say any more.

Both stood by their replaced instruments feeling sad and disappointed. Mrs Newton wondered what had happened to the grave little boy who had been afraid of dragons. Geoffrey had forgotten the quiet, calm mother who would so gently bathe a cut knee, give comfort over a disappointment. All he could remember now was a stubborn old woman who would not grant his wish, thus condemning him to domestic discord.

Neither of my children has the least affection for me, she thought, returning to the sitting-room. All they want is the capital I represent. And though Jennifer, in her hour of need, had come home, it wasn't love that had brought her; it was shame. She had run to the one place where she could hide and be protected.

"Did you have any lunch?" she asked her wayward child.

"I forgot," said Jennifer.

Mrs Newton knew that there was a Captain's Pie in the freezer. There were also some frozen peas. They would make an adequate meal. She went to put the pie in the oven. The peas could be done in the microwave. Then she placed a glass and a bottle of tonic water on a small tray for herself, adding two cream crackers on a plate. It was time Jennifer learned that there were limits to her mother's endurance.

"I'm going back to bed," she said. "My jaw is very painful and I have a headache."

By morning she might feel able to cope with whatever must be done to help Jennifer escape the most serious consequences of her actions.

It would never do for her to go to prison. Apart from the horror of such an experience, she would emerge convinced that she was a martyr. No, that must, at all costs, be avoided.

Jennifer thought that she wanted nothing to eat until the faint aroma of Captain's Pie came wafting from the kitchen. Of course it was her mother's duty to see that she was fed, especially after all that she had been through. Why else had she come home, if it was not to be looked after? Her mother had taken care of her through measles, tonsillitis, a broken collar bone, failure to be selected for the school tennis team, and other vicissitudes. Tears of rage and frustration filled her eyes and she stormed about the sitting-room, not quite daring to break her mother's china ornaments but flinging cushions around, finally throwing herself on the sofa in a gale of noisy weeping which her mother should be able to hear; then she would feel guilty and reappear in her role of ministering angel.

This did not happen, and in the end Jennifer could not ignore the call of the pie. She sat up and looked for a tissue. Her mother always kept a box in a drawer of the small chest beside her chair. Jennifer pulled out a handful, blew her nose and went to attend to the peas. There would be sherry in the house; was there some wine? She searched and found some Entre Deux Mers white wine sold by the supermarket; that would do.

Jennifer quite enjoyed her meal, eating it at the kitchen table, waiting for Daniel to telephone, as of course, in the end, he would.

But he did not, and as she sat there, expectant, Jennifer began to think of her mother's words: she had said that Stephanie was not to blame; it was Daniel who had been responsible for their separation.

Jennifer was still convinced that if Stephanie were removed from the scene, he would return; it was a simple equation. But her mother had a point. He had been unfaithful; he should have sent Stephanie packing, resisted her advance. Even admitting that, however, what could she do to bring him to his senses? As long as Stephanie was around, Jennifer could not be sure of getting him back, and even if she did succeed, it could happen again. Someone else might come along and tempt him; men were so weak.

If she could not have him, no one else should.

Mulling it over, knowing that if she went to bed she would not sleep, Jennifer went for a walk.

Upstairs, Mrs Newton heard her leave the house. Presumably she'd still got the spare key. It must be replaced; it was easy to lock oneself out by accident. Where was she off to now? Mrs Newton listened in case she took the car, but there was no sound of its engine being started. Mrs Newton had removed her sleeping pills from the bathroom cupboard as a precaution, though she thought Jennifer was too angry to swallow an overdose, unless she decided it was the only way to win sympathy and then she would mean only to alarm other people, not seriously damage herself.

I do care, thought her mother sadly. I want to see the eager, bright person she once was return, but I want her to be responsible for her own mistakes, not to lay them upon me, or the unfortunate Stephanie. She had hoped that in the end Jennifer and Daniel would marry; he was so calm and steady and he might settle her down. She sighed. What sentence would the magistrates mete out? At best it would be a fine, and being bound over to keep the peace. If she reoffended, she could receive a custodial sentence. What she had done was certainly worse than stealing a packet of biscuits from a supermarket, and people were sometimes sent to prison for that sort of crime.

Had Jennifer really intended to hurt Stephanie? Where had she gone now? Had she taken off again, left as suddenly as she had come?

Mrs Newton almost hoped that she had.

14

Next morning, Geoffrey telephoned William to let him know that Jennifer was safely in Middle Bardolph.

"My mother will look after her," he told the solicitor, reassuringly. "I imagine you'll get her off the hook at the resumed hearing?"

"I can't guarantee that," said William. "Naturally I'll do my best to ensure she doesn't go to prison but a great deal depends on the magistrate."

"But a first offence—a woman with her background—" Geoffrey began.

"Class doesn't come into it," said William. "In fact it can work the other way. Certain magistrates would suggest she should have behaved better because of that."

William did not like this case. If Jennifer would not accept advice it could get nasty, and there was the underlying element of sexual jealousy which the gutter press would love, if they heard about it. There was no guarantee that Jennifer might not do something even more extreme than throw stones, but at least while she was in Middle Bardolph her mother would, presumably, control her.

"Will you be speaking to Jennifer?" Geoffrey asked.

"Not immediately," said William.

"I told my mother you said she ought to see a psychiatrist," said Geoffrey. "Maybe she'll get her to one," he added, not sounding very hopeful. "I suppose there's no chance of Daniel having second thoughts? About Jennifer I mean. About it being on again?"

"None whatsoever, in my opinion," William answered. "Perhaps when the hearing is over she could go away for a while. Have a holiday. Visit relatives. Is there anyone who might invite her?" You, for instance, he was thinking.

"I don't think she'd do that," Geoffrey said. "And anyway, she'll need her friends' support."

What friends, thought William; Jennifer might have some at the office but away from it she had devoted herself entirely to Daniel.

"She'll need her family," he warned. "You'll come down for the hearing?"

"I'll try, but I'm a very busy man," said Geoffrey.

In other words, you'll find some excuse to stay away, thought William. He put his troublesome client from his mind while he dealt with other urgent matters which, because of her, had had to be postponed.

At some time in the night, Jennifer had returned. Mrs Newton, wakeful, had heard her coming up the stairs, running a bath, moving about the landing. When the house was quiet, at last she fell asleep and in the morning, though her head still ached dully, she knew that the worst of her migraine was over. If she took things gently it would lift, helped by analgesics and the strong coffee which was anathema to some sufferers. She went downstairs in her dressing gown and put the kettle on.

The newspaper had come, thrust through the door by the boy who did the round before catching the school bus to Wintlebury Comprehensive. She appreciated its early arrival and always read the news at breakfast.

She drank some coffee and ate a piece of dry toast. That should help the tablets work. Her jaw felt a little easier today and the swelling had subsided slightly. Fortunately, as the gap was at the back, she would not need a denture.

Turning the pages of the paper, reading about the alarming state of affairs in the Middle East—always, she remembered Frederick saying, a most unquiet place—she saw a small paragraph under the heading WOMAN THROWS STONE AT RIVAL.

> Jennifer Newton, 37, was remanded on bail for a week after being charged with throwing a stone through the bedroom window of Stephanie Dunn, 23, her former lover's fiancée. Friends reported Miss Dunn to be unhurt but shaken.

Daniel was not mentioned. As the incident had been reported in this sober newspaper, it was likely to be given greater space in the tabloids, thought Mrs Newton, unaware that it had attracted attention only because a sensational assault case was due to follow. Her own address was not disclosed, however; the press would not pursue Jennifer down here.

She took a little time to calm down after reading this public proclamation of their troubles. Then she cleared the kitchen. Jennifer had eaten the entire Captain's Pie, which would have fed Mrs Newton twice, and washed up, which was something to be grateful for; she had always been a tidy girl but in her present state, who could tell what she might do? The spare front door key was lying on the table, and when Mrs Newton had washed and dressed, and done her face, she went outside and replaced it in its hiding-place.

Returning to the house, she made fresh coffee and toast and took a tray up to Jennifer in bed.

The dark hair protruded from the bedclothes but no word was said as Mrs Newton drew back the curtains and made a comment on the weather, which was overcast and chilly.

Downstairs, she took the sweeper out and began to clean the sitting-room. She always did this on Fridays, ready for the weekend, not that she was likely to ask anybody in, but routine in life was essential.

Later, William rang. He sounded calm, and, to his ear, so did Mrs Newton. He named a London doctor who might be helpful to Jennifer's case and suggested making an appointment before the hearing, so that his report could be used in her defence, and Mrs Newton understood that this was good advice.

"She may do it again," she said. "Or something worse."

William noted with relief that she did not question Jennifer's guilt, or her unstable state of mind.

"I know," he said.

Lucy Moffat had seen the item about Jennifer in a different paper. She noted the name of the assailant, Jennifer Newton, and only slowly remembered her new acquaintance whom she had revived with coffee and sympathy the day before. While they looked at Lucy's work, Mrs Newton had mentioned that her daughter had enjoyed pottery as a girl but had never followed up this minor interest. It seemed clear that the daughter had no real artistic bent and that Mrs Newton was merely trying to meet Lucy on some shared ground. She worked in London, Mrs Newton had revealed when Lucy asked about her, and she had referred to her as Jennifer.

What a strange coincidence, thought Lucy, and how bitter were the consequences of jealousy. A guilty pang hit her as she remembered her own illicit lunch with Tim in London. It had been fun, a natural thing to do, since she happened to be there, or so she had told herself then; but there had been spice in their meeting, excitement, potential for more had things been different. She had known Tim for years, had had a brief affair with him at university before she and Simon started going out together. You never forgot the first, it was said, and for her there had been only two, Tim and Simon. If she and Tim were shipwrecked on a desert island, fidelity to Simon would be impossible. She still found Tim attractive, and she liked him; he felt the same, she knew, despite Susan and their three children. This was how affairs began, gathered momentum, involved other people and could destroy them.

She shivered. She wanted nothing like that to endanger her life. She loved Simon, even if he was often vague and sometimes dull. He worked hard and had worries at the lab to do with financial restrictions, the ambitions of his younger staff, and the passionate love life of one of his technicians who, before now, had fallen asleep at his bench.

She finished her coffee and went back to her workroom to continue working on the necklace she had been commissioned to make as a silver wedding present for the wife of the mayor of Wintlebury. She had only the catch to finish; then it could be exhibited tomorrow at the craft fair which was to take place in the town hall, and where she would have a stall.

After her mother had left the room, Jennifer drank her coffee and ate her toast and marmalade, which was home-made. The tray had been laid attractively, the butter and marmalade arranged in small glass pots. Her mother never dropped her standards, Jennifer reflected, and that had to be admired. Her own were high, too; Daniel could never complain about her in that respect—nor in any other. Oh, true, she found him slow and would needle him, trying to prod his ambition. He could rise to the very top if he tried, she told him. Sometimes she devised schemes in which they would start their own business and he had laughed and said he did not want ultimate responsibility.

"We're in good jobs, with good salaries and prospects," he had said, and had taken her off to France for a bargain weekend break.

She had not been content. She had wanted change, excitement, and to feel important. At work she would never rank among the high-fliers; she was capable, and until recently had been accurate; she had energy, but in the eyes of her employers her judgement was uncertain and she could be abrasive, making her sometimes difficult to get along with, though in other moods she was amusing and good company. She was aware that she could easily be replaced by someone just as able and this sapped her confidence, but work had come second to Daniel. He had been her prime concern. They had shared chores; he was a good cook and liked being in the kitchen, and he had ironed his own shirts, but she had done most of the cleaning and polishing, and willingly, loving to care for the things they had bought together, and enjoying entertaining. She wore the role of hostess with some grace because to play it filled her with pride, and Daniel always praised her afterwards. She saw herself as a social asset to him as he rose up in the hierarchy of, if not his present firm, another. She would be equal to any demand that might be made of her and in due course there would be children—two, at most. They were part of the trappings of the prosperous life she aimed at for them both, as would be, eventually, a place in the country, even if only for weekends.

She had not thought in detail about the children. She did not know many and rarely saw her nieces. Babies were quite sweet, especially when asleep. She imagined that nature contrived for you to like your own and when she heard of wakeful nights and toddler tantrums, she dismissed such problems as caused by poor infant management.

Now there were going to be no children. Could she have held on to him by becoming pregnant? It was not too late, if she could get him into bed again. Then he would have to stick by her; he'd want to. All that nonsense with that silly girl would end and need never be spoken of again. She dwelt on this appealing prospect for some time, almost convincing herself that she could make it happen, and to order.

But if it failed, she didn't want a baby on her own. Some women did, but Jennifer was not among them. She would lose her liberty, and much more besides.

Her mother had a point about the break-up being Daniel's fault as much as Stephanie's. She had thought about it, walking in the night around the lanes that made up the village. Perhaps she was punishing the wrong person. She lay in bed, pondering, and then her mother tapped on the door and entered the room without being granted permission. She stood at the foot of the bed gazing down at Jennifer, and spoke.

"I want to know exactly what you did," she said. "You said there was an argument and you broke a window. Your solicitor has been on the telephone. It sounds serious."

Jennifer sat up in bed and stared at her mother who had the odd impression that inside the mature woman who was her daughter, there lurked a ten-year-old who was still afraid of the dark and of being baffled by her homework.

Last night, pacing the neighbourhood in the darkness, Jennifer had passed houses whose inhabitants were unknown to her, as anonymous as those in London. Here and there a light had burned at an upstairs window or in a porch; the shop had a glow from somewhere at the back. One car went past her, and a motorbike. She had wild thoughts of getting a stick and poking it through windows, needing to shatter the complacence of the smug sleepers, as she imagined them to be. She was unaware of asthma, bereavement, money worries, chronic antagonisms harboured beneath the quiet roofs. She had strayed into the churchyard and sat on a cold tombstone waiting for ghosts to appear but the only spectres she saw were those in her mind. The church itself was locked; had it been open, she might have spent the night inside it, so that in the morning her mother would be alarmed by her absence. Why should she, Jennifer, be the only one to suffer? How could her mother, toothache or not, go up to bed and leave her to get her own supper and spend the time alone? They had never been close, thought Jennifer, whilst acknowledging the quiet efficiency which had ordered her childhood: the neatly sewn nametapes; the games clothes always spruce; the excellent tea for her friends; the French exchange arranged and returned with painful politeness on both sides.

The coldness of the night had at last driven Jennifer to return to Yew Cottage and it had taken her some time, despite a bath and the electric blanket in her bed, to get warm again. No wonder she felt like death this morning and here was her mother bent on lecturing her.

"You told me you had an argument and broke a window in—er—Stephanie's flat," said Mrs Newton.

"Well?"

"I believe you threw a stone at the window," said Mrs Newton.

"So what?"

"I thought the damage was caused by accident," said Mrs Newton. "But it was deliberate."

Jennifer did not answer.

"You could have hurt someone. What if broken glass, or the stone itself, had hit someone in the room?"

"Pity it didn't," growled Jennifer.

"You can't mean that."

"Why not?" Jennifer was defiant.

"There was an argument," Mrs Newton persisted. "How did that end with throwing stones?"

"There was only one stone. The argument, as you call it, came first," said Jennifer. "Earlier," she added. "Several hours earlier," she elaborated, to make it clear.

"You mean you waited outside the house and then threw the stone?"

"I went back," said Jennifer sulkily.

Mrs Newton felt slightly faint.

"Violence solves nothing," she said. "It's destructive."

"Stephanie's destroyed my life," said Jennifer.

"You're destroying it yourself," said Mrs Newton. If she had immediately agreed to lend Jennifer the money she had wanted, would this crime have been prevented? At this rate, it might be needed for her defence if she went on behaving recklessly. "You must accept what has happened. Daniel has found someone else he means to marry. The rest of your life lies ahead of you. Perhaps you should change your job, get to know new people, maybe move to another part of the country. Scotland, perhaps," suggested Mrs Newton, unaware that Jennifer had mentally moved her up there, and for one of the same reasons: the cheaper property, which Mrs

Newton now mentioned. "It's healthy," she added. "Bracing."

"You've never been there," Jennifer answered curtly.

"Oh yes, I have," said Mrs Newton. "During the war."

She never talked about that time. Jennifer felt quite startled to hear it mentioned now.

"You're trying to get rid of me," she said. "You want to banish me."

Lying in bed, she felt at a disadvantage, as if she was a naughty child sent there for punishment, though to be fair, that was something her mother had never done. She had been sent upstairs only until she felt able to return "feeling pleasant," as her mother had put it. Her room had never doubled as a prison.

"That's foolish talk, Jennifer," said Mrs Newton. "I want you to find enough courage to put the past behind you and begin again. First, though, you've got to get through this court business safely. Your solicitor suggests that you should see a doctor who would say that you have been under strain recently and so obtain tolerance for you from the bench."

"Did he really say that? Were those his actual words?" asked Jennifer.

"Not precisely," said her mother. "They represent his meaning."

Suddenly Jennifer began to giggle.

"How pompous," she said. "How legalistic," and as she laughed her mirth wobbled over into hysteria. She writhed in the bed, out of control, half laughing, half weeping.

"Jennifer!"

Mrs Newton watched her quivering form, back arched, hands clutching the duvet cover, and wondered how to bring her back to sanity. A slap would not be right; a bucket of cold water poured over her would be more effective but was impractical; why soak the bedding?

Hysterics were a means of craving attention. Deny it, and without an audience, there would be no point in continuing.

It was no good speaking. Jennifer would not hear the words. Mrs Newton collected the tray and went out of the room, closing the door behind her. She stood on the landing listening to the sobs which now exceeded the guffaws. She was trembling herself. What if this went on? What if Jennifer did not calm down?

After a while it occurred to her to telephone her doctor, whom she seldom saw but whom she had consulted several weeks ago when she cut herself badly and required three stitches.

"I was careless," she had told the doctor. "I was cutting something in the kitchen and the knife slipped."

The doctor had put the stitches in, and removed them several days later. He was a man of forty or so whom she had seen previously for a bad cough and for a stomach disorder which would not settle down. He knew she was no malingerer.

She telephoned him, being firm, insisting on speaking to him, not the receptionist, telling him that her daughter was in rather serious trouble and was now upstairs, hysterical.

He promised to come round as soon as surgery was over, and by the time he arrived Jennifer had ceased her weeping, though she had not found the courage to come down and face her mother. She was sitting in her dressing gown looking out of her bedroom window at the wintry garden scene, where the leaves were off most of the trees, and beneath the brooding shadow of the heavy yew some sparrows hopped about seeking nourishment.

Mrs Newton took him upstairs and knocked on Jennifer's door, opening it immediately.

"Here's Dr Brewster. Please let him help you, Jennifer," she said, and left them to it.

At sight of the doctor, Jennifer's face had changed, lighted up, and she had become almost beautiful. Now she had a stranger to impress, thought Mrs Newton, someone who was not familiar with her moods. This was the face she had shown

Daniel in the beginning; this was what he had loved. Why could she not be like that all the time?

She went downstairs to wait for the doctor's verdict. Probably he would tell her nothing. When your child became an adult, she had rights to privacy; but then, reflected Mrs Newton sadly, surely parents also had some rights?

The doctor had given Jennifer a sedative.

When he came downstairs, Mrs Newton met him in the hall.

"What can you tell me?" she asked.

"I'll make out a prescription," he said. "Something to calm her down."

He followed Mrs Newton into the sitting-room where he sat down and began scribbling on his pad.

"Tranquillisers," she said.

He nodded.

"Necessary for the moment," he said. "Some counselling would be a good idea. Many practices have counsellors attached to them now. We have one who's excellent."

"Did she tell you what she'd done? That she's on remand, on bail?" asked Mrs Newton.

"No," said the doctor. "Oh dear!"

Mrs Newton briefly explained.

"She's been advised by her solicitor to see a psychiatrist who may help to get her a light sentence," Mrs Newton said.

"That seems a good idea," said the doctor. "When would this be?"

"Early next week, if she can get an appointment," said Mrs Newton. "Her solicitor has recommended someone."

"Well, I suggest she takes the tranquillisers in the meantime," said Dr Brewster. "They'll make her feel easier." He frowned. "This is difficult for you."

"Yes," agreed Mrs Newton.

"In a way, this burst of weeping and so on may have been useful," said Dr Brewster. "Her anger may have spent its force."

"I hope you're right," said Mrs Newton.

"If she needs the counsellor, just telephone," he instructed. "Perhaps afterwards—" he let the sentence dwindle away.

"No one seems to be encouraged to help themselves these days," said Mrs Newton. "Counsellors come in at the first hint of trouble."

"Sometimes people can't get themselves back on course," he said. "Then damage can be done. Serious damage."

"I know." Mrs Newton sighed, and squared her own thin shoulders. "Thank you, Dr Brewster. I'll ring you if she needs more help."

She saw the doctor out, then looked at the prescription he had left. She would fetch the tablets. The remedy must, at least, be tried.

She went upstairs. The curtains in Jennifer's room were drawn and she seemed to be asleep. Dr Brewster must have given her an injection. Sure enough, the discarded needle and some swabs were in the wastepaper basket. Mrs Newton gathered them up to throw them away. Then she went off to Wintlebury in the car. As she drove off, she looked for the young man, Neil, next door, but the site was deserted. Work must be finished. She was quite surprised that he had not come round touting for more odd jobs.

In town, she collected the tablets and bought sole from the fish van which parked on Fridays in the space near the library, then some fresh fruit, and two bottles of Beaujolais which Jennifer might drink as a tonic. Frederick had been keen on a good red wine as a restorative. When they were first married, he had opened a bottle every night for dinner, unless they were eating fish. She bought some white wine, too, for Jennifer, ever pernickety, would want that with the sole.

Perhaps drink should not be combined with the tranquillisers, but if so, Dr Brewster had not mentioned it.

Walking quickly round the town, Mrs Newton looked out for Lucy Moffat, but she did not see her. Her own sore gum and swollen face still troubled her. She'd take sherry for that, she thought, and went back to buy another bottle. She almost laughed, looking at the contents of her basket, so concentrated were they on medicine and alcohol. She bought some grapes and a pineapple to set the balance straight.

When she reached home, Jennifer was still in her room, and she stayed there all day. Mrs Newton took her up her radio and cassette player, and some tapes of books she had borrowed from the library: Jane Austen and Thackeray: Mrs Newton liked the classics. Modern novels were too introspective, and detective novels far too preoccupied with violence; there was enough of that in real life without reading about it, she thought, and real life did not, as in fiction, provide tidy solutions to every problem.

Jennifer made no acknowledgement of these offerings, but when her mother went in later with a bowl of home-made soup and some toast, the radio was on.

All the afternoon, Mrs Newton worked at her tapestry. She had a second radio; accustomed to her solitary life, she had the props necessary to connect her with the world and to keep her company, and back-ups in case of failure of essentials. Sooner or later, Jennifer would emerge, would come downstairs, would have to talk.

At half-past three, Mrs Newton telephoned the London psychiatrist whom the solicitor had recommended, explained the situation to his secretary and was granted an appointment for Jennifer for the following Tuesday, two days before the hearing. If she could persuade Jennifer to keep it, the whole thing might be cleared up at some expense but without further trouble. If not, perhaps the solicitor could obtain an extra period's grace on remand.

By the end of next week Jennifer herself might be capable of creating a good impression in the dock; she might even have begun to take steps towards her own recovery.

But her mother doubted it.

15

It rained on Saturday morning.

Mavis Smith was preparing to go off and do the shopping; pork, she'd planned, for Sunday dinner. She began bundling Jason into his pushchair to take him with her.

"Poor little kid, he'll get soaked," said Neil.

"He's got his plastic cover," Mavis replied.

"I'll mind him," offered Neil. "He'll be better in the warm. Got a cold, hasn't he?"

It was true. Jason had been snivelling the previous day, and during the night had woken everyone with his crying. This morning Roseanne was working and had left already. Kevin wasn't up yet; he had come in very late. No doubt he'd be going out later.

His car was not parked in its usual spot outside the house, though there was space for it. It was unusual for him to leave it up the road. Neil's van occupied the drive and Kevin, who was always last in and last out, parked beside the gate, sometimes blocking it so that Neil had to push the Merc to get the van past. He never drove Kevin's car.

After his mother had gone, Neil settled Jason in a big armchair, wedged in with cushions, and put the television on.

Children's programmes were in progress. Propped up, Jason could watch the bright, crude cartoons. Soon he'd be crawling, moving around, and couldn't be left dumped; mobile, he'd become more of a problem, but he'd start chatting, turn into more of a person. Neil looked forward to that. He'd take him for proper walks, show him the nice things in the country, pigs and cows and ducks, help him to grow up healthy. They'd walk along hand in hand. It would be almost like having a kid of his own. Neil didn't expect ever to do that—have his own wife and family. The hurdle of finding a girl must first be overcome and he would never have the courage to go looking for one. At school he'd found girls strange, alien, difficult to talk to, although Roseanne's friends had liked him. They thought him quiet and interesting—too quiet, perhaps, with little to say and he never wanted to go bowling or to discos, spending his time tinkering with that old scooter he had. Then he went out of circulation. He was suspect after that, though a few girls thought he'd acquired glamour with his record. One invited him to a party and he refused because he had promised his mother he'd be home by ten. He became known as a mummy's boy, but he didn't mind that; it was safer to stay quiet, away from trouble. His one aim was to buy a set of wheels; working on his car, when he bought it, would give him something to do. He liked driving around, going to river banks to watch the fishermen; that was a good sort of sport, he thought, practised alone, with no fuss, and it took you away from folk who tried to hassle you. He thought he would like to take it up, take Jason with him, fit him up with his own little rod and line when he was bigger.

The boy already enjoyed going out in his van. He'd got one of those proper little seats kids had to have and fitted it to the passenger seat when he took Jason with him. He faced backwards, head towards the dash, and they could talk, or Neil could talk to Jason, who would gurgle back.

When Jason could toddle, they'd play ball. He might grow up to be a footballer if he started young enough. Already Neil had tasted the pleasure of vicarious living.

Mavis was glad that Neil had taken Jason off her hands this morning, although she never minded having the little lad along; she was so used to bundling him round in his pushchair, a wire basket on her arm. She shopped little and often, unable to carry home the heavy loads of those who came in cars, and watchful, also, of the budget. Kevin hadn't been giving her as much as usual lately; he said he was on short time at the works but she'd seen nothing about that in the local free paper, which gave you all the news, and no one else had mentioned it to her, though there had been talk of laying people off. It was happening everywhere just now. That wouldn't happen to Kevin, though; he was too useful. He had a responsible job in the stores department and had been earning well. It was this recession that was the trouble. She was thankful that she had weekly rent to pay and not a mortgage, but that new tax they'd introduced had hit them hard; everyone except Jason was eligible. They were paying in instalments; it seemed the easiest way.

That afternoon she hoped to go to the craft fair in the town hall. She liked looking at all the things laid out, even though she couldn't buy any of them. She wondered if young Jane Moffat would help her mother at her stall; usually when she came home she brought a pile of books and spent hours working in her room. Those two Moffat youngsters were the same ages as Neil and Roseanne, yet they were not earning. Was it worth it, all that studying? None of hers was clever enough to have gone to university, but all were practical. Neil's plans to become a mechanic might have worked out if he hadn't got himself into trouble; he seemed to like the carpentry, however, and maybe there was a future there for him. Roseanne's plight could have happened to anyone; indeed, Mavis herself had got married because Kevin was on the way, and in those days, that was what you did, made it legal, though later you often regretted it, as she had done. Still, that was life, and most people, then, had made the best of things, not like these days. She had her compensations;

she loved her children, and they her; they helped each other out and Roseanne was very grateful for the support they gave her with Jason. It did you good to see how fond Neil was of the little chap, and it was mutual. Jason would stop crying for Neil, laughed when he saw him, and already tried to move towards him though he couldn't sit up yet. It was a treat to see them together. Of course it was time Neil showed an interest in girls, but he would, when he grew more confident. That spell inside had set him back, and no wonder. Mrs Smith couldn't understand how such a dreadful thing had happened. Well, he'd learned his lesson; he'd do nothing like that again. It had been good of Len to give him a chance. He'd done it for old time's sake, he'd told Mavis, meeting her in The Bell when she was behind the bar. He still brought her home once a week, making a detour on the way. On rare occasions, when the house was empty but for Jason, he came to see her and in the summer there was a copse they knew of which was quiet. She was fond of Len. He said his wife wouldn't let him touch her but they got on well otherwise, and they'd never split up now. Mavis wouldn't want that to happen, she hadn't time for any more and she liked running her own show, the family dependent on her. Len, full time, would be a complication.

She put them all out of her mind as she toured the supermarket, trying to remember everything they needed.

Neil was just going to start his usual weekend labour of cleaning the van when Kevin came and asked if he could borrow it for the day.

Neil had been planning to prop Jason behind the wheel so that he could pretend to be Nigel Mansell while he washed and polished, then take him for a spin.

"Sorry, no, Kev," he said. "It's not insured for you to drive."

"Don't worry about it," said Kevin. "I'll keep it safe. I've promised to move some stuff for a guy—he got this load of electrical stuff cheap and he's got a buyer. I'll get a good cut for coming up with the wheels and I'll pass some on to you. Safe as houses, it is."

"But where's the Merc?" asked Neil.

"The brakes went. It's being fixed," said Kevin.

Neil protested a little more, but in the end, as Kevin had known he would, he gave in.

"You'll see it back soon, none the worse," Kevin promised.

He took the keys Neil gave him and set off, whistling.

He had had to dump his own car.

He had been out on a job the previous day with a man he had met in a pub in Crimpford, and it had gone wrong. Kevin had been out of work for three weeks, but he had stuck to his normal routine, leaving home at the usual time as if nothing had changed. He was afraid of telling his mother he had been sacked, and with every day it became harder to do so. He had been unemployed before but had always found something else very quickly; this time, it wasn't so easy. He didn't want to do ill-paid work of a humdrum nature; good money was what he needed. He liked what it could buy and was used to spending lavishly, eking his wages out, as he'd always done, by jobs on the side when he lifted goods and sold them on. He liked impressing women he met by waving a full wallet around; he had learned how to have a good time—drink, sex, weekends abroad—without responsibility. There were plenty of willing women about with motives much like his, and he could soon spot the other sort, the kind who had security on their minds, which meant a wedding ring and a mortgage, and a good deal for them if later it all fell in ruins. At the back of his mind he had the idea of running a firm of his own, something legitimate, with maybe a few rackets on the side when the chance arose, but at the moment it was hard to see where the best openings lay, and he thought he might need a partner. He'd even considered a second-hand car business, with Neil in to help, for the kid knew a lot about cars and was quite a mechanic. The snag was that he was so immature and wouldn't want to be mixed up in anything that was the slightest bit bent. Anyway, this was no time to be setting anything up, with interest rates so high, but better days would come. Life was a seesaw and recession would be followed by a boom time, as sure as day followed night.

But things had taken a bad turn when he joined up with Frank Todd to rob a building society in Crimpford. Kevin hadn't expected it to be such heavy action; Frank had planned to raid a radio and television shop next to the building society just after lunchtime, when it wasn't busy and the second assistant was off having his break. Frank had a dummy gun. It had seemed a bit of a laugh, dressing up in a combat jacket and balaclava mask and all that: Kevin had done nothing like it before; his scams had been monetary deals when he passed on stolen goods to someone else, except for the few times he'd cut out the third party and made his own sale.

The radio shop was unexpectedly busy; they'd seen that, standing outside, masks in hand, ready to put on at the last moment. It got the old adrenalin going, waiting on the kerb. They were going to raid the till and scoop up any small items they could carry; Frank would go after the cash and Kevin had a large plastic bag for the goods. The Mercedes was parked close by, ready for their getaway; they had waited for the spot until a woman shopper had at last driven off in her Golf. But that day the shop had a special offer, a ten per cent cut on all stock, and customers were crowded inside. They'd had to change their plan and Frank had decided they'd hold up the building society instead. He'd looked in and seen that there was only one customer inside, an elderly woman with white hair, dressed in a brown coat, and as soon as she emerged, Frank had put on his mask and gone in, waving his imitation gun, while Kevin sat in the car with the engine ticking over, ready to leave in a hurry. In advance, he'd smeared mud on his number plates, obscuring the letters and figures; he hadn't equipped himself with false plates because this was, for him, uncharted territory.

Frank had only been in the place a few seconds when someone else entered behind him, a young woman this time, in jeans and a white jacket. Kevin didn't think twice: he'd reacted instinctively, pulling on his mask and leaping out of the car. He'd burst in and caught the woman by the arm, twisting it behind her while at the same time putting his hand over her mouth. Meanwhile money was being meekly handed over to Frank at the counter.

The woman writhed and tried to kick Kevin. He twisted her arm still further and she made muffled sounds of pain; then he cuffed her on the side of the head, by which time Frank was ready to leave. Kevin threw the woman across the room so that she stumbled and fell as he, too, fled.

The two of them sprang into the car and drove off. Once on the edge of town they split up. Frank gave Kevin a wad of notes, then got out of the car and sauntered off up the road.

"Get rid of the car," he instructed. "You hurt that bitch."

Kevin knew he had; his own strength had surprised him as he flung her away, but she was light and slight and he was a big, burly man. He drove into the country, alarmed but also exhilarated. The physical danger, new to him, had stimulated him, made him come alive, and it was only after he had gone some distance that he took in what Frank had said about the Merc. He'd have to dump it, and that was a horrible thought. Where would he be without the car? And it represented all his capital.

He'd get another later, when things were quiet. He'd steal one, alter the plates and the colour. Now he had begun on this kind of thing, all he needed to do was to get clever. He took the Merc to a patch of waste ground near a rubbish tip, and there he set it alight, putting a match to the upholstery and then standing back to watch. It didn't take long. He knew kids stole cars and burned them, just for fun; to Kevin the blaze which ended the life of his Mercedes was a funeral pyre and it filled him with sorrow. Once it caught, it blazed fiercely. He walked back to the main road and hitched a ride back to Wintlebury where he spent the evening drinking. He still had the black balaclava, and he wore the combat jacket under his leather one.

Of the haul from the building society, Frank had given him only seventy pounds, mainly in fivers.

The raid had attracted attention and was reported on the local radio. Kevin heard it in a pub. A woman had received head injuries and a broken arm; she was detained in hospital. Two men were being sought.

He hadn't broken her arm. He'd twisted it, yes, but it hadn't snapped. He appreciated women, didn't believe in roughing them up and had never done so before; still, he'd had to prevent her from screaming and raising the alarm. She'd mend, and she hadn't seen either him or Frank without their masks.

Frank had cheated him. The news had said that five thousand pounds had been taken in the robbery. While Kevin was busy driving away, Frank had stashed most of the haul in his pockets, concealing the success of the raid from him and giving him peanuts, with no compensation for the loss of his car. He'd put that right one day. Let Frank wait. Kevin would get even.

Now, the next day, he drove around for a while in Neil's van. Its engine ran smoothly; even the windscreen wipers were reliable. The kid certainly tended it like a mother. As rain pattered down, Kevin wondered how to begin the day which he planned would include a visit to Middle Bardolph. No one would look twice at Len Harding's van there, accustomed as they were to seeing it on the site next to where the old girl, his target, lived.

At The Prince Hal, he missed the turning and drove on through Upper Bardolph until he came to the village of Little Nym, a cluster of cottages strung out in a line, with a few bungalows set amid them, and one shop. It was raining, and no one was out in the street. On impulse, Kevin stopped outside the shop and glanced inside. It was empty of customers.

The chance was too good to miss. He put on his balaclava mask, picked up an adjustable spanner which Neil had left in the dash shelf, and rushed into the shop.

A woman assistant, her back to him, was stacking bottles of mineral water in a rack at the rear. She turned as he came in, ready to smile a welcome, and Kevin lifted the spanner threateningly.

"Empty out the till," he growled, his words muffled by the black wool across his face.

The woman, who was about forty, gave a squeal and cringed back against the shelves.

"Empty the till, I said," Kevin repeated, and she very slowly moved to do so, then cowered back again.

There were notes in some sections of the drawer; coins, sorted as to value, lay in others. Kevin pulled out the notes and the pound coins, shoving them into his pocket, then, from the corner of his eye, he saw that the woman had picked up a bottle from the floor and raised it as a weapon. Without a moment's hesitation, he lifted the spanner and hit her upraised arm as hard as he could, knocking the bottle from her grasp and causing her to give a scream of pain. She clutched her hurt arm with the other, hugging it to her, beginning to whimper.

"Shut your gob or you'll get another," Kevin warned, and he ran from the shop, jumped into the van and drove off.

The woman, alone in the shop and with no one in the house beyond, took a few moments to pull herself together before she could raise the alarm and seek help for herself. Kevin, with his single blow, had smashed her wrist.

Meanwhile, he was driving off, well pleased with this opportunist snatch. Unfortunately for him, there had not been much money in the till because it was emptied every night and so far little had been taken that day. When he stopped and counted it, he found it was less than thirty pounds. So far his robberies had not been very profitable, considering the effort and risk they had involved.

He'd do the old girl next. She'd have loads of loot in that place and he could take his time if he parked his van on the site next door. She might be out, which would make things easier, and he could soon get in, using the key Neil had mentioned. But if she was there, he'd still do the place. If she kept quiet, he'd not hurt her, but if she got stroppy, well, she'd have only herself to blame, like the woman in Little Nym.

Jennifer slept late that morning. Mrs Newton had encouraged her to come downstairs the previous evening, but after watching the news on television and eating her sole, which she seemed to enjoy, she had begun yawning and had gone upstairs again. Her mother attributed her sleepiness to the doctor's treatment, welcoming it as the best remedy for her wound-up state, and felt she should have realised sooner that Jennifer's apparent acceptance of Daniel's defection was superficial. With proper rest, she would feel better about it all, Mrs Newton decided; she could not bear to contemplate what would follow if this did not happen. Meanwhile, Jennifer upstairs in bed was safe, not out in the streets breaking windows.

How should they spend the weekend? Mrs Newton's own physical problems were much easier today; her swollen jaw had subsided and the gum was much more comfortable; her head was clear. She wondered if Geoffrey would decide to come down to confer about Jennifer's difficulties. Her attitude to this was divided; she wanted him to come because it would demonstrate concern and mean that he was shouldering his duty; on the other hand, he would pontificate, be pompous, lecture his mother on her obligation to solve his and Jennifer's financial worries for them, and they might all end by quarrelling.

He telephoned at nine o'clock.

"I can't come down," he said, before she could ask him to do so. "I realise you need some help, but I've important matters to attend to here, and I'm sure you're managing. You've always done so."

Sweet talk, thought his mother, and a sour taste rose in her mouth.

"Oh, I'm managing," she assured him, but she would not give him the dispensation which she knew he wanted by telling him that all was well.

"How is she, then?" he was obliged to ask.

"Sleeping a lot," said Mrs Newton.

"Have you called in Dr Brewster?"

"Yes."

"What did he say?" Her brief replies infuriated Geoffrey. Why couldn't she be more reassuring?

"He's prescribed tranquillisers. Short term, I'm sure that's wise, as long as she doesn't become dependent on them," Mrs Newton said.

"What did he say about her?"

"He can't say much to me. He may have said more to her," said Mrs Newton.

"But you're her mother!"

"She's adult. She has a right to confidence," said Mrs Newton, and then weakened enough to repeat what Dr Brewster had said about the counsellor, and added that Jennifer had an appointment with the psychiatrist recommended by her solicitor.

"I hope she keeps it," Geoffrey said. "Will you see that she does?"

"I can try," was all Mrs Newton could guarantee.

Their conversation ended with relief on both sides, and Geoffrey told her to ring him if he could help in any way.

Unaccustomed tears stood in Mrs Newton's tired eyes when she replaced the receiver. He did not mean it; if he did, he would be on his way to Middle Bardolph at this very moment. He was only going through the motions. She knew he had troubles of his own; Lynn was probably giving him a hard time and he could be fighting to save his own marriage, but he must manage that, or not, without his mother's aid. If only she could feel some warmth from him, some true affection. Once he had been a sturdy schoolboy with chapped knees scarred from tumbles off his bicycle. Now he was an overweight middle-aged man with a tendency to drink too much and an extravagant wife and two daughters whom she, their grandmother, barely knew as individuals.

She took Jennifer up some breakfast and was greeted with a mumbled "Good morning." That was something: an improvement on previous form. The small mellowing cheered Mrs Newton; Jennifer might have turned the corner.

"It's raining," she said, but in a brisk tone. "The forecast says it will brighten later. Perhaps you'd like to go out to lunch somewhere? There's a nice pub at Grayling by the river. We could go for a walk there, if it clears up." She had been there with the Blaneys.

"I don't think so," said Jennifer, and added, "Thanks all the same. Haven't you got things you want to do? I don't want to interfere with your social life."

Mrs Newton had no social life, and Jennifer knew it. She sometimes looked in at functions in the village, the odd coffee morning, the summer fête, but she neither gave nor attended drinks parties. Long ago she had resolved never to get involved, to make no ties she could not easily break, to give no part of herself, to protect herself from pain. She had always moved on before even the most casual friendship became more; no man, woman nor child except her own had been allowed to come close to her and if occasionally she felt tempted to relax this rule, as had happened very rarely, she had put up an invisible barricade around herself to ward off the danger.

She went downstairs and found the post lying on the mat. There was a bill and Jennifer's petulant letter posted before she threw the stone.

Mrs Newton tore it into tiny pieces and threw the fragments in the dustbin.

16

Jennifer felt as if she was in a dream—aware of what was happening around her but detached, as if watching from some remote viewpoint. She knew she was at Yew Cottage; if she looked out of her bedroom window she would see the big old tree on the lawn. She remembered what had happened to make her run here, but it was as though someone else had smashed the window, been to court, caught the train. She knew she would have to go to court again and yet it seemed impossible that she would do so. It was also impossible for her to spend the day in her mother's company, and she could not go back to the house in London for no one else would be there; it would be just Jennifer, alone.

Daniel should be there, waiting for her. She pretended that he would be, letting herself drift into an anticipatory dream of desire until into her mind's eye came images of Daniel with Stephanie, and the dazed feeling induced by exhaustion and the doctor's tablets began to recede as once again the hatred she felt for the other woman surged within her. Then she remembered what her mother had said about Daniel's part in this; how he, not Stephanie, was to blame.

Was she right? Jennifer considered it, and could not agree.

Daniel had been weak; that was all. It was Stephanie who was shameless and bold, pursuing him until he found himself unable to resist; she had the charm of novelty, Jennifer allowed. But it was she whom he loved; he had proved it by helping her when the police made such a meal of a mere accident with a stone. Why, they had carried on as if she was a football hooligan or yobbo vandal. No real harm had been done; surely the whole thing could have been ignored? But no, the wheels of bureaucracy had begun to grind and she was charged.

Unable to let it go, Jennifer worried at her jealous misery like a terrier with a rat. It must be possible to dismiss Stephanie and to bring Daniel to his senses.

Lying there in bed, her pulse beating more rapidly, the fresh dose of medication due but now forgotten, Jennifer worked out that Daniel and Stephanie would be out of London for the weekend. Had she heard him mention that they were going to Wiltshire, or had she imagined it? Had she heard him tell William that was where he would be, or did she just sense that it was so?

It did not really matter. If they were not in London, they would be in the country, and without a shared base it was easy to work out where they would go; she knew they went there often at weekends for she had watched them leave, had seen Daniel collect Stephanie from the office just as he used to collect her, and drive off. One weekend Jennifer had hired a car and followed them, learning the address from the telephone directory. She had located the grey stone manor house in a small village where people kept horses and life was, or seemed to be, peaceful. She had prowled round the village, noticed the single shop, had lunch in the pub hoping they would walk in, but they hadn't. She'd thought of ringing the bell at the house, crashing in, demanding a showdown, but in the end had turned away, afraid of what she might be taking on.

She'd do it now. She had nothing to lose.

She swung out of bed feeling suddenly energetic, quickly

washed and dressed and went downstairs looking bright and
perky, quite different from the pale, jaded woman who had
arrived on Thursday.

Mrs Newton, in the kitchen, wondering what to feed her
on over the weekend, looked up in surprise as Jennifer came
in.

"You won't mind if I borrow the car," said Jennifer, not
asking, but assuming.

Where did she want to go? Mrs Newton bit back the question which might not receive a truthful answer. Probably she
simply meant to go to Wintlebury, or possibly Crimpford, for
things she might be lacking if she meant to stay until the
hearing.

"Will you need it for long?" she asked. "There's a craft
fair in Wintlebury this afternoon. I'd planned to go to it."
She'd meant to visit Lucy's stall.

"I might be back," said Jennifer. "I'm not sure." She
hadn't worked out how far it was to the Wiltshire village
where Stephanie's parents lived. "Will you mind very much
if you miss the fair?"

"No," said Mrs Newton, inured to disappointment, and
she added, "It goes on till five o'clock." Implicitly, she had
consented to Jennifer taking the car. "Don't rush back from
wherever you're going," she said, and wondered if Jennifer,
on tranquillisers and overwrought, was in a fit state to drive.
But how could she stop her, except by denying her the car
keys? She seemed much better this morning, almost too
bright: febrile.

There was plenty in the freezer: chops, bread, frozen vegetables; she did not need the car for shopping. She would settle
down with Jonathan Raban, and get on with her sewing; she
might finish the cushion cover she was working on.

"I just thought I'd like a day in the country, on my own,"
said Jennifer, relenting slightly. "I don't know what time I'll
be back, so don't start worrying." She might not return at
all. Daniel might sweep her back to London, she thought,
forgetting about her mother's car in this version of the future.

"You'll need some petrol," Mrs Newton warned, and was going to reach for her purse, to give Jennifer the money, when her hand was patted firmly.

"I'll pay," said Jennifer, and went upstairs to fetch her jacket.

When she came down a few minutes later, her mother was watering the chrysanthemum on the hall table. Jennifer had brought her breakfast tray down; she had forgotten it earlier. She left it on the kitchen table, putting the used crockery on the draining board. Then she opened one of the drawers, and took out a kitchen knife, running her fingers over its length before selecting it from among several others. It was very sharp, and had a long, thin blade. She slipped it in her big pocket.

"Can I do any shopping for you, Mother?" she asked, returning to the hall, and when Mrs Newton said no, there was nothing she needed urgently, Jennifer resolved to buy her some flowers.

But of course she forgot.

Kevin reversed Neil's van into the driveway next to Yew Cottage. He could get away fast if that was necessary; he could easily take his loot across the fence, breaking one of the hurdles he and his brother had so painstakingly put up. He glanced round the renovated house, peering in through the windows; old fittings had been ripped out; the kitchen alone must have cost a bomb. All the window frames had been replaced and two small rooms on the ground floor knocked into one. Whoever had bought it was in the money and might be worth visiting, once they'd moved in; Neil didn't seem to know anything about them; business people from London, he thought; they'd scarcely been near the place while the work was in progress. It was a pity Neil was so dim; he'd a good chance, with a job like his, of knowing where there were likely to be pickings, even of finding keys— at least he'd been sharp enough to note the old woman's hiding place. Kevin could see that a well-planned visit to empty premises could be lucrative. He did not think of his earlier thefts as crimes; no private individuals had been affected as the goods had been taken from factories or in transit. If he hadn't lost his job, he'd have stuck to that kind of thing, but now, he reasoned, he had no choice, and he had lost his good car into the bargain.

This old girl would have plenty of stuff. She'd got silver displayed, and there'd be more in cupboards and drawers. She'd have jewellery, and there'd be cash, too, and a cheque book: all that. He'd do well here. The china ornaments she'd got might be worth a lot and he'd have to store them until he could find out where to take them. Hideous bits of china were worth hundreds of pounds, as he knew from the Sunday television programme his mother liked watching. Afterwards she'd look at the few pots and jugs they'd got in the house that had belonged to her mother and imagine them to be worth thousands. It wasn't very likely. Mrs Moffat, at The Old Vicarage, had a lot of stuff about, too; that place might be worth a visit and Kevin knew that Mrs Moffat was going to be at the craft fair that afternoon, but Dr Moffat would probably be at home and he was something else, a big man with a large, bushy beard, and no weakling. Kevin didn't fancy tackling him.

He walked along the fence separating the renovated house from Yew Cottage, past the new hurdles to the end. There, shrubs and bushes shielded Mrs Newton's garden from the field beyond. A post and rails fence marked the boundary and strong mesh wire kept rabbits and other stray creatures from invading her property. The field was down to grass which the farmer was planning to sell off as turf for lawns, a fact Mrs Newton did not yet know.

From the corner, Kevin could see Yew Cottage, its windows glinting in the pale winter light, all the curtains drawn back. What would the old girl be doing? Was she even at home? He could have telephoned to see if she answered, but he didn't know her name; maybe Neil hadn't mentioned it. She hadn't got a dog, which was something; there was no risk of noisy barking or snapping jaws when he entered. He glanced at his watch. It was only ten-fifteen; perhaps she'd be out at the shops; most people went shopping at weekends, didn't they, like his mother?

He slipped over the post and rails and, using as cover the shrubs which grew beside the fence he had helped to repair, he moved towards the house. He had his balaclava hood on now, and he wore gloves. There was the water butt which Neil had mentioned and somewhere below it was the key which would mean easy admittance. He'd take the old girl by surprise, frighten her into sitting tight while he ransacked the place. He frowned behind his wool mask which made his face itch; he should have brought some cord to tie her up with and a mock gun like the one Frank had used. But there'd be tights or something else in the house which he could use to bind her, and a cuff on the head would quieten her down if she gave any trouble.

Then he heard a sound. It was the garage doors opening. She was going out. What a break! He heard the car's engine start, and, peering cautiously round the side of the garage, saw the rear of Mrs Newton's Vauxhall, which Jennifer had turned in the small gravel space in front of the house, disappear towards the centre of the village and the road to Wintlebury.

He grinned. The job would be a cinch, for she lived alone and now he had all the time in the world: or at least, until she came back.

He went to collect the key. Once he was inside and had assembled his takings, he'd fetch the van round for easy loading; he didn't want to leave it outside the door for too long, in case it was seen there, whereas no one would question it where it was now, since it had been parked there every day for weeks.

Mrs Newton was upstairs, sorting out Jennifer's room. When she opened the window to air it, Kevin was already out of sight and round at the front of the house. Across the fence, she could see Neil's van parked next door and wondered why he was working on a Saturday; she thought the place was finished and had quite expected the new neighbours to move in at once. People lost no time these days, with bridging loans so expensive, even when you could get them. There had been a rumour that the new owners were renting a place while the work was done; perhaps they were in no hurry.

Jennifer, usually tidy, had left the bed unmade, the duvet flung back, the long tee-shirt she wore instead of a nightdress crumpled on the pillow. Mrs Newton folded it, frowning in distaste at such an unaesthetically pleasing garment.

Jennifer must learn, as she had done, to protect herself from being hurt. Now, Mrs Newton found it hard to remember the pain she had suffered more than forty years ago; it was as if all that jealous rage and grief had been felt by somebody else. Afterwards, she had met Frederick who had shown no curiosity about her life before they met, had accepted the little she chose to tell him and had brought her contentment.

Now she should be able to help Jennifer, but only if Jennifer herself were to make some effort.

Mrs Newton puffed up the duvet and pillows and remade the bed, pulling on the spread which matched the curtains. She would fetch the vacuum sweeper and a duster and give the room a quick clean; then it could be left until Monday, when Jennifer's plans might become clearer.

She closed the door so that the open window should not cause a draught and came downstairs, one hand on the banister rail. Once she had slipped, sliding painfully down the last few stairs and bruising the base of her spine; luckily she had not hurt herself seriously but since then she had moved more slowly, taking care, knowing that because she was so thin and slight she might have brittle bones which could break in a fall.

Dusters and sweeper were kept in the cupboard under the stairs. She never saw the man who hit her on the head with the pot of chrysanthemums from the hall table, lifting it high with both hands to bring it down with the maximum impact.

17

It took Jennifer nearly two hours to reach the Wiltshire village where Stephanie's parents lived, and she almost forgot the petrol, remembering it only when she saw a Little Chef café and went in because her bowels and bladder were reacting to her nervous condition and she needed to relieve them. Coffee would set her off again, she thought, and, not liking to leave without ordering something, she asked for tea and drank half a cup. Then, switching on the car's ignition again, she saw that the tank was almost empty.

She felt calmer now, and filled it up at the neighbouring service station. Her mind became detached from the purpose of her journey and she concentrated on finding the way. By this time she had settled down behind the wheel; as she had no car of her own, she very rarely drove. Before Daniel and she moved in together, she had a third-hand Metro, but she used it so little then that she decided to sell it and use the money to buy things for the house.

The day was grey and damp; moisture clung to the bare-branched trees, and the grass in fields that she passed was more grey than green; the nadir of the year approached. Eventually she found herself driving across Salisbury Plain, the area split by artillery ranges and other military zones, then becoming open country where clumps of trees sat on rounded hills and the straight main road ran west. She missed the turning to the village she sought and had to loop back to return to her proper route. Now she slowed down, going carefully along the narrow lane with its banks and high hedges on either side. When she arrived, what did she mean to do?

Why, march into the house and demand to see Daniel, of course. He would immediately put his arms round her and tell her it had all been a dreadful mistake; then they would leave together.

This fantasy kept her going as she drove through the village, past flint cottages with thatched roofs and one small shop, then the pub where she had been on her other visit. She passed a pond and an old tiled barn, then took a turning to her right. There was her goal, the long low house with the mullioned windows and the grey tiled roof.

Jennifer paused by the gates. Would it work out as she had already decreed? If it didn't, if Stephanie was there, triumphant, there was always the knife, which was now in her bag. The thought strengthened her resolve and she put the car in gear again and drove up the drive, past trim lawns to a wide macadam sweep in front of the house where she parked outside the heavy old oak front door. There was no other car in sight, but at one side, in what must have been stables, was garage space for at least three cars. All the doors were closed. Daniel's Audi must be behind one of them.

She rang the doorbell.

There was the sudden sound of a dog's bark: two deep yelps and then no more, and seconds later the front door opened on silent hinges. An elderly man of medium height, with a balding head and a small grey moustache, stood regarding her over a pair of half-glasses.

"Yes?" he said, enquiringly. He knew by sight most of the residents in the village of some three hundred souls but failed to place this caller. She was not a Jehovah's Witness; they hunted in couples. She must be collecting for something, he supposed, but it was odd that she had come by car, and where was her tin? With her pale haggard face she looked in need of charity herself.

"I've come to see Daniel," she said, and her defiant tone, combined with her appearance—"She looked distraught," he told his wife later—warned him instantly of who she was. Stephanie's parents had had to learn about Jennifer's assault on the flat, though her trailing of Stephanie for the past weeks had not been mentioned.

"You're Jennifer Newton," said Brigadier Dunn. "You'd better come in," and he opened the door wide, standing back to admit her.

Jennifer stepped into a large square hall with faded oriental rugs on the golden polished floor. A long case clock ticked loudly; a black Labrador dog stood gently waving its tail some yards behind its master. On the wall hung some oil paintings, dark landscapes reminiscent of Constable.

Jennifer's heart was pounding. Soon she would see Daniel. She followed Brigadier Dunn across the hall to a half-open door which he pushed and then indicated that she should precede him into the room beyond. It was a drawing-room, of a good size, with leaded windows looking out on two sides to the garden where a lawn sloped down to some fields which bordered a stream. A log fire burned in the hearth, the pile of ash demonstrating that it seldom went out. Facing the fireplace was a long, four-seater sofa, its soft cushions covered in rose-coloured linen printed with a floral design. Several armchairs of different sizes and shapes stood about, some covered in the same fabric, others in plain rose-coloured velvet. There were rose velvet curtains at the windows, and a soft green carpet, worn in patches, covered the floor. A copy of *The Times*, folded at the page the brigadier had been reading when she rang the bell, lay on one chair. Several cushions on the sofa were dented as though someone had been sitting there recently. Critically, Jennifer thought they should have been plumped up when the person or people left.

Daniel was not in the room; nor was anyone else.

"Sherry?" offered the brigadier.

"What? Oh no," said Jennifer, then added, "Thank you."

"I should have some," advised the brigadier. "You must have had a long drive."

Where, in fact, had she come from? Last night, after Stephanie and her mother had gone up to bed, he and Daniel had had a frank talk, the brigadier anxious about his daughter's safety, Daniel clearly wanting to allay his fears but worried, too. He had said that Jennifer had run off after the hearing and disappeared. Both men had wondered if she would do something foolish, Daniel fearful that she might harm herself. Brigadier Dunn had thought that she was more eager to hurt others than herself, but did not give this opinion aloud.

"I want to see Daniel," Jennifer repeated.

"He's not here just now," said the brigadier. "Why not have the sherry?" and he crossed to a table behind the sofa where, on a silver tray, stood some decanters and glasses. "Dry or medium?"

"Oh, I don't care," said Jennifer crossly.

The brigadier poured her a glass of Amontillado; she looked dry enough already. Unless this unhappy woman could somehow be brought under control, Stephanie's future happiness was threatened. He was not sure that Daniel, whom he liked well enough, was worth all this upset, but he knew that he would probably find no man worthy of his daughter.

"Do sit down, Miss Newton," he said, directing her towards a chair by the fire. He placed her glass on a table beside it.

Jennifer did not question his presumption of her identity. She felt the chair against the backs of her legs and folded herself down to perch stiffly, sitting forward, her thin hands clasped on her knees, her legs pressed tight together, feet side by side, toes touching.

She was oddly dressed, thought the brigadier: more like a student than a mature woman in those thick black tights, the boots and the long black skirt. He saw that she seemed to be shivering, so did not suggest that she remove her jacket. He poured himself a glass of Fino and sat facing her, moving *The Times* from the arm of his chair to a long low stool which stood before the fire. The Labrador had followed them into the room and now lay at the side of the brigadier's chair.

Brigadier Dunn raised his glass towards Jennifer but could think of no apt toast, so he simply took a sip, and Jennifer, unnerved by his matter-of-fact courtesy, reached out for her glass and did the same. Her hand wavered about and she bent her head to her glass so that it did not spill.

"Daniel," she said. "Where is he?"

"He and Stephanie have gone over to lunch with friends in another valley," he replied. "It's all valleys here, Miss Newton. Did you know that? A friend may live only a handful of miles away as the crow flies, yet you may have to drive thirty miles to find a bridge before you can visit."

Jennifer was not aware of this.

"Oh," she said.

"Are you familiar with this part of the country?" he asked.

"No."

"It's very beautiful," he said. "You'll have seen that, driving over. We've lived here a long time. I bought this house years before I retired from the army. Now I'm retired altogether. I worked for a charity until a year ago," he informed her.

She reached out for her glass to sip more sherry, and he saw that her hand was steadier. He would not give her more: one glass might settle her, a second could tip her out of her fragile control.

"I like to think of all the people who have lived in this house before us," he went on, his voice calm and level, compelling attention. "It was originally a farm. Generations of families have worked the land, were born and died in this place, all working out their destinies, leaving their imprint."

"Yes," said Jennifer, only partly understanding what he was saying. "My mother has moved a lot," she volunteered.

"Oh? And where does she live now?" asked the brigadier, who knew the answer.

"In Middle Bardolph," said Jennifer. "It's a small village near Wintlebury. There's a craft fair in Wintlebury today and my mother had planned to go."

"Really?"

"She can't now. She lent me her car," said Jennifer, and a curious expression, a look almost of satisfaction, crossed her face. At last she relaxed a little, softening so that he saw what could have drawn Daniel towards her in the beginning, and some of it was due to chivalry; he had wanted to protect her. Poor woman, she was in a bad way. What was the mother doing about it? What, in fact, could she do?

"Perhaps a friend will give your mother a lift to the fair," he suggested.

"What? Oh, no, she has no friends," said Jennifer.

"Surely that can't be so?"

"She's moved a lot, you see. She was always moving. She doesn't like people encroaching."

"And how did you feel about that? About moving?" asked the brigadier, who in his military career had moved more times than Mrs Newton.

Jennifer shrugged.

"I wasn't consulted, nor my brother. We were just told," she said.

"Army families move a great deal," said the brigadier. "Every three years or so. Children are always changing school, leaving their friends. It can help them to become adaptable. Are you adaptable, Miss Newton?"

"I don't know," said Jennifer. "When will Daniel be back?"

"Oh, not for hours," said the brigadier, and invented, "After lunch they're going on into Salisbury to see how the Cathedral restoration work is going and meet other friends."

He spoke so evenly. Jennifer could not bring herself to accuse him of lying about Daniel's plans for the day, and it was certainly clear that there was no one in the house now apart from the two of them and the dog. Brigadier Dunn was not in the least like her father, but he was a man in control.

"Where else have you lived?" he asked her.

Jennifer found herself stumblingly telling him about the various homes she had known, almost all fairly modern though there had been an Edwardian villa, semi-detached, early on, but they had stayed there only a year for her mother had not liked sharing a wall, though the place was so solidly built that they had heard very little from their neighbours. She told Brigadier Dunn about this, and about Yew Cottage which had been built, she said, just before the war; it was stucco-faced, light and airy inside, with this huge old yew tree in the garden.

"Mother is good at curtains and things," said Jennifer vaguely.

"She was widowed young?" asked the brigadier.

"She was about thirty-eight," said Jennifer.

Not much more than Jennifer was now, he thought; not a child: not without experience. He had come across plenty of much younger widows during his career.

"Who lived next to you, in the semi-detached house?" asked the brigadier. "Can you remember?"

"I remember a man. A man with dark hair and glasses. He came round sometimes," said Jennifer. "I didn't like him."

"And his wife? Was there one?"

"I suppose so. I don't remember." She frowned. "There weren't any children. I suppose he could have been a nuisance," she said, suddenly recollecting her mother refusing to answer the door to the man's ring.

"I expect your mother was a pretty woman. Perhaps things were sometimes difficult," said the brigadier.

"I hadn't thought of that," said Jennifer. "She never had a —well, I suppose they weren't called boyfriends then. Not that I knew of, anyway," she added. Why was she telling him all this? She had come here to see Daniel, to get him back, and she was talking to Stephanie's father about her mother. It was obscene.

She set her lips and stiffened in the chair, and the brigadier changed tack. She had talked a little about the house where they had lived when her father died, too big, she had admitted, for them on their own, but clearly moving from there very soon after his death had added to her distress at the time. He was curious about the mother; he knew little more about her now than at the start of their conversation.

"You'll be wanting to get back to your mother," he told her. "I won't tell Daniel you came." He waited. How would she take this?

Jennifer stared at him, plaiting her fingers together on her lap, her body now as tense as it had been when she first sat down.

"I want—" she began.

The brigadier plunged.

"You want him, you think," he said.

"I know I do. He loves me," Jennifer said.

"He did love you. He could still be fond of you, if you let him. He could remember your years together with pleasure and affection," said the brigadier. "Things pass, though, and we change. What we think of as love isn't always for ever. A love for a child can be—it will survive all sorts of storms and tempests—but other loves are less durable and people need different things as they go through life." He gazed at her steadily, his thick white eyebrows knitting above his deep-set blue eyes and the small snub nose. Stephanie was just like him, Jennifer saw, with a shock of recognition. "I was married before," he said. "My first wife died, after an illness, and I thought I could not survive her loss. I immersed myself in my army career and it satisfied me for a long time. Then I met Stephanie's mother. By then I was over forty." He paused, to let that fact penetrate Jennifer's mind, if she were capable of accepting subtle information. "She was not at all like my first wife," he went on. "And she was fifteen years younger than I was." Just as Stephanie was a lot younger than Daniel, he meant Jennifer to understand. "I was lucky. I had a second chance of happiness, very different from my first. What I felt for Stephanie's mother did not diminish what I had felt for my first wife. The two things were separate."

He waited. Would she understand? Was she even willing to try to relate this to herself or was she past all reason?

Jennifer did not want to take in his message; nevertheless, he saw understanding in her face.

"Things can be destroyed, though," he pressed on. "Suppose that after her death I had found out that my wife had had a lover, or been a thief, or something else damaging. That could imply that our life together was a sham, founded on something that never was. I should have felt betrayed."

There was a silence. He waited. Would she speak?

"You're telling me that Daniel hates me," she whispered.

"I'm not, but I'm asking you to protect your dignity and let him go without adding pain to his guilt about you."

"He should feel guilty," said Jennifer, scowling.

"He does," said the brigadier. "But how would anything be improved by his pretending to something that was no longer true?"

"What about my pride?" said Jennifer.

She had not said, what about my heart.

"What sort of pride? Is it worth incurring a possible prison sentence? Letting the whole world know that a man has withdrawn his love from you and transferred it elsewhere? If you behave well—however painful it may be for you—you will be admired."

Had he gone too far? He rested his wide, stubby hands on the arm of his chair and regarded her. She was looking at the fire. The logs needed attention and he rose to add a new one and stir up the rest. His movement broke the tension and Jennifer sat back a little as his steady gaze was removed from her. She looked at his sturdy back, the Harris tweed jacket, the twill trousers, the shiny brogues. You would know at once that he was a retired army officer.

Having arranged the fire to his liking, he turned slowly and, his back to the hearth, looked down at her. She had turned her head away and he saw that she had begun, very quietly, to cry.

Brigadier Dunn crossed the room and gazed out of the

window where two swans in the distance sailed majestically down the stream. They nested here every year; their current crop of cygnets—only two had survived—must be somewhere near the faithful parents. Lifetime matings were possible despite depressing statistics; swans paired for life and were known to mourn if one died.

Was Daniel worth all this? Would he make Stephanie a good husband? He had not behaved too well to Jennifer but it would have been much worse if he had gone on to marry her. How long would that have lasted? He seemed kind and even-tempered, and Stephanie adored him. The brigadier, experienced with men, would have welcomed him to the mess. He was practical—could saw logs, mow the lawn, had helped paint a bedroom on one weekend visit. He had not deceived Jennifer for long, telling her very quickly after they returned from Italy that he wanted to sever their relationship, as it seemed fashionable to call such arrangements, so little different from a marriage except that no vows were exchanged; legally, there could be immense problems, as witness this difficulty over the house. There was a lot to be said for the old morality, thought the brigadier. In this house, Daniel occupied the spare bedroom and Stephanie her own, and if one of them tiptoed along the corridor in the night, the brigadier did not want to know about it.

He gave a little cough, then turned. Jennifer was rummaging in her handbag, looking for a handkerchief.

"I think you should have something to eat before you leave," he said. "I'll just go out to the kitchen to see what my wife has left for my lunch. She's away visiting her mother in hospital today. I'm sure there will be plenty for two," and he moved towards the door. Then he turned again. "There's a cloakroom just across the hall," he said. "The door in the corner," and he walked out of the room, leaving the door open.

The Labrador rose from his warm spot near the fire and followed.

18

The brigadier had carved large, moist pink slices from a piece of gammon which his wife had cooked. There were beetroot salad and celery, cheese, and home-made bread. There was fresh fruit. There was mineral water in a bottle chilled in the fridge. All this was placed before Jennifer at the kitchen table. The brigadier began to tell her about his dog, which was the son of an earlier one he had owned. Then he spoke about France where he hoped to go in May.

The thought of Stephanie's wedding, planned for that month, hovered in the air between them but the brigadier's conversation never faltered. He touched on Nantes and its treaty, and Huguenots in general, saying that his wife's family was descended from them, then mentioned various cathedrals and chateaux, about all of which he seemed to know a great deal. Jennifer half listened to what he was saying while she ate the ham he had placed before her, toyed with the beetroot and almost enjoyed the Stilton with the crusty bread. Then he asked her if she knew France well.

She didn't. She had been to Greece several times years ago, but with Daniel had usually gone to Italy with the same friends in the summer, and skiing in the Austrian

Alps in winter. They had, however, been to Paris more than once.

"Then you've a lot to look forward to," said the brigadier. "What about your mother? Does she like France?"

Jennifer could not remember her mother ever going abroad. She said so.

"Then she must begin," said the brigadier. "Have you considered taking her there? You could take her car, or fly and drive if you wanted to visit the south. Aix-en-Provence, for instance: that's a most interesting town in a lovely area and I defy anyone not to enjoy a visit there."

Jennifer mumbled something. Taking her mother away with her would never have occurred to her, and she was not attracted to the notion now. She was not reconciled to going anywhere without Daniel.

The brigadier made coffee using coffee bags in mugs, and when she had finished hers he escorted her to the car and opened the driver's door for her. She slid in behind the wheel without a word, then muttered an ungracious "Thanks for the lunch" before driving off, treating the gearbox rather roughly. He watched her out of sight, and as she disappeared fatigue swept over him. He had known that Jennifer had come with murder in her heart; he had disarmed her, but for how long?

How lucky that the others had been absent when she arrived. Daniel and Stephanie had gone out to lunch, as he had said, but they had no plans he knew of for the afternoon and could be home at any time. He had intended to go with his wife to see her mother, but had suspected a cold was coming on and so had remained behind, anxious not to carry germs to her.

He gave an enormous sneeze as he began clearing up in the kitchen. What would Jennifer Newton have done if she had found the house empty? Thrown more stones? Set it alight? She was desperate enough for anything and he felt very anxious. What was it that made people so obsessed with someone that they could not relinquish that person when feeling on one side had died? It was not love; love desired the other's growth and happiness, wanted to give and not to plunder. Jennifer had laid a burden of what she thought was love on Daniel; the brigadier could understand why he had wanted to help her, to protect her: how he might have found her dependence on him at first appealing. What a fool he had been to get in so deep, to buy the house with her, so making a commitment which was near marriage, and now he needed a near divorce to free himself from bonds that had grown unbearable. Was this going to prove good for Stephanie? Daniel would bring the baggage of the past with him but at least he had no brood of children to whom she would be an instant stepmother. If it had not been for Jennifer's vendetta against Stephanie, the brigadier would have been unconcerned; a man Daniel's age must have some sort of amorous past; but if Jennifer failed to get over this, she could cause a lot of trouble. Of course, the law would deal with extreme actions, but she might do something worse than throw stones, and serious punishment could come too late.

He hoped she would get back to Middle Bardolph safely. A road accident would solve nothing and only increase Daniel's sense of guilt.

No more could be done now. The brigadier decided not to tell his wife about the visitor until Daniel and Stephanie had left for London, which would be the following day. Meanwhile there was racing on television. After the dog had had a run, he would settle down to watch it.

Jennifer went back along the lane, past the pub and the village shop towards the main road. She drove instinctively, her mind a blank, and she was inattentive. Rounding a corner, she almost ran into a car travelling the other way and had to stamp on the brakes, trying as she did so to pull in to the left; the other driver was more cautious and had time to stop, then reverse to a wider spot to allow her to pass. He glared at her as she went by but Jennifer was impervious to anything outside herself.

The near escape shocked her, though, and she realised that her journey had been fruitless. She had not seen Daniel. Even so, she could not wait outside the Dunns' house until he chose to return. In some odd way the interlude with the brigadier had altered her, but she could not understand why or how.

I want a father, she thought. That's what I really want, but I can't have one. It's too late.

At this, she began to cry again and drove on with tears pouring down her face. She wept until at last it seemed no more tears remained to be shed, and once again she stopped at the Little Chef she had visited earlier to wash. Again, she ordered tea. When she drove on, she ran over in her mind part of her conversation with the brigadier. He had suggested she took her mother on a touring holiday. Other people did that sort of thing, she supposed, but not Jennifer. She had always gone away with her own contemporaries, even before she met Daniel.

There were singles groups you could join, or cultural tours. She might look into the possibilities. She would have to be out of the country at the time of the wedding. If it took place.

Perhaps she could get married herself before they did: that would show them. She could go to a dating agency, take the first offer that came. The idea sustained her for twenty miles.

What a little tin box this car was after Daniel's Audi; it was all a question of what you had grown used to, of course. Driving round France in something so small would be gruelling, she decided, though the hired car they had had in Italy last year was no larger, but that was different. She reached the outskirts of Wintlebury and took the new bypass that had opened four years ago, freeing the town from much of the traffic that had clogged its narrow streets for years. By now it was dark. She had not thought ahead to what would happen when the weekend was past; Sunday must be survived in some way first; she supposed she would spend the day in Middle Bardolph. On Monday she would return to the office for want of an alternative, and she needed her job for if she left it, how would she keep up the mortgage payments?

Jennifer came to the crossroads where the lights of The Prince Hal glowed in the evening murkiness. She turned off and drove past the shop and the school. The Blaneys' old house, now dazzlingly renovated, was in darkness, and so was Yew Cottage. That was odd. Her mother must be out. Perhaps after all someone had taken her to the craft fair.

Jennifer put the car in the garage and went round to the water butt for the key. She had not replaced it but had left it where her mother would see it; no doubt by this time she had returned it to its usual place. It wasn't there. She frowned, feeling anger begin to flare. How thoughtless of her mother to go out without leaving her a means of entry.

As she passed the back door she tried the handle and it opened. That surprised her, for her mother was scrupulous about locking up. How very careless! Perhaps she was beginning to go senile. Jennifer turned on the light. She went through the kitchen to the hall, where her foot scrunched on something, a piece of terracotta flower pot. It was a few seconds before she observed that the chrysanthemum which had stood in a china pot by the telephone was no longer there, and only seconds more before she sensed that something was very wrong.

She went into the sitting-room and immediately saw that the television set was missing. The flap of her mother's desk was open and some papers lay in disarray. All the paintings from the walls had gone. An uncomfortable choking sensation rose in her throat as she ran upstairs and found that her mother's dressing-table had been ransacked; her leather jewel case had been taken. But where was her mother? She must be at the fair: while she was out some thief had tried his luck and broken in, easily done with the unlocked door an open invitation. Both radios had been stolen, too, and silence prevailed in the house; a menacing silence; the weight of it pressed on her ear drums.

The police wouldn't do a thing about it, of course; they never bothered about burglaries of this kind though they were quick enough to hound you for merely heaving a stone at a window. It wasn't worth reporting, except that the insurance people would insist, thought Jennifer, walking slowly back down the stairs.

Maybe the telephone line had been cut. She tried it, and found that it was working, so she dialled 999 and asked for the police, then reported the burglary. As an afterthought she added that her mother was not at home and she did not know where she was, unless someone had taken her to the craft fair in Wintlebury.

An officer would call, she was told, and as she replaced the handset she thought that really her mother might have left her a note to say where she had gone and when she could be expected back.

Very slowly it dawned on Jennifer that her mother certainly would have done this. Perhaps the thief had destroyed the note. As these thoughts went through her head, her gaze travelled towards the staircase and the cupboard beneath. It fastened with a drop latch, like the cottage-style doors throughout the house; Jennifer thought them pretentious, since the house was not really old. She glanced down at the floor, wondering why the thief had taken the flowers. Was the pot valuable? Then she saw something dark on the carpet close to the door, as though paint or some other substance had trickled underneath it. Her mother must have replaced polish or cleaning fluid carelessly; really, she was beginning to slip. Jennifer lifted the latch and opened the cupboard door.

Mrs Newton lay in a heap, bundled inside, and the substance was blood which had poured from a wound on her head.

After he had hit Mrs Newton with the pot, Kevin had frozen, watching her crumple and fall to the ground as he dropped the pot, which shattered. He kicked her, but she was silent; not even a moan escaped her and he pushed her into the cupboard and fastened the door. Then he collected up the broken pieces of pot. Both the original earthenware one and the china container had broken, and Kevin put the fragments and the plant in the bin in the kitchen. It was empty except for some scraps of paper. By this time he was nervously sweating, but he was not going away empty-handed. He fetched the van and reversed it up the drive, then loaded in the television set and the pictures. He rifled the desk, looking for cash, and found fifty pounds in a drawer. Then he went upstairs, took a pillow case from a bed and filled it with anything that might be of value, including the jewel case and some silver which was in the dining-room: candlesticks and cutlery. Before he drove off, he closed the garage doors; leaving them open might attract attention to the house.

He sold the two radios and the television set within the next hour. Then he telephoned home to see if anyone was there, but there was no reply. Even Neil must be out. That meant it was safe to return and stash the rest of his loot until he could decide how best to turn it into money. He'd put the things where Neil would not see them, for there might be a fuss when the old woman got out of the cupboard. It wouldn't take her long to do that but there was nothing to connect him with the theft.

He left the van in its usual spot and caught the bus into Crimpford where he went to a football match and made sure that the people around him took notice of him, would recognise him, would say he had been there all the afternoon.

Before leaving the house, he left a ten-pound note under Neil's hairbrush on the dresser, to pay for the use of the van.

The evening paper was on sale when the match ended. Its headlines screamed that there had been a hold-up at Little Nym. By this time Kevin had almost forgotten his early adventure, the forerunner to his visit to Yew Cottage.

He decided that this was a night to spend with the boys, and he had money. As well as the cash in the desk, he had found sixty pounds in Mrs Newton's handbag, and he had her credit card and cheque book. What a pity the banks were shut.

It was strange that someone else had gone off in her car.

19

The woman hurt in the robbery at Little Nym that morning
had not been able to give a very clear description of her
attacker except as to his size and general build. He had
worn a combat jacket and a black balaclava hood, and his
eyes were, she thought, but could not swear to it, brown, but
then again they could have been blue. She said it would take
a cooler head than hers to notice details at such a time,
shuddering as she spoke. She had not seen any vehicle he
might have come in, and enquiries were proceeding in the
village in the hope of finding witnesses, or reports of vehicles
parked near the shop. His victim had been taken to hospital
where her wrist was put in plaster; it would have to remain
encased for five or six weeks and in that time she would be
existing under difficulties. She lived alone; how was she to
wash, dress, cope with her life, while the villain went free to
frighten and hurt other people?

By the time Mrs Newton was discovered in her cupboard,
little progress had been made with the earlier crime but it
was possible that the two attacks were made by the same
individual, and he was dangerous.

* * *

Neil had taken Jason out.

Without the van to clean, he had no busy task to perform and felt restless. After a while Jason, snuffling with his cold, had begun to whine, so Neil had bundled him into his padded suit and wrapped him up in blankets in the pram. He pulled the plastic cover over the child. At least it kept the weather off but it turned him into a small plant in a mobile conservatory, Neil decided. Jason wailed as they walked along and Neil was unable to cheer him up with chat, or by pulling faces or tickling his toes. He wondered if it would be possible to alter the handles on the pushchair so that it faced the other way. Walking along the street, he noticed other similar conveyances, some more luxurious, padded; others held two children and stretched across the pavement. Then he saw one where the child faced towards the mother. Such things were made, it seemed. He wondered what they cost.

After a while the motion sent Jason to sleep and Neil pushed on through the drizzle, which stopped eventually. He walked down to the river which flowed beside the graveyard and sat there on the bank, damply content, while Jason slept. When the child woke up, Neil threw stones into the river to amuse him. He liked the splash. Neil towed him back into town, the plastic cover pulled back now, walking beside the pushchair, talking to him. On the way he bought some chips at the fish and chip shop and gave one to Jason to suck.

By the time they reached home, his van was back, apparently unharmed. Neil inspected it and saw that it was dusty; there were two new deep scratches on the floor.

He took Jason into the house and changed him, then made him a bottle. Jason drank some of it, burped, and decided he had had enough so Neil took him out to the van and strapped him into his seat while he cleaned the whole thing out. He used his mother's vacuum attachment, sweeping it thoroughly, then washed and polished it tenderly. Jason did not mind the whine of the sweeper; he had been accustomed to it all his short life. Later, Neil took him for a little spin, anxious to make sure Kevin had not harmed the engine. He noticed that he had travelled nearly eighty miles and was surprised to see that he had gone so far; probably to Crimpford, fifteen miles away, he thought, but where else? The petrol was low; he must fill it up on Monday morning at the pump where Len Harding ran an account.

The ambulance arrived at Yew Cottage before the police.

Jennifer had dialled 999 again as soon as she had found her mother. She was sure her mother was dead, but knew you should not move an injured person, so she fetched a duvet from upstairs and wrapped it round the thin body, making small mewing sounds of mingled panic and distress as she did so. Should she try to force some brandy between her mother's lips? Instead, she picked up one cold, limp hand and caressed it, muttering and mumbling to herself, unaware of what she was saying. She was still there on her knees when the ambulance arrived, and the driver had to peal the bell to be admitted.

She stood back then, trembling, her hands to her mouth, while the attendants—one man and one woman—gently inspected Mrs Newton and carefully lifted her out of her prison. They were not yet ready to hear Jennifer's story of how she had found her mother locked in the cupboard, and the burglary; and it was some minutes before the woman detached herself from helping her colleague to give her some attention.

"She's dead, isn't she?" said Jennifer.

"No, not quite," said the woman, and had asked what happened.

Jennifer told her, explaining how she had already rung the police before noticing the bloodstain on the carpet. It was clear that she was very shocked.

"You'd better come with us," she was told. "We can get a message to the police. Fetch a coat. Quick."

Jennifer was reduced to the capability of a young child. She obediently went upstairs to find her jacket, then managed to remember that she had flung it off downstairs when she discovered that the house had been entered. She put it on and climbed into the ambulance.

The ambulance passed the police car which was answering Jennifer's first call. When the two officers reached Yew Cottage they found the house deserted, but the lights were on. The back door was unlocked and they went in. The scene in the hall indicated immediately that violence had occurred; there was clearly a bloodstain on the carpet and more inside the cupboard, whose door stood open. There were marks on the back of it, scratch marks, as they later realised, made by Mrs Newton when briefly she regained consciousness and found herself virtually entombed. This was not the simple burglary they had been sent to investigate.

Between them, Jennifer and the ambulance attendants had destroyed much of the evidence which the police might have expected to find at the site of whatever had happened. Very soon, however, a message came through to explain to the officers that the victim and her daughter were on the way to Crimpford Hospital. Routine procedures were begun, the detectives who followed their uniformed colleagues to the cottage cursing because there had been so much walking about and trampling in the area.

They found some clues, however.

Jennifer, at the hospital, had completely gone to pieces and had to be sedated, but she had supplied her brother's name and telephone number first. Someone telephoned him.

Geoffrey was at home. His wife was giving a dinner party at which were present among the guests a Member of Parliament and his titled wife and a minor television personality with her current husband. Geoffrey had only a short battle with his conscience before he let it win against the inevitable fury of his wife.

He told the hospital caller that he would come at once, and he did not even stop to pack a bag, only grabbing his wallet before driving southwards in his dinner jacket. As he sped onwards through the night the thought came to him that if his mother died, his and Jennifer's financial problems would be solved.

It was a base thought. He did his best to banish it from his mind.

Mrs Newton was in intensive care. Hypothermia and lack of oxygen had caused more damage to her than the actual blow to her head, though she had severe concussion, and possibly a hairline fracture to the skull. She had also sustained three broken ribs and considerable bruising as a result of Kevin's kicks. Much would depend, said the doctors, on her own strength and stamina.

Geoffrey thought she had a lot of both.

"Or did," he said. "She's not had an easy time."

He said this in surprised tones, as if the idea had only just occurred to him. His mother looked so frail, so small and thin, unmoving, very pale without her make-up. Her hair, unbound, spread round the pillow, and wires and tubes connected her to various pieces of machinery. He felt a sudden visceral pain, an intimation of her mortality. He had been badgering her to move for reasons of his own and not, as he had maintained, with any intention of helping her at all and now he was ashamed. In that instant he decided that Lynn could whistle for her mansion and if she didn't like what he provided for her, she could do the other thing. Quite what he meant by this he did not define, but at the back of his mind was the confident figure of Jack Bridges whom he had abandoned at the dinner table with the other guests.

Perhaps at this moment he was still at the house, alone with Lynn.

Geoffrey found himself quite untroubled by the notion.

Police officers hovered in the hospital corridor. There was a uniformed woman constable whose duty seemed to be to keep guard over Mrs Newton and there were two men in plain clothes, the younger of whom, a tall thin man with sparse dark hair, introduced himself as Detective Inspector Wilson, and his colleague, fair and thickset, as Detective Sergeant Bennett.

Jennifer, it seemed, had been able to tell them nothing useful. She had been out somewhere, and returned to find her mother shut in the cupboard. She was too upset to provide more details and anyway was unlikely to have useful information.

Geoffrey proceeded cautiously. He wondered if the police officers knew that his sister was on bail on a charge in London.

If they did, they did not say so. Best that they should not find out, he thought; it might lead to their doubting her reliability as a witness. The fact that he had no faith in her either was by the way; he must help her now to get a grip on herself so that what she might reveal would be of value.

Jennifer was lying fully dressed on a bed in a side ward. Though drowsy, she was not asleep. She seemed very calm but he was shocked by her pallor and by the fact that she had lost so much weight since the last time he had seen her. She was always slim; now, he thought, she was positively gaunt and looked a hundred. What on earth had got into her, acting so insanely, running round London breaking windows? She must have lost her mind.

She blinked as he appeared beside her bed.

"Hullo, Geoff. You came," she said, speaking slowly, her voice slurred.

"Of course," he said. "Naturally. At once."

"You look awfully smart," she said, and giggled weakly.

"Lynn had guests for dinner," he said acidly.

"You didn't come for me," said Jennifer, plucking at the coverlet on which she lay.

"No—well, you hadn't been attacked. Left for dead," he said defensively. Looking at her now, so thin, so white, his failure seemed inexcusable. She had needed support, and where else should she find it but from her brother?

"She's dead, isn't she?" Jennifer said sadly. "No one will tell me."

"No," he answered. "She's not. She's hanging on. It depends really on her recuperative powers."

"Recuperative powers," Jennifer repeated, nodding like a mandarin. "What a phrase."

"Yes, well, it's what they said," he countered. "The police say you couldn't tell them much, but I can see you're doped up to the eyeballs."

"I feel rather drunk," she said. "All vague and swimmy."

"Well, tell me what happened," he said.

"Nothing, much. Just I came home and she wasn't there. Then I saw the blood. Not a lot of it. A bit seeping under the cupboard door." Jennifer's face suddenly crumpled as if she were about to cry. "How long was she in there?"

"No one's said," he told her. "Perhaps they don't know. She can't tell them. She's unconscious. Jennifer, you seem to be making a bit of sense now. If I get one of those policemen in, will you make an effort to tell them everything?"

"All right, but there's nothing to tell. I simply found her. That's all. There'd been a burglar. She left the back door open."

Geoffrey went off and spoke to a nurse, who reappeared with cups of tea for both of them, and then the detective sergeant came in to coax a statement from Jennifer. Speaking slowly, concentrating hard, she related how she had borrowed her mother's car to visit friends in Wiltshire and had stayed to lunch, returning about five or maybe later; she hadn't seen the time but it was dark. The house appeared to be empty and as her mother had mentioned a craft fair in Wintlebury, Jennifer had assumed that that was where she was. Then she had realised that there had been a burglary and that the thief had entered by the unlocked back door.

"I thought my mother had been very careless, going out and leaving it like that," she said. "But I didn't realise she was there all the time. Of course she wouldn't have locked it—not until the evening, anyway."

"You had your own key?"

"No. A spare was kept outside, under a water butt in the garden," said Jennifer. "I used it when I came down on Thursday. It hadn't been replaced when I went to find it after I got back. Then I discovered the door was open."

"So you hadn't put it back and neither had your mother?"

"No. I left it for her in the kitchen."

"So the thief could have walked in through the back door?" asked Bennett.

"I suppose so. Then he must have seen mother—" Jennifer paused. "But why did he steal the chrysanthemum?" she asked. "Was the pot valuable?"

"What chrysanthemum?"

"There was one on the table in the hall. A pink one, in a china pot. That's how I realised something was wrong. I stepped on a bit of flower pot in the hall." She frowned, unable in her dazed state to connect up this detail to the fact that the pot had been used to strike down her mother.

Bennett was making notes. Much later, scenes of crime officers at Yew Cottage found the plant and the broken shards of earthenware and china in the waste bin, but not the key that she had mentioned. They also found the fragments of a torn-up letter and a keen detective, using tweezers, pieced it together well enough to get the gist of it: a begging letter from the daughter, offering a motive.

"Did you see anyone hanging about when you drove away?" asked Bennett. "Any car in the road, for instance?"

"No, I don't think so," said Jennifer. "Oh, there was a van parked at the house next door. I didn't take much notice of it. Builders have been there doing it up. It was one of their vans, I suppose."

"Did it have a name on?"

"I didn't see that."

"What colour was it?"

"Sort of brown. Nothing special," said Jennifer.

"What sort of size?"

"I don't know. Post office size, perhaps."

"Large post office or small?"

Bennett went on questioning her patiently, trying to discover what else Jennifer might have noticed but there was little more. He established her approximate time of departure for Wiltshire, which meant that the attack came afterwards. Clearly, tracing the brown van would be the best way to find a lead.

When Bennett left, one of the nurses in the corridor was talking to another.

"That's the woman who threw stones at the girl's flat who's taken over her boyfriend," she was saying.

"What's that?" asked Bennett, and the nurse, looking somewhat sheepish, repeated what she had been told when Mrs Newton came up from casualty. Someone there had read about it in the paper.

It didn't take Bennett long to check the story out and confirm its truth.

"That means we've got to consider her as a suspect," he declared. "She's got a violent nature."

"But the robbery?" said Detective Inspector Wilson when he posited the theory.

"She could have done that as a blind. Taken the stuff off in her mother's car and dumped it," Bennett said.

"Maybe," said Wilson. "Maybe that does put her in the frame. And are you going to get her for the job at Little Nym as well?" He grinned at Bennett, a dogged officer who ignored no possible line of enquiry.

"Who can say what gets into the head of a woman of a certain age," said Bennett grandly.

Wilson thought that age did not come into it, but Jennifer Newton's movements during the day must, as routine, be investigated.

20

Although the scenes of crime team had not yet finished at Yew Cottage, they had decided that they would get no more useful information from the hall area and were packing up till morning. Geoffrey was told that he could take his sister back there for the night, but the cupboard itself was sealed to await further examination, and the sitting-room and Mrs Newton's bedroom. They could use the rest of the house, which appeared to have been untouched.

It was possible to reconstruct what had happened. That the flower-pot had been the weapon used was clear; there was blood on some of the pieces discovered in the cupboard; other splinters had been found in the beige cardigan which Mrs Newton was wearing. She had probably surprised her attacker, who had used the nearest thing to hand to strike her, whereas at Little Nym the assailant had armed himself with an adjustable spanner. If the two incidents were linked, Mrs Newton had been lucky; the spanner would have done more damage than the pot.

Geoffrey led his sister out to the car, wishing the hospital had decided to keep her overnight; indeed, he had implored them to do so but they had said she might rest more tranquilly at home. Their mother was still unconscious. Geoffrey felt unequal to coping with Jennifer who, walking along the hospital corridor beside him, travelling in the lift, meekly accompanying him to the car, seemed quiet and composed, almost like a zombie. Geoffrey helped her into his Rover and reminded her to fasten the seatbelt. Then he got in and started the engine. He drove carefully through the outskirts of Crimpford into the country. It would be just his luck to be stopped by the police and breath-tested; naturally he had had a few drinks at home, bracing himself up before the party and while acting as host, never expecting to have to drive anywhere that night, but they reached Yew Cottage without adventure, and almost in silence. He asked Jennifer where she had been that day, and she simply said, "Out." After that she seemed to doze.

A police officer was at the cottage when they got there. He let them in, since between them they had no key, and departed after making clear the restrictions on which rooms they might use. The other doors were sealed with tape.

It seemed strange to be in the house without their mother. When the policeman had gone, Jennifer sat on the stairs and shivered.

"It's as if she was dead," she said.

"Well, she isn't, not yet," said Geoffrey. They had time to prepare themselves for that, he thought, aware that the doctors had avoided saying anything definite either way. Meanwhile Jennifer must pull herself together. It wasn't Stephanie's fault that Daniel had dumped Jennifer for her. Why couldn't she just let it go? His own reaction to Lynn's wanderings—he knew she was having an affair with Jack and thought this was not the first time she had strayed— was not jealousy; he simply felt a great weariness and a sense of failure.

He was too tired to think about it now. The next day would be demanding and he must concentrate on getting Jennifer into shape to face it.

"Have you got some stuff to take to make you sleep?" he

asked her, though she seemed almost out as he persuaded her to go up to bed.

"They gave me a jab at the hospital," she said. "And I've got some pills from Dr Brewster. I wonder if they'll mix?"

"I should think so," he said firmly, but he supervised her as she swallowed one of the tablets, then confiscated the bottle. "What about a bath?" he asked her.

"In the morning," she said.

"Some Horlicks or something, then? It might help the pill to work."

"All right," she said, and began taking off her clothes.

"I'll make some," Geoffrey said, and he went heavily down the stairs.

He had not been to the house for months. Searching in the kitchen cupboard for whatever his mother might have in the way of a bland nightcap, he tried to remember when it was; nearly a year ago, he decided, when he had attended a seminar in Oxford. He had called in on the way and had had tea, sitting stiffly in the sitting-room telling his mother about the girls' progress at school and with their riding lessons. Then his mother had spent Christmas with them, an uneasy visit during which she seemed to shrink daily, retreating more and more into the large wing armchair designated as hers, only coming to life when playing a game with the children; she was quietly serious in Scrabble and grew animated teaching them Cheat. He never remembered her playing that with him and Jennifer; in fact he could scarcely remember her playing with them at all, and he had felt resentful. When he was a child, after his father's death, she had always been so busy; from that time she had never had help in either the house or the garden and though he had tried, as he grew older, to do the man's jobs about the place as he saw them—fetching coal, chopping wood—and she had been grateful, there seemed to have been no time for fun. Fun did not figure high on his mother's list of priorities, he thought; perhaps she had forgotten how to enjoy herself.

Each summer since his father died, they had stayed at

boarding houses in Cornwall for two weeks by the sea. He and Jennifer had caught shrimps, sailed boats, made sand castles, and when they were too old for such activities she had taken them to various places of interest—Tintagel, Exeter Cathedral, museums and potteries. While they swam or played on the beach, she slept or read, sitting in a deck-chair, often with a rug around her for she felt the cold. Now he perceived that she must have been extremely weary. She had never had anyone to depend upon except herself—and the remote, unseen solicitor, Mr Booth. There had been godparents, distant friends of their father's who had sent occasional presents but who had slowly faded out after he died and who never visited; there were no grandparents, no aunts or uncles. He remembered his mother sewing every evening, stitching away at tapestry cushions; belatedly he realised that she sold them, that her work bought treats and holidays and that their constant moves may have been a means of making money. In those days it had been a safe thing to do as property had steadily, sometimes spectacularly, increased in value until recently.

He found Ovaltine. The thought of his mother drinking it alone at night was suddenly pathetic. He imagined her in her woollen dressing gown stirring a ritual cup. There was milk in the fridge, and he made a drink for Jennifer. Then he sought out the bottle of brandy he knew his mother kept for emergency use; that was what he needed now. He might take one of Jennifer's pills with it, he thought.

When he took her up her drink, she was in bed and he thought she was asleep, but as he tiptoed in she opened her eyes. Now she looked rather pretty, her face pointed, looking at him in a dazed way. Here he was, mothering her; Daniel had taken care of her, too; there was something defenceless, vulnerable about her, despite her brittle, assured manner. Inside, she was terrified, just as he was as he juggled his life to keep everything in motion, appeasing here, controlling there, offsetting one action against another and always hoping that one day things would somehow become simpler, more straightforward. Geoffrey had never got real satisfaction from his work; any business successes he achieved brought him relief, not elation, and he was perpetually fearful of failure.

He should not be in business at all; he should have become a farmer, or a lighthouse keeper, he thought fancifully.

He went into the spare bedroom and turned down one of the twin beds. He and Lynn had never stayed here and nor had the girls, though his mother had planned the room with them in mind. She had had so little joy from them: Lynn had clung to her children, not wanting to share them with this grandmother though they often visited her parents, who lived in a large house in Solihull and who also owned a villa in the Algarve.

He stripped down to his boxer shorts and got into bed. Both beds were kept made up and aired as though sudden guests might arrive unheralded. Had that ever happened in the whole of his mother's life? He knew so little about her, about her youth before she and his father met. She had never talked about that time and now it was probably too late to ask.

What was he going to wear in the morning, with only his evening suit and the short trench coat he had grabbed as he left the house?

It was no good worrying about that now. Forgetting about the pill he had planned to take, he climbed into bed and in four minutes he was asleep.

Geoffrey had left his door open in case the hospital called during the night; there was a telephone in his mother's locked room, and he put the one in the hall as close to the stairs as its flex would reach, but in fact it was the doorbell which woke him up at eight o'clock.

His room overlooked the front of the house and he opened the window to see who was outside. On the step stood the stocky figure of Detective Sergeant Bennett.

"I'll be down in a minute," he said, and withdrew his head. Of course they'd come in person to break bad news; it wouldn't be given over the telephone. His mother must have died while he slept, and now the police were dealing with a murder hunt. He put on his evening trousers and his trench coat and went down to admit the detective.

But the man had brought no news from the hospital. He wanted to find out if Jennifer could remember anything more about the van seen in the neighbouring drive the day before. It seemed that a brown van had been noticed near the shop in Little Nym at much the same time as the attack there; this positively linked the two incidents, if corroborative evidence could be found.

Incident, thought Geoffrey: what an inadequate word to use about a criminal assault which could turn out to be a murder.

"We'll find the van," said Bennett confidently. "But the sooner the better. I've got officers making door-to-door enquiries in the village asking if anyone else saw it."

"Well, that's a start, I suppose," said Geoffrey grudgingly.

He felt foolish, standing there in his evening trousers and his trench coat, and depressed because whoever had done these things might not be caught.

"Miss Newton," prompted Bennett.

"She's still asleep," said Geoffrey. "I'm not keen to wake her."

But Jennifer had heard their voices and was awake. She appeared at the top of the staircase, clad only in her curious long tee-shirt.

I'll wear that, thought Geoffrey. It was a harmless garment in her usual black, without a legend printed on the front, and would be better than his frilled evening shirt. He rubbed his hand over his chin. Luckily he had shaved before the dinner party so his stubble was not as long as on a normal morning. He would have to buy a razor, unless his mother had one stashed away; then he remembered that it was Sunday and he was stuck with the limitations of his wardrobe.

"Sergeant Bennett wants to talk to you about the van you

saw," he called up to Jennifer. "Put something on and come downstairs."

It would have been quite in character for Jennifer to ignore this instruction and come down exactly as she was, her long thin legs revealed almost to the crutch, but she made some mumbling reply and turned away, and Geoffrey led Bennett into the kitchen, where he put the kettle on.

Jennifer reappeared in her old dressing gown. Her hair stood out round her head in a fuzz; it looked unwashed, unkempt, and she, having made him think of her as old the night before, now, in Geoffrey's eyes, seemed about twelve.

"I told you about the van," she said. "Brownish. Medium sized."

Bennett had brought photographs of various types of van. Jennifer scrutinised them while Geoffrey made them all mugs of coffee. In the end it was decided that it might be a Ford Transit, but it could be smaller. You couldn't decide the size from photographs, she said.

"Now, Miss Newton," Bennett said, "I'd like to know exactly how you spent the day. What time did you leave? Who did you visit?"

"I went to see friends in Wiltshire. I told you that," said Jennifer.

"Their name and address, please," he insisted.

"But they're not involved."

"No, but they can prove that you were with them," he said. "Otherwise we've only got your word for where you were when Mrs Newton was attacked."

"But you can't think—" As she understood why he asked this question, Jennifer's face went ashen pale and she set her lips in a line. "I'm not going to tell you," she managed to utter. "It's private."

"Sergeant, are you implying that my sister might have attacked our mother and stolen all the things that are missing?" Geoffrey was outraged. "That's grotesque."

"Miss Newton is already on remand on a charge of causing criminal damage," said Detective Sergeant Bennett. "She is allegedly capable of violent behaviour and she needed money. A letter from her protesting because Mrs Newton had refused to provide it was found in the rubbish bin.''

"Don't talk about me as if I wasn't here," said Jennifer angrily. "How can you think I'd do anything to harm my mother? That's slander, and I refuse to say where I was."

"Miss Newton, we will be discreet," said Bennett.

"For heaven's sake don't make a mystery, Jennifer," said Geoffrey. "Tell the sergeant where you were and he can stop wasting police time on this mad theory."

"I don't see why I should," said Jennifer.

"Because if you don't, he'll start trying to prove you bashed Mama on the head, and I daresay with your finger-prints all over the house, he could make a case," said Geoffrey. "Though what he thinks you've done with all her possessions I don't know. It's nonsense."

"It may seem nonsense to you, Mr Newton, but it's routine," said Bennett reprovingly.

"Well, I'm not going to satisfy your curiosity," said Jennifer, folding her arms across her chest.

If she'd dumped the stuff, it would be discovered, Bennett thought. She'd have tipped it in a field or some ditch to make it look as if there had been a robbery.

"If you won't tell me here, I may decide to take you down to the police station where you might change your mind," said Bennett. "And we'll need to take your fingerprints. And yours, Mr Newton, for comparison with those we found here last night."

"Well, of course you found some. My mother's and my sister's, and I expect my mother had visitors at some point," said Geoffrey. "I doubt if you'll find mine, as it's a while since I visited. And I can account for where I was last night, if you're interested, with witnesses to prove it."

Jennifer had a sudden idea.

"I had tea at a Little Chef," she said. "I've probably got the receipt."

"Where was it?"

"On the way back from Wiltshire, of course," said Jennifer. "I suppose you'll let me go and look for it without arresting me?"

Why hadn't the sergeant decided that Jennifer could have attacked her mother before she left the house on her mysterious expedition? Unless she regained consciousness and was able to describe what happened, with a hint as to the time of the attack, there was no way of proving how long she had been confined in the cupboard. Geoffrey decided not to point that out to the bloody-minded policeman: sarcasm would make things even worse for Jennifer. And where could she have been? Why wouldn't she say? Was she just being contrary? He stared after her as she went upstairs to look for the bill.

"She was probably just driving around," he told Bennett. "She's—er—she's had a difficult time lately."

"So I believe," said Bennett. "So she might have done anything."

"Certainly not. She'd have no reason to attack our mother, and do you seriously think she could have carried out quite a large, old-fashioned television set on her own?"

"That's as may be," said Bennett. "Perhaps there was a burglary, and she returned to find things gone, and then attacked Mrs Newton with malicious intent."

"But why? Why should she do such a thing?"

"Two reasons. She needed money and she probably blamed her mother for her problems," said Bennett.

"You've been reading too many text books on psychology, sergeant," Geoffrey, who also needed money, said in disgust, as Jennifer returned with two flimsy slips of paper which she had thrust, unheeding, into her jacket pocket, the receipts for both the pots of tea which she had ordered.

"The girl might remember me," she said, shrugging. "Who knows? But you don't care about finding out the real truth, do you? About what really happened and catching the right person, as long as you make an arrest?"

Bennett had not really intended to pursue this so far, but

he was annoyed by Jennifer's hostile manner, he knew what she had done in London, and he thought she could do with a little of the treatment. It was at this harmonious point in the interview that a detective constable arrived with news that a woman on her way to do the flowers in the church had noticed the brown van outside what had been the Blaneys' house at about eleven o'clock the previous day. It had been facing outwards and there was no one in it. She had also noticed that the garage doors at Yew Cottage were open and that the car was out. She had thought it rather strange as Mrs Newton always closed them when she went anywhere by car.

"Didn't you shut them?" Geoffrey was quite angry. "You should have done. Mama always did. The garden tools might have been stolen."

"Perhaps they were," snapped Jennifer. "Has anyone been to look?"

"I'll do that now," said Geoffrey. "You get dressed."

Weren't they going to ask her if she found the garage closed when she returned? They didn't, and she decided not to tell them that it had been unless they thought of doing so.

Geoffrey was anxious to separate Jennifer and Detective Sergeant Bennett before the man charged her with obstructing the police or some other offence. He could see that she was smouldering with rage and he was nearly incandescent himself. No wonder the police got such a bad press if this was how they dealt with the innocent. What if Jennifer had been an inarticulate member of society and entirely blameless? Jennifer had been guilty of a previous offence, though she had not yet been tried and convicted, but that was no excuse for Bennett's conduct. She had irked him. Of course, he had seen her skimpily dressed; maybe that had had some effect on the man. The notion made him feel uncomfortable.

He went out to the garage with the detective, where as far as could be ascertained nothing was missing. The mower and the other things that were kept there were in place, clean and neatly stacked. There was no garden shed.

"My sister had a dreadful experience, finding our mother

in that state," he said. "I hope you're not going to badger her about her movements yesterday. As I've already reminded you, she's been under a lot of strain apart from this."

"All the more reason to be cooperative now," said Bennett. "I suppose she was meeting some man whose wife was unaware of their affair." There was contempt in his tone.

"That's hardly likely, sergeant, since she's been accused of lobbing a stone through the window of her boyfriend's fiancée's flat," he said.

Bennett had not known this detail, merely that she had thrown a stone through a London window. He would not recant, however.

"We'll see," he said shortly.

Bennett left, and Geoffrey, having arranged that he and Jennifer, on their way to the hospital, would call in at the police station to be fingerprinted, went to seek out his sister. She was in the bath.

"Have you got a razor?" he asked her through the closed door.

She hadn't. There might be one in the bathroom cupboard, she said; he could come and look.

"I'll wait till you've finished," he said, embarrassed. "I'll have a bath too, if the boiler will run to it."

There was a small neat razor in a plastic case, and using ordinary soap he managed a shave of sorts, after which he felt better. Jennifer offered him the trousers of a tracksuit which was in her room, but they were too small. He put on her black tee-shirt and his evening trousers.

"You have changed your image," she said. "Won't Lynn bring you down some clothes? You'll be staying for a bit, won't you?"

"We'll see how things go," he said, answering neither question. He had telephoned the hospital while she was in the bath and had learned that their mother was comfortable and stable. At least she was no worse.

They were not kept long at the police station. Jennifer felt clammy and her heart began to pound while they were dealt with by a polite detective constable. This was the second time within a few days that she had been in a police station, having never entered one before in her life.

On their way out of Wintlebury, on the Crimpford road, they passed a farm where a car boot sale was being held.

"You might get some trousers there," said Jennifer.

"Really?" Geoffrey braked. He had never been to a car boot sale.

"You never know. They sell all sorts of things," said Jennifer. "It's worth a stop, I'd say." She smiled, and he had a sudden memory of a small girl catching shrimps, eagerly counting her spoils and chortling because she had more than he. She had not always been this grim, dour woman with the strained look.

They turned in to the farmyard and found a place to leave the car, then walked through the field gates to where rows of cars were drawn up with their boots open. Some people had small tables with their goods arranged invitingly upon them. There was a woman selling hand-knitted sweaters, and Geoffrey bought one, knitted in shades of dark blue and maroon. He put it on over Jennifer's black tee-shirt.

"It's great. It does a lot for you," said Jennifer. She had thrust her hands into her pockets, and though her face was still very pale, her eyes had lost their dazed expression. Geoffrey began to feel more optimistic about her eventual return to normality. At least she was thinking of someone other than herself.

They found a man selling tracksuits and Geoffrey was able to buy himself a pair of baggy black trousers.

"That will be better," he said, writing out the cheque. "Where can I put them on?"

"There'll be a barn or somewhere," said Jennifer.

They found a stable, empty and unlocked, and he quickly made the change, then rejoined Jennifer who was looking at a shaggy pony in a field. As he had rejected her tracksuit, she was wearing it today, with her black jacket.

"We're like twins now," she said.

He gave her arm a squeeze. For once he was with someone who, though all snarled up herself, was not antagonistic towards him and the experience was novel; even at the office he felt that he was among foes, forced to struggle for survival. But this wouldn't last; once things were back to normal, he and Jennifer would drift apart again.

When they reached the hospital they were told that their mother had regained consciousness briefly, but lapsed back again into what was now more like a normal sleep. She was rallying a little; her pulse had steadied and she had been taken off all the machinery except for a drip feed.

How frail she looked, thought Jennifer. Her face was grey, and her hair was in disorder, though she was clean and otherwise tidy and the bed was neat. Her thin arms lay over the bedclothes, the skin fleshless, hanging away from the bones; her wrists looked gaunt, her hands, surprisingly, a little red, the nails broken. She realised, with a sickening shock, that her mother must have come round while in the cupboard and struggled with the door, trying to get it open. How dreadful!

"You won't go home, will you?" she said anxiously to Geoffrey. "It is Sunday, after all."

"No, I'll stay," he reassured her. "I might give Lynn a ring." Jennifer's earlier suggestion that Lynn should bring him down some clothes was perfectly reasonable. He would ask her to do so.

But there was no answer when he telephoned, and he left no message on the machine.

Where was she now? And where were the girls?

Those were both questions Jennifer would have liked answered, when he told her that no one was at home, but she did not say so. Now was not the time to stir things up.

21

Neil was at home when the policemen came.

A fine smell of roasting came from the kitchen, where the piece of pork was in the oven. Neil had been peeling potatoes; he liked cooking and often helped his mother. Roseanne, who had the day off, was sleeping in. Kevin had come down at half-past nine, which was very early for him on a Sunday, and had gone out after eating a plate of Sugar Puffs and some toast thickly buttered and spread with Marmite, which he loved. In response to a shouted question from his mother, he had said he would not be home for the midday meal and this annoyed her as she had catered for him when buying the meat, and had made an apple pie, using fruit Mrs Moffat had given her. The Moffats had also supplied leeks and a savoy cabbage; Mavis gained a lot by working for them.

Jason, in his pushchair, was parked in a corner of the kitchen surveying the company when the doorbell rang.

Neil answered it. He knew at once, though they were in plain clothes, who the callers were, but his conscience was clear; he had done nothing wrong and he smiled at them enquiringly.

"Neil Smith?" asked one.

"Yes." Neil's smile faded and a sick feeling began to develop in his stomach. They could stitch you up without a bit of bother, if they wanted to; everyone knew that.

"This your van?" They pointed to it, gleaming clean outside the house.

"Yes. Well, I drive it. It belongs to my boss," said Neil. They could plainly read Len Harding's name painted on the van.

"We'll just step inside," said one of the officers and he pushed past Neil into the narrow hall, his colleague following.

Neil retreated behind their advance and his mother, hearing voices, appeared in the kitchen doorway, a tea towel in her hand. Her hair, just washed, was done up in rollers under a pink scarf and her round red face shone.

"Oh Neil," she said, in dismay. "What have you done now?"

"Nothing. I've done nothing," Neil protested.

"We'll talk about it, shall we?" said Detective Sergeant Bennett. It had not taken him and his colleagues long to discover the name of the builders working on the site next door to Yew Cottage, nor the fact that one van was kept overnight by Neil Smith, who had a record. "We'll go in here," he said, and propelled Neil into the front room which the Smiths called their lounge. "That will be all, Mrs Smith," he added dismissively to Mavis.

Neil almost went to pieces straight away. He stood in a corner of the room, twisting his hands together, while Bennett asked him how he had spent the previous day. He denied going out in the van at all until the afternoon, after he had cleaned it.

"You went out in it in the morning," he was told. "You went to Little Nym, and then to Middle Bardolph."

"I didn't," Neil declared. But maybe Kevin had. If Neil said that his brother had taken the van, both of them would be in trouble, he most of all, for letting Kevin drive it. If

Kevin had caused an accident, it wasn't for Neil to drop him in it.

"I stayed at home looking after Jason. That's my nephew," he said. "He had a cold, and it was raining. You can ask my mum. He stayed with me while she went to the shops. When it stopped, I took him for a walk. We went to the river and then we bought some chips and ate them in the park. Well, Jason's got no teeth yet so he sucked his," he added, with a nervous laugh.

"Oh yes?" asked Detective Constable Conway. "Anyone see you there?"

"Plenty of folk," said Neil stoutly, though the park had been deserted on such a damp afternoon. "My mum'll tell you," he added.

"You've just said your mum was out shopping," Conway observed.

"She'll tell you I took care of Jason."

"Maybe you did," said Conway. "You can take the kid in the van, can't you?"

"Yeah—I did, in the afternoon," said Neil. "That was after."

"After what?"

"After I'd cleaned it. I told you," Neil replied.

"What would you say if I told you your van was seen in Little Nym, at about ten o'clock in the morning, during a robbery in the village shop when a woman was attacked with a spanner and badly hurt?"

Neil said nothing. Kevin couldn't have done that; it wasn't possible.

"And some time later you drove to Middle Bardolph, to a house where you've been working. You parked there and attacked an elderly woman living in the house next door."

"I didn't!" Neil gasped his answer.

"She was very badly hurt," stated Bennett. "And the place was done over."

At this point, he cautioned Neil, and he was arrested.

"But what's he supposed to have done?" asked Mavis, her rollers now removed and her hair arranged in bouffant curls.

"You'll find out," was Bennett's curt reply.

They found Neil's adjustable spanner in his van and put it carefully into a polythene bag, ready for testing. The van itself was also removed for close examination; naturally it would be covered with Neil's prints.

Mrs Newton was very confused.

For some reason Geoffrey and Jennifer were standing by her bed and seemed to be holding hands. They were dressed casually, Jennifer in her usual black. Geoffrey's face was rather red and Jennifer was pale. What were they doing in her bedroom?

She closed her eyes. Her head ached and her whole body felt sore and bruised. Where were her spectacles?

"My glasses?" she tried to say, but the words would not come out.

Someone held her wrist, to take her pulse, and she saw it was a nurse. It dawned on her that she was in hospital, but why? Had she had a stroke?

"What's the matter with me?" she asked, in a clear high voice made audible by desperation.

A new voice spoke, and she saw a policewoman in uniform.

"Mrs Newton, you were attacked," said the policewoman. "Someone came into your house to commit theft. Can you remember seeing anyone?"

"No." Mrs Newton frowned. "I don't remember anything." She turned her head to look at Jennifer and Geoffrey. "Nothing," she added.

"I went out, mother. You let me take the car," Jennifer prompted.

"Oh. Oh yes." Dimly some remembrance of this came back to Mrs Newton. "The craft fair," she said vaguely. "I didn't go."

"No."

"Mrs Newton, someone locked you into the cupboard under the stairs, and your daughter found you there in the evening, when she came home from Wiltshire."

Wiltshire? What was Jennifer doing in Wiltshire?

"Did she?" asked Mrs Newton.

"Had you had lunch, do you think?" prompted the officer, keen to pinpoint the time of the attack.

"I don't know," said Mrs Newton.

The policewoman tried another tack.

"Mrs Newton, for some time now there have been workmen at the house next door."

"Yes. That's right. I remember that," said Mrs Newton, like a pleased child producing the desired answer in the classroom.

"Can you describe any of them?"

"Oh yes," said Mrs Newton. "There was one called Neil. He mended my fence when it blew down."

"Did he come to your house?"

"To the door, yes, more than once." He had been importunate, she recalled. "Never inside," she added. There had been his brother, too, whom she had seen somewhere before. She felt too tired to mention this.

"Thank you, Mrs Newton. That's a great help," said the policewoman, just as the nurse made ready to send her away.

Mrs Newton paid no heed, lapsing back into unconsciousness. As she drifted off she remembered the car wash incident and the man who had been so rude, but she did not hold the thought long enough to make the connection.

There seemed no point in staying at the hospital but Jennifer felt it would be wrong to leave her mother there alone all day.

"Not that she is alone," she said to Geoffrey. "Far from it." The policewoman, for instance, was still there.

It was agreed that Geoffrey should go home and fetch enough clothes to tide him over for a few days, and after he had gone a nurse advised Jennifer to visit the hospital shop.

It was staffed by the Friends of the hospital, and she would be able to get a cup of coffee and a sandwich. It seemed a good idea and she set off, following signs along the corridors.

Someone had left a paper on a chair at the table where she sat with her coffee and cheese sandwich, and she picked it up. It was a tabloid which she never saw; the headlines heralded a lubricious story about a minor Royal and, mildly curious, Jennifer turned to the appropriate page to read the allegations.

Below the story was a paragraph under a headline.

MOTHER OF JILTED WOMAN ATTACKED, she read, and saw her own name. She read on.

> Mrs Eleanor Newton, 69, lies unconscious in Crimpford Hospital following a vicious mugging attack during which her house was stripped. At her bedside keeping vigil is her daughter Jennifer, 37, on bail on a charge of causing criminal damage. Jennifer's former boyfriend, Daniel Ferguson, was not available last night for comment.

Reading it, Jennifer felt sick. How had they got on to this? Weren't the Sunday papers set up in advance? Some other story must have been killed to give space to this one. Did the paper expect it to run and run? If her mother died, they could blow it up into a major feature lasting weeks. She tore the page out of the paper and crumpled it into her pocket. None of this should be happening, and it wouldn't have if Daniel had kept faith. At this moment she blamed him for the attack on her mother, and her anger, muted for the past hours, began to rise again. She left the shop and managed to lose her way trying to return to the ward. By the time she reached the right landing she was almost weeping with frustrated rage, but the nurses thought this was due to filial concern and they greeted her with sympathy.

It was the policewoman who came to the rescue. A man had been arrested for the assault and it was not necessary for an officer to remain at the hospital. If Mrs Newton were able, at a later stage, to remember something about the attack, she could be interviewed again. Meanwhile WPC Locker was leaving to return to Wintlebury. A squad car was on its way to pick her up.

"Why don't we take you, too?" she suggested. "You can't do anything here as things are, and you look shattered."

"I am," said Jennifer, and added, weakly, "I'm in trouble, too."

"I'd heard," said WPC Locker. "Well, we all do silly things sometimes, don't we? I expect you felt better, after."

But Jennifer hadn't. She had only added to her misery.

"I would like to go home," she said. "Thanks."

She obtained an undertaking from the hospital that they would telephone at once if her mother's condition worsened, and she'd ring Geoffrey when she reached Middle Bardolph, hoping to catch him before he started back.

"I should settle down and watch telly," advised WPC Locker when they were in the car, being driven by a male colleague whom she called Tom. "There's often a good film on Sunday afternoon."

"I can't do that. The set's been stolen," said Jennifer.

"Oh dear, I'd forgotten that," said WPC Locker.

"You said someone's been arrested," said Jennifer. "Who is it?"

"Young fellow who's been working on the site next door," Tom told them, for WPC Locker knew no details. "Used his boss's van, it seems. He's wanted for the job in Little Nym as well."

Jennifer had not heard about that and asked what had happened there. The two officers explained. They were pleased with this speedy resolution of both cases.

"Well, at least that sergeant of yours will stop accusing me of beating up my own mother," said Jennifer bitterly.

"He didn't," said WPC Locker, but her voice rose questioningly.

"Wanted to know where I'd been, when, why. None of his business," said Jennifer.

Neither WPC Locker nor Tom wanted to pursue this aspect of the investigation.

"Young chap's got a record," Tom told his colleague.

Jennifer, in the back of the car, stopped listening to them, closing her eyes, wishing she knew one way or the other if her mother would survive. Once you knew, either way, you could adjust.

When they reached Yew Cottage, the scenes of crime team who had returned that morning were just finishing. She could have the run of the house.

The two officers came in with her, and WPC Locker made some tea, which they all drank sitting in the kitchen.

Tea, thought Jennifer. Some people think it's a remedy for everything.

22

It was quiet in the house after the police had gone. Jennifer had told them what she thought was missing: the pictures, the silver, the jewellery, the television and radios, and now, of course, she had no artificial means of breaking the silence.

She had described her mother's engagement ring—a sapphire set with diamonds, and valuable; she rarely wore it. There were also a gold pin, a silver bracelet, an old-fashioned bar brooch mounted with a pearl set between tiny diamonds. Mrs Newton had been wearing her pearls, which were cultured, and they had been left untouched; some villains, it was implied, would have torn them from her. Her attacker had left her watch, too. This indicated that he was not a professional thief; someone accustomed to robbing people of their possessions would have known that there would be valuables on the victim.

Jennifer found it strangely difficult to open her mother's bedroom door, afraid of the disorder she knew she would find. Dust used to detect fingerprints covered every surface and various drawers were still open, but nothing had been tipped out; the thief had merely riffled through the contents and there had been no vandalism. She began tidying up the disturbed clothing, replacing handkerchiefs, tights, underwear in tidy piles, but with a sense of intrusion. Her mother wore chain-store nightdresses with sleeves and high-buttoned necks. She would need some in the hospital, Jennifer thought.

No, she wouldn't. She was not going to recover, and these things might as well be packed up ready for Oxfam.

Jennifer shook herself. It was too soon to think like that. She put everything away neatly, then looked in the hanging cupboard where it seemed as if nothing had been touched. There was a jacket she could borrow; though taller than her mother, she was just as slim. She slipped her arms into the garment, a navy-blue single-breasted reefer coat, very useful, she would have thought, but she did not remember seeing her mother wearing it; she was almost always in beige. Jennifer would save that for herself. She tried on a long, loose cardigan. There was no scent to it, no reminder of her mother, no personal fragrance.

Eventually everything had been put back and Jennifer fetched the vacuum and a duster and polish. The room must be cleaned even though she was sure her mother would never use it again. She did it all thoroughly, moving the bed, under which there was not a speck of dust or fluff. Then she went down to the sitting-room where the desk drawers had been opened and papers disarranged. Cleaning up the mess left by the fingerprint men took some time and the silence, as she worked, was oppressive. It was a relief to switch on the vacuum sweeper and have its noise as a sort of company. Confused thoughts kept running through her mind as she worked. She did not like thinking about her mother looking so fragile and old in the high hospital bed. She had never been in hospital herself and the size of the place, the enforced surrender of self to the authority of others made her uncomfortable and afraid.

Tidying files in a drawer, she came upon three photograph albums and took them out. There were black and white snapshots of herself and Geoffrey as small children, some with their father sitting between them, his large calm face smiling. Seeing him like that brought tears to her eyes. She thought she remembered him clearly, but perhaps her memory was only prompted by the photograph her mother had given her after his death, which she kept in her room. The album held pictures of their tree house in the Bournemouth garden, and of picnics on the beach or in the New Forest, where they sometimes went on Sundays. Those had been safe days. There were very few photographs of her mother, and after her father's death they ceased altogether although Geoffrey as a schoolboy had had a camera. Where were his family snaps? At his own house, she supposed.

Were there no albums dating back to the time before she and Geoffrey were born? What about her father's youth, and her mother's? She knew almost nothing about either, nor how her parents had met, and until now had felt no interest. There had never been grandparents in her life. Jennifer knew that her mother's parents had been killed in an air raid on London. Her father's parents must also have been dead. There were no wedding pictures, nothing from the earlier times.

Surely that was very strange? Sitting there at the desk, the albums spread before her, Jennifer felt a slow curiosity stir. Her mother's maiden name was Harris; that she knew; it figured on her own birth certificate. Who were the Harrises? Where were they from? Her mother must have something about them here—some papers from the past.

She began to lift out more envelope files from the desk. Eventually they would all have to be gone through, like the clothes, and the final task would be simpler if she did some checking now.

So she quietened any prickings of conscience as she opened each file and looked inside.

One envelope related to investments; they were clearly listed on a stockbroker's valuation sheet and went back over many years. There were details of the pension that her mother drew; one paid by her father's insurance and not index-linked. Didn't she also draw the state widow's pension? Or was she

widowed too young? Even so, she must be entitled to a
pension on her own account. The figures Jennifer had found,
however, demonstrated that her mother had needed to make
money from her house moves to keep pace with the cost of
living and explained why renovations and furnishings had
been done economically, for short-term gains. The investments had prospered; it seemed that Mr Booth, the solicitor
in Bournemouth, had overseen them, employing a broker
whose advice had been sound. There were methodical details
of the sales of embroidery in recent years; her mother had not
made a great deal from her tapestry cushions but, supposed
Jennifer, it had given her something to do and earned a little
extra income.

She found her mother's birth and marriage certificates.
There was no passport, but then her mother had never, to her
knowledge, left the country. That was extraordinary, nowadays, when people were so mobile. She read so many travel
books; you'd think she'd want to visit some of the places she
had read about.

In the centre of the desk, which had been her father's, there
was a small door between the pigeon holes where writing
paper and envelopes were neatly stacked. This section contained an address book with very few entries, a ball of string
and a pair of scissors. On either side of the little door was a
fluted piece of wood, scarcely more than an inch wide, separating it from the pigeon holes. Sitting there, Jennifer had a
sudden memory of her father seated at this desk; she saw him
inserting something sharp—a paperknife?—into the side of
one of these columns and then pulling. He had taken something from the desk and sat reading it while she, unobserved,
perhaps forgotten, was sitting on the floor nearby, colouring
in a book.

There was no paperknife in the desk now but Jennifer went
to the kitchen for a sharp bladed knife. She had one in her
handbag, she remembered, but there were others. She pushed
its point into the column on the right side of the central door,
but nothing moved though she prodded it in several places.

She tried the other side then, gingerly, fearful of scarring the desk though if her mother died she would never know what Jennifer had done. There was a tiny movement, infinitesimal; she levered the knife slightly downwards and saw that what was here was, indeed, a hidden drawer concealed behind the dummy fluted front. It took time to free the movable section; it was stuck so fast that she felt sure it had not been moved for years.

She held in her hand a box drawer open at one end. Inside there was a large envelope in which were contained a smaller envelope and some yellowed, ancient newspaper cuttings.

The telephone rang in the afternoon.

Jennifer did not hear it at first, so intent was she on what she had learned from the papers in the desk. It rang and rang, and at last she rose to answer it.

It was Geoffrey, calling from the hospital to which he had just returned. She had entirely forgotten her original plan of catching him at home.

"Oh Geoff—sorry to keep you waiting," she said, while she tried to pull her mind away from her discovery. "I left," she added. "Mother was unconscious again and there seemed no point in staying."

"I thought we'd agreed that one of us should be there," he said. He sounded cross.

"Is she worse?"

"No," he admitted, grudgingly. "She's a little better, actually. She's had a natural sleep, it seems."

"Well, then," said Jennifer. "That's good."

"Are you coming back?" She could use the Vauxhall.

"I don't think so." She must put all these papers away before Geoffrey came; there was no need for him to know about them. "I've been busy clearing up," she said. "The police had made an awful mess."

"I hear they've got the chap," said Geoffrey. "A nurse told me."

"Yes. Some workman who'd been doing up the Blaneys'

house," said Jennifer, speaking warmly now, wanting to keep him in a better mood. "I'll expect you later, then," she said.

She went back to her reading. She had at least twenty minutes in hand before he could arrive; time enough to go over the story again, take in the astounding details of her mother's past. No wonder she never alluded to the years before she had met Jennifer's father.

The shock of what she had learned was devastating; even when she finally put the papers away again in the hidden drawer, Jennifer could scarcely believe that it was the truth.

It was, however. And her father had concealed the proof.

23

Mavis Smith could not believe it: not again, not after all that had happened before. She had been so sure that Neil had learned his lesson and would have gone to the stake for that belief, but all the time he had been using Len's van to go on little trips knocking things off.

After arresting him, the police had returned to ask her if she had any objection to their searching the house. She was told that if she had, a search warrant could soon be obtained.

"I'm sure we've nothing to hide," said Mavis in her most regal manner, and her surprise and shock was clearly genuine when they beckoned her up to the room Neil shared with Kevin and showed her the cupboard with the goods in boxes which had not got there by any legal means. They looked in the loft, too, where they found objects which they were sure would prove to have come from Yew Cottage. Under a floorboard in the bathroom they discovered Mrs Newton's jewel case containing her ring, her brooches, and some other items. Her initials, EN, were on it, stamped in gold.

Detective Sergeant Bennett and a detective constable left, carrying out polythene bags full of their haul.

"Your lad'll be gone a long time for this lot," she was told, as they left.

The roast pork was scarcely touched. Even Roseanne had little appetite and Jason wouldn't stop grizzling. His cold was worse.

"He's missing his uncle," said Roseanne, trying to persuade him to take his bottle but Jason didn't want it.

"How could he do it?" Mavis said. "He'd got a good job. He was trusted. We'd all stood by him. He was saving for a car." What would Len think about it? Neil had let him and all of them down so badly. And those poor women who'd been hurt; that was terrible.

"Perhaps he got impatient," Roseanne said. "He met all sorts inside, Mum. He may have learned bad ways."

This would finish her chances with Mike, her boyfriend; when he heard about Neil he wouldn't want to know her. She sighed; she liked him.

"He attacked some woman in a shop in Little Nym," her mother said. "Broke her wrist, Neil did. And may have killed that Mrs Newton over at Middle Bardolph. It's the one that was Mrs Moffat's friend. I met her. A nice sort of person— very stiff in her ways." Suddenly her round red face puckered and she began to cry, tears pouring down her cheeks and spilling off her nose like tap water. "How could he?" she wailed.

"There, there, Mum. Don't take on," said Roseanne, and she plucked a piece from a roll of kitchen towel to mop her mother's sodden face. "Poor Neil, he was always weak. That's what led to the other business. I don't suppose he thought of this on his own." He was no Mr Big. Then something else struck her. "And he was minding Jason. He must have taken him with him. Left him in the van while he— he——." Words failed her, and as she stopped speaking Jason joined his grandmother in a storm of weeping. Mavis, too, was aghast at the thought of her infant grandson witnessing Neil's crimes.

"Maybe he left Jason behind. Put him to bed and went off," she said.

"Oh, he wouldn't," said Roseanne. "He wouldn't leave Jason alone. What if the house caught on fire? He loves that child."

"If only he could tell us what he knows," sobbed Mavis, gazing at Jason whose face was now redder than her own. Roseanne had transferred her attentions to him and was patting his back, crooning to him, trying to calm him, but Jason was past comforting. "Why had he to do it yesterday? Why offer to mind Jason if he'd got this planned?"

The two women stared at one another, unable to answer the question.

"We'd better tell Mrs Moffat what's happened," sniffed Mavis at last. "About Mrs Newton, I mean. They were sort of friends. Better we tell her than she learns from the telly or that."

"The telly!" Roseanne stared at her mother. "They'll be here. Reporters. Cameras," she said. They'd been spared all that before; Neil's previous crime had been small beer compared with this one. "Do you really believe our Neil's violent?" she asked.

"He wouldn't hurt a fly," said his mother.

But he had, and had served his sentence. And now he had done it again.

After darkness fell, Mavis went round to The Old Vicarage. For once Jason was being cared for by his own mother, who was not working that night. She walked up the dark drive and rang the doorbell.

Dr Moffat opened it. He held a glass of beer in his hand and beamed amiably at her. She did not usually care for beards, but his, large and bushy though it was, seemed to enhance the kindliness in his face.

"Ah—Mavis," he said, and allowed a note of surprise to enter his voice, for she never came on a Sunday, nor made

social calls. This visit was for a purpose, and she was all
dressed up, he saw, as she stepped over the threshold into the
hall wearing a purple hip-length coat and a short black skirt.
She had very muscular calves and narrow ankles; he had
noticed this before. "Well," he encouraged her. "What can
I do for you?"

Mavis saw no point in a gradual approach.

"It's about our Neil," she said. "Well, not really him.
Only in a way. It's more about Mrs Moffat's friend in Middle
Bardolph."

"What friend is this?" asked Simon. "I didn't think she
knew anyone in Middle Bardolph." Belatedly, Simon realised that Mavis was in some distress. "Come into the kitchen,
Mavis," he said. "Lucy's in there. Jane's still here."

"Yes—well, I'm sorry to bother you, but I reckon she'd
want to know," said Mavis, and she bustled off towards the
kitchen at the rear of the hall.

Simon followed, a bear-like presence, comfortingly large,
and Mavis had an impulse to turn and cast herself on his broad
chest in its dark blue guernsey sweater. But that wouldn't do
at all. If she were to receive any comfort over this, it would
have to come from Len, and he might easily turn nasty at the
way Neil had repaid him.

Lucy was making sandwiches for Jane to take on the train
she was due to catch later. Her face was flushed and she
looked happy. One reason Mavis liked working here was
because the atmosphere was always pleasant; she felt no envy,
merely basked in its warmth.

"Mavis has a problem," Simon said. "Like a drink, Mavis?"

"I wouldn't say no to a sherry. Ta," said Mavis, who
knew there were two bottles in the sideboard. "It's about that
Mrs Newton," she told Lucy.

"Sit down, Mavis," said Lucy, who disliked people hov-
ering while she worked. She spread mustard on the piece of
bread she had just buttered and began arranging ham in thick

slices; she was sure Jane never ate enough while she was away from home. "What about Mrs Newton?"

Mavis gulped, then told her bluntly.

"She's in the hospital. She's been hurt. Mugged. Maybe killed," she burst out.

"No! You can't mean that!" Lucy halted operations, then placed a second slice of bread on the first and pressed it down while she bisected the sandwich. "Whatever happened?" she asked.

"Seems someone attacked her at home. Took a lot of stuff. Hit her." Somehow Mavis got the words out. "Left her for dead but she isn't, not yet." That was the part Mavis found most difficult to reconcile with Neil's conduct, the bundling of the old woman into the cupboard, locking her in. The police had made quite sure that she knew this part of the story.

"How dreadful!" Lucy was very shocked. "Where is she? Crimpford General?"

"Yes."

"Is her family with her? She's got a daughter, and there's a son, too, I think."

"The daughter found her," said Mavis. "Luckily enough, or she'd be lying there yet, shut in the cleaning cupboard under the stairs."

"Oh no! You mean whoever did it shut her up like that?"

Mavis nodded.

"There's more," she said. "My Neil's been arrested. They think he did it."

"Oh, Mavis! But they must have got it wrong. He wouldn't—he couldn't—" That mild, inoffensive young man, scarcely older than a boy, wouldn't do such a terrible thing. But Lucy knew about Neil's earlier conviction; what had happened once could be repeated, often was.

"His van was seen out there. He says he stayed with Jason all day, but who's to say?" Mavis now began to weep, and she took a tiny lace-edged handkerchief out of her pocket to dab her eyes. Lucy, who only ever used tissues, had time to be amazed. "There was another job done, in Little Nym. Someone was attacked there, as well. They say he did that, too."

"And did he? What do you think?" Lucy asked.

"I don't know what to think," said Mavis. "I couldn't credit it the time before, and yet it happened."

During this exchange, Simon had returned with a glass of sherry for Mavis.

"Have some," he advised, thinking brandy might have been more appropriate.

Mavis obeyed. She liked a drop of medium sherry and often had one when a customer stood her a drink at The Bell. Then she told the Moffats about all the things which the police had found stored at the house.

"He must have been taking stuff for weeks," she said. "He'd have the chance, you see, driving around as he does, and he was often home alone with just Jason. That would give him time to move it without the rest of us knowing."

"But does he spend a lot?" asked Lucy. "Flash it about, I mean? If he's been stealing things and selling them, he'd be using the money."

"No, but he's saving for a car," said Mavis. "He loves them. That's what started it before—he saved for driving lessons first, then he got a taste for thieving." She mopped at her face, swallowed the rest of her sherry and stood up. "I thought you'd want to know about Mrs Newton, poor old soul," she said. "There's sure to be something about it in the paper tomorrow." Mavis, immured indoors all day with her troubles, had not seen a Sunday paper.

"I'm so sorry, Mavis," Lucy said gently. "You were brave to come and tell us. It's awful for you. Perhaps it's all a mistake and it'll turn out someone else did it."

"They found her jewel case in the house," said Mavis. "It had her initials on in gold. How could he be so stupid?"

It looked as if another storm of weeping was on the way, but Mavis hung on to her control.

"I'm on duty at The Bell tonight," she said. "I mustn't look all blotchy in the bar."

"Has Neil got a lawyer?" Simon asked, more for Mavis's comfort than for Neil's; if he had done this thing, he deserved no mercy, but he was entitled to his rights.

"I rang up the man who looked after him before," said Mavis. "He said he'd look into it. Neil knows not to say anything, though," she added, not without a touch of pride.

After she had gone, Simon said, "Perhaps Neil should do a bit of talking. If he didn't do it, he should account for his movements."

"He must have done it," Lucy said. "Who else? He drove that van, didn't he? His boss is Mavis's boyfriend."

"How do you know?"

"She let it fall. She didn't tell me directly," Lucy said. "Poor Mavis—she's no age, you know, and a grandmother already. I'm glad to think she's got something going for her. Or had," she added. "He won't be so keen now, will he? I wonder what I ought to do about Mrs Newton. I hardly know her." She didn't want to tell Simon how they met.

"You can't do anything," said Simon. "You heard what Mavis said. She's probably beyond all human aid by now."

"I could try ringing the house," said Lucy. "The daughter might be there. I want to know, in any case. I felt sorry for Mrs Newton. She was so buttoned up, so timid, in a way."

Simon was more interested in Neil's part in the affair.

"I'm disappointed in that boy," he said. "I really thought he'd go straight."

"So did I."

"The other boy's all right, anyway. That's something. He'll be a great help to Mavis now, I'm sure," said Simon. "He'll prop her up."

He hoped Lucy wouldn't have to do it; he was off, himself, on Tuesday, to a conference in California, so he would not be involved in what must follow, but Lucy had a kind heart and was given to impulsive gestures. He hoped she would not end up supplying moral support to Mavis and her family, and Mrs Newton's daughter.

Roseanne, alone at home, was fretting. She was so used to being able to pop out for a drink or to see her friend Tracy when she wasn't working; staying in, with so much trouble and Jason her only companion, was frustrating. She'd be stuck now, with Neil gone. She and her mother would have to work out some system for sharing the baby-sitting. It was too bad of Neil to get into trouble again; he'd put them through enough the last time. Kevin would have something to say about it, when he came home. What had he thought about that stuff in the bedroom cupboard? He must have noticed it.

For the first time since Neil's arrest that morning, a tiny seed of doubt crept into Roseanne's mind, only to be dismissed. It had to be Neil; he was the one who'd done it before. Anyway, Kevin could speak for himself when he came in.

She was in bed and asleep by the time that happened.

Kevin saw that the van was not outside the house, but he knew nothing of the latest events. During the day he had managed to forget everything about his Saturday activities. He had fallen in with a crowd he met in a pub. Among them they had three cars, and he had been with them to Bristol where they'd found some girls, drunk a lot and had what they considered to be a good time. One of his new friends had dropped him off in Wintlebury on his way back to London.

He might go there himself, Kevin thought. If that old girl snuffed it, he'd better get away, not that anything could be pinned on him.

When he went upstairs he saw that Neil's bed was empty; that was very strange. Then he discovered that the things he had stored in the cupboard had gone. Had Neil taken the van and the loot and gone off? It was most unlikely, but in a sudden panic he went to the bathroom and prised up the carpet tiles, to lift the loose floorboard where he had hidden things before and where Mrs Newton's jewel case was stashed.

His mother came in while he was scrabbling around. In her quilted nylon satin dressing-gown, with grease on her face, she stood staring down at him.

"It was you," she exclaimed. "You took Neil's van. You did it."

Kevin stared back at her. Then he slowly rose to his feet. The open floorboard gaped below them both.

"What are you talking about?" he said.

"Neil's been arrested," she said. "Charged with murder, as like as not, by now. They took the van away for testing, but it was you driving it, wasn't it?"

Kevin looked away from her and laughed. It was not a nice laugh, and when she heard it she understood what it meant to say your blood had turned to ice.

"You did it," she repeated.

"Prove it," snapped Kevin, and he pushed past her and rushed into his room, where he locked the door.

He heard her go down the stairs. She'd think about it. Would she ring up the police? Would she shop him for Neil?

Kevin was not going to wait and see. He seized a soft holdall from the top of the cupboard and stuffed some clothes into it, then picked up his passport, which was in a drawer. At least the police hadn't taken that, but then they were after Neil, not him. He still had Mrs Newton's cheque book and her credit card. He'd used the card today, signing with a flourish, E. Newton. Luckily her stupid first name—Eileen, Edith—whatever it was—was not spelt out in full, and the pub where he had used it had been satisfied. His new friends were quite impressed by his generosity. He'd spent most of the cash he'd managed to collect on his two raids but when the banks opened in the morning, he'd use the cheque book to get hold of more.

He needed wheels. Now he lamented the cremation of his Mercedes. What a loss! He'd missed it every day since it went up in flames, and he couldn't claim from the insurance because he'd failed to pay the last premium.

Would he find a car in town with its keys in, waiting to be

stolen? Neil was the one with the skills to liberate a car; he'd
told Kevin a bit about it; a screwdriver was all you needed,
but he hadn't shown Kevin exactly what to do.

He couldn't sit here wondering. There was no time to lose.
Kevin left the house through the bedroom window, lowering
himself on to the flat roof over the shed and so to the ground.

Meanwhile Mavis was still trying to make up her mind
whether to ring the police. She never heard him go.

He might try The Old Vicarage for a car. The Moffats were
careless about security and he'd seen that old car of the
doctor's left outside with the windows open and the keys in
before now, when he'd been up for vegetables.

He went straight there, to find the car drawn up on the
gravel sweep. The keys were in it. They deserved to lose it,
he thought, getting in, an opinion which the police shared
when the loss was discovered and reported in the morning.

24

When Mavis discovered that Kevin had left the house, his guilt was confirmed.

A sick despair, so great that she felt as if a huge weight had been tied to her heart, filled her. There was real physical pain in her chest, so that she wondered if she was having a heart attack. She was too shocked even to cry, but crying had never been Mavis's way and her earlier tears had been the first shed for many months.

Of course Kevin had gone to give himself up, she told herself, rallying. He wouldn't let Neil go down for something he hadn't done. Yes, that must be why he'd slipped out and soon Neil would come home, at latest in the morning. She would not listen to the voice which told her Kevin would have openly declared what he was doing, telephoned the police station, asked them to fetch him, if that had been his intention. And why would he have packed a bag if he had been going to confess? He knew you weren't allowed any personal possessions once you went inside.

Kevin wouldn't have done that on his own: hurt that woman at Little Nym and then done Yew Cottage over, shutting that poor soul up in her own cupboard. He must have been helping

221

a mate of his, someone he'd met at work. Her Kevin, who was so generous, treating them to trips abroad and meals in restaurants when he was in the money, wouldn't go mugging women.

When he was in the money: but he hadn't had so much lately and it was a long time since he'd stood treat. Of course, the repair to his car must be going to cost a lot. It had been gone some days now.

He hadn't sold it, had he? Told them all a tale? Why should he, when he had been earning good wages with overtime to account for his extra funds.

But there were the things the police had taken away: items not stolen from Mrs Newton, boxes they'd brought down from the loft and from the bedroom Kevin shared with Neil. Kevin, not Neil, had stolen them.

Utter weariness crept over Mavis as she lay in the large bed, now sagging in the middle, in which she and Len snatched a comforting interlude if they got the chance. She had tried so hard with the children, yet now all of them had been in trouble, though Roseanne's was of an all too human sort, and no offence against the law. How could she have foretold that Jason's father would run out on her? And Neil had not, after all regressed. That knowledge slightly eased the aching pain that wouldn't go away. But now both the boys would have records and Kevin's crime was very serious. Where had she gone wrong in their childhood years? What had she failed to do that might have stopped them both from sinking into wickedness? For what they had done was wicked: both of them had been violent, had hurt another human being, and in Kevin's case deliberately and badly. She had no illusions about that; the woman in Little Nym had been hit with a spanner, so they'd been saying in the bar at The Bell, where there had been a lot of talk about both the episodes. Though it was known that a man had been arrested, as he had not yet been charged his identity had not been disclosed. She was safe from pitying looks and whispered murmurs for a few more hours. What about later? With a son facing a murder charge, she might lose her job. And Roseanne hers.

Mavis could not face such a thought immediately. She banished it, and tried to think of something happier, ending up reciting nursery rhymes in her head until at last she slept.

In the morning, Roseanne brought her a cup of tea in bed.

"Is it my birthday?" she asked, sitting up, heavy-eyed.

"I thought you could do with a treat," said Roseanne. "I was up with Jason. I think he must be teething. It seems so quiet. Kevin's out. He can't have come back all night, not that it's the first time. But he won't know about Neil. Maybe we can get hold of him at work."

Mavis accepted the tea, then patted the bed beside her.

"Get yourself a cup, too, love, and come back," she said. "There's something you've got to know."

When the Moffats discovered Simon's car missing from outside the house, at first Lucy thought he must have put it away, then forgotten that he had done so.

"I didn't," he said.

He'd taken Jane to catch her train, felt his usual pang on parting from his pretty daughter, feared for her in the company of the lecherous males he imagined would be on her train, not to mention surrounding her every day at the university. Telling himself all fathers felt like this about their daughters, he had driven home anxious to get to bed and Lucy's welcoming arms, which he would miss in his two long weeks in the States.

She had come closer in recent days. There had been a spell, back in the summer, when he had felt her drifting off, not quite present when he talked; he had begun to wonder if she was bored with him; it would not be surprising, for he thought himself very dull. Was she nosing round, looking for adventure? Perhaps he had imagined it. In America, he would have opportunities, if he chose, but he would not so choose; he loved Lucy, had vowed himself to her for life, had meant it, and had never been seriously tempted to stray. Besides, it was so difficult to manage; there were lies, and energy as well as guile was required. Moreover, what did you do about your socks and pants? And it would be so unaesthetic: he was used to Lucy, and she him; she didn't mind his pot belly and said she liked his bald patch.

She was cross now, though, as she ran out to check the garage, which, of course, was empty.

"Did you leave the keys in?" she asked.

"Oh no," he said.

But he had. He had done it before, often enough, and got away with it, as you would expect in quiet Wintlebury, but even here, precautions should be taken. They made quite certain, before ringing the police, looking in the bowl on the hall chest where keys were left by each of them so that they were never lost.

Damping down her anger, Lucy telephoned the police, who were in no great hurry to investigate this routine crime. Car theft was increasing all the time, and if people were stupid enough to invite a passing thief to steal their car they must take the consequences. They were very busy at the moment, with several break-ins to investigate and two cases of assault, one of which might end up as a murder enquiry.

There was no reason for the police to suppose that the theft of the Moffats' car was in any way linked to the crime at Middle Bardolph; cars were stolen in large numbers every day, all over the country. When at last an officer arrived, Simon had gone, glad to escape to his laboratory, taking Lucy's car, which she was none too pleased about.

"See that you bring it back tonight," she said curtly. He had an important meeting; she had to lend it to him.

Reporting the details was soon done. Then Lucy rang the insurance company and discussed hiring a car if it had not been recovered when Simon returned from California. The police had not been optimistic about finding it.

"Youngsters torch them," the constable said. "Go for a spin and then set them alight. It's a new craze. That's if they don't crash first and maybe kill somebody." It was quite clear that if this happened, the officer would consider Simon, because of the keys, responsible for the fatality.

Who were these youngsters, wondered Lucy; were they the ones she saw hanging around in the streets at night, with nothing to do and nowhere to go except, if they were old enough, the pubs? They didn't necessarily want to spend the evenings in small cramped houses or flats with their parents. Wintlebury no longer had a youth club. Would they attend it if another one was started? They needed somewhere to meet, to play snooker and darts and buy soft drinks.

She gave up speculating, and went to telephone Mrs Newton's daughter. As she was now deprived of her own car, there was nothing active Lucy could do to help her, which was a relief.

A high brittle voice answered the telephone.

Lucy gave her name and went on, "I know Mrs Newton slightly. I'm so shocked at what has happened. How is she? Is that Jennifer?"

Jennifer was wary. If this woman knew her mother, she might also know about Jennifer's own troubles.

"Mother hasn't mentioned you," she said coldly. "She's in what the hospital calls a stable condition but then that's what they always say."

"She's still unconscious?" Lucy asked. At least she wasn't dead.

"She came round, then she dropped off again but it may have been more sleeping," Jennifer said. "She's very weak," she added. "My brother's here. Would you like to talk to him? We're going to the hospital quite soon."

"Oh, he doesn't know me," said Lucy. "Look, we had a car stolen last night, and my husband's taken mine to get to work so I'm stuck, but I just wanted to offer sympathy and find out how things are. Let me know if I can help at all."

"Well, you can't, can you?" said Jennifer. "Goodbye," and she put the telephone down.

Geoffrey had heard her end of the conversation.

"Who was that?" he asked. There had been several calls from newspapers that morning.

Jennifer explained.

"She was a friend of Mama's. Why were you so rude?" he said.

"She was being nosy," said Jennifer.

"She wasn't. She was showing concern and you snubbed her."

"She knew she couldn't help. Her car was stolen last night," said Jennifer.

"Well, you never commiserated with her about that. Why do you have to be so hostile all the time? Why do you think everyone's got it in for you?"

"Because they have," said Jennifer in a sulky voice.

"What nonsense. This Lucy woman was being kind. She may be fond of Mama. It's not impossible," he said.

"You let everyone take you for a ride," Jennifer accused him. "Lynn, the girls, the people at work. You should look after yourself, like I do."

"And look where it's got you!" He had to say it. "You always lash out, regardless. What about looking inside Jennifer for a change and seeing what's wrong there?" and he turned on his heel and went out into the garden where he stumped about looking at the tidy plants and neatly trimmed lawn until he had cooled down.

Well, she had it coming to her, he decided, and if she'd gone upstairs and cut her wrists because he'd been unkind, too bad.

But he'd better go in and make sure that she hadn't.

When the police produced some of the items they had taken from the house, Neil simply stared at them, dumbfounded. He had never seen the ring, nor the brooch, nor the silver, nor the pictures. He did not know what to say so he kept silent. That was always safest; he had learned that during his time inside. It was the way to avoid being trapped into making a damaging remark, if not a full confession. Kevin had done the job, that was obvious, and all he, Neil, had to do was wait for Kevin to come forward, which of course he'd do as soon as he heard that Neil had been wrongfully accused. It might take a little while, but it would happen.

The arresting officers were not harsh, but they were firm. They were sure they had found the perpetrator, and when confronted with the evidence, this thin gangling villain would not take long to break down and admit to his new offences. Taken to a cell after a lengthy preliminary session in the interview room during which Neil had supplied no information beyond his name and age, which they already knew, he had sat hunched on the narrow bed, his head in his hands. Jason knew he had told the truth about how he had spent Saturday, but Jason could not say so.

Kevin had carried out these two attacks, using the van he had borrowed. That was the hardest thing to accept. Kevin had deliberately attacked the woman in Little Nym, and Mrs Newton. When Neil hurt that other old lady, the crime for which he had been justly sentenced—Neil knew he deserved to be punished and bore no grudge—it had been an accident because he panicked. Kevin had carried the spanner from the van into the shop in Little Nym, and maybe he had used that at Middle Bardolph too. It was Neil's own spanner, not Len Harding's, and that made it worse.

Now he understood that the various boxes and packages Kevin had sometimes brought into the house must have been full of stolen goods. He'd been stupid not to catch on to that before, but he'd always looked up to Kevin, thought he could do no wrong, never seriously imagined he'd been into thieving, much less violence.

Neil wasn't going to tell them. He wasn't going to grass on his brother. Besides, even if he did, they wouldn't believe him. No, it was up to Kevin to put things right, and he'd do it.

He was interviewed a second time, after an interval. Under

the new rules, the interrogation was timed and recorded but Neil was barely aware of that.

"What did you do after you'd hit Mrs Newton?" he was asked.

"I didn't hit her."

"What did you hit her with?"

Silence.

"What did you do with the flower pot?"

"What flower pot?"

When they asked him what he would do if he broke a plant pot, he said, "Sweep up the bits and throw them away, I suppose."

"Where? In a bin?"

"Yes."

"Ah, so that's what you did, then."

"No, you asked me what I'd do if—" Neil began. Then he stopped talking. They were tricking him.

In the morning, Kevin would come, Neil assured himself. By that time he had agreed that he had been to Mrs Newton's house when he repaired the fence and had often spoken to her.

"I'm sorry she's been hurt," he said once. "How is she?"

But they wouldn't tell him.

"It's convenient to have a cupboard under the stairs, isn't it? Maybe you've one at home?" they asked.

Neil said they had.

"It might get a bit stuffy in there, if you were to shut someone inside?"

Neil thought it might. Only gradually did he understand that this was what Kevin had done to Mrs Newton after hitting her on the head. Where the flower pot came into it, he did not learn.

What Kevin had done was dreadful. But he hadn't meant to be so rough, of course, it was just that he was scared. Neil knew all about that.

At last Neil summoned up the sense to ask for a solicitor. After that he would not say another word.

* * *

Roseanne needed no convincing that the police had arrested the wrong brother.

"But Neil must have seen that stuff upstairs. Wouldn't he have wondered what it was?" she asked her mother.

"Kevin would have had an answer for him. Said he was taking care of it for a friend. Something like that," said Mavis. "Neil's very trusting."

"But he'll say Kevin took the van," said Roseanne. "That must be what happened."

"If he did, and they believed him, the police would have been round here for Kevin by this time," said Mavis.

"You mean he won't say?"

"He'll wait for Kevin to own up," said Mavis.

"And he's not going to do it. He's going to let Neil take the rap for him," said Roseanne. "Oh, Mum! What are you going to do?"

"I'm going to go down to the police station where they took him," said Mavis. Neil was in Crimpford. Wintlebury had no lockup cell.

"I'll come with you," said Roseanne. "Maybe Sandra would have Jason." Sandra was a neighbour who had three small children.

"I wouldn't trust him with her," said Mavis. "No, you're on this morning. You must go to work as usual." She did not want to alarm Roseanne by mentioning aloud that both their jobs might now be on the line. "Jason will be company for me on the bus. It's a good thing he's too young to notice where he is. Let's hope it's the first and last time he enters one of them places."

"He might find a lost purse and hand it in one day," said Roseanne, and was rewarded by hearing her mother chuckle.

"You're a good girl, Roseanne," said Mavis. "You deserve better than to have two brothers like this."

"Neil isn't bad," said Roseanne. "We both know that. And it'll be a relief to Len, too, won't it? Neil'll keep his job and Len won't have been let down."

"Len won't like him letting Kevin take the van," said Mavis.

"Kevin may not have asked. He may have just taken it," said Roseanne.

"I hadn't thought of that," said Mavis.

"Do you think the police will believe you? About Kevin, I mean?"

"I don't see why not," said Mavis. "Why would I make it up? They're both my sons." She was quiet, then went on. "Of course, I might leave it for a while. See if Neil can get out of it on his own. Then, if Kevin gets away—"

"You can't do that, Mum. Kevin might do it again. Kill someone else," said Roseanne. "He's dangerous. Neil isn't."

"I don't suppose he meant to hurt those women," Mavis said.

But Roseanne remembered playground tussles where Kevin's sheer size had been all that was needed to give him dominance. He had been a swaggering bully, though she hadn't seen it like that at the time. She was so much younger that they had barely overlapped at school, but no one ever gave her any serious trouble because they knew that if they did, Kevin would be after them. Roseanne wondered about Jason, still so small and helpless; how would he turn out? Would he be diffident, like Neil, or able to stand up for himself, which he must learn to do? How could any mother be sure of anything?

"We can't let Neil take the blame for Kevin," she said.

25

During the night Mrs Newton's condition had deteriorated and for a time she had seemed to be hallucinating. A nurse heard her say, "I won't let you do this. No, no," and a curious dry sobbing had shaken her thin body. Then she called the name "Jimmy" several times in a loud, clear voice. After that she had lapsed into unconsciousness again.

When Geoffrey and Jennifer arrived on Monday morning she was still apparently sleeping. A nurse asked Geoffrey if he was called Jimmy, saying that Mrs Newton had been asking for him by that name.

Geoffrey looked startled.

"No," he said. "My name's Geoffrey."

"Ah. Her husband, perhaps," said the staff nurse.

"No," said Geoffrey. "My father's name was Frederick."

"Never mind," said the nurse. "She was probably dreaming." She paused. "There was something else," she said. "The nurse who heard her made a note of it. Something about Mary catching her if she didn't move. Some childish game, perhaps, in her dream."

"Probably," said Geoffrey.

They sat down, one on either side of the bed, Jennifer very quiet and thoughtful, Geoffrey anxious. He thought that if they were not brother and sister they would not have any interest in common, would never seek each other out. But they seldom did that anyway, he remembered, sadly. Kinship, however, imposed obligations.

"Lynn's found someone else," he said suddenly.

"Oh Geoffrey!" At this, Jennifer was jolted out of her withdrawn stillness and she looked really sorry. "How awful for you," she said.

"It isn't really," he said. "It's not like you and Daniel. I'm not besotted with her. I doubt if I ever was, but I was chuffed at getting her. She was pretty. Quite a catch, I thought."

"But you loved her," said Jennifer.

"I thought I did. What is love? It's nature pulling a con trick to propagate the species, that's what it is. We dress it up with romantic labels but it all boils down to lust in the end. And after a time even that ceases to appeal."

"Not always," said Jennifer.

"Often," Geoffrey answered.

What would he say if she told him what she had discovered from the papers hidden in their mother's desk? What would he say if he knew that their mother was a widow when she married their father, Frederick Newton? And that she had killed her first husband because he had had an affair with another woman? How would he feel about that? Would he be as shocked and as stunned as she had been?

It had happened during the war when her mother had married James Talbot, a captain in the army at the time of his death. He had been rescued at Dunkirk and had later been sent to the Western Desert with the Eighth Army. After being wounded during the Battle of Alamein he had come home and had been posted to Scotland. Meanwhile Eleanor, a clerk in the ATS, was stationed in Yorkshire and they rarely met. She had been recommended for a commission, which delighted her as she was very conscious, one of the newspaper articles implied, of her other-rank status. Wanting to surprise James with her news, she had obtained a weekend pass and, without warning him, had travelled up to Scotland.

At the mess, where she had been before and was known, she learned that James was away on an overnight pass. He had left a telephone number—this was mandatory in case of curtailment of leave—and Eleanor rang the number from a call box in the village. A woman answered, and some instinct made Eleanor, instead of asking for James, enquire who was speaking. The woman, Mary Campbell, gave her name and with icy calm Eleanor apologised for making a mistake over the number.

There were several Campbells in the telephone directory. Eleanor found the address, five miles distant.

She went back to the mess and bluffed her way into the block where James lived: as she was in uniform and known to some of the company, it wasn't too difficult. From a drawer in James' room she extracted a pistol he had brought back with him from Africa as a souvenir. He had shown it to her, proudly; he had taken it from an Italian major. It was a Beretta, a neat little weapon which held seven rounds and he had even offered to give it to her, for self-defence, but she had said she did not like guns and had questioned his wisdom in keeping such a souvenir. He had laughed and said people had brought all sorts of trophies back with them and it might come in handy one day. He kept it loaded, ready for use.

James had always been reckless. This had attracted her when they met but now it was to prove his undoing.

She hitch-hiked some of the way to the address she had traced and walked the last mile. It was September, the days still long so far north. Eleanor walked unobserved up the short drive to the grey granite house with its slate roof, built to withstand the gales. She peered in through the front windows and saw two children playing with a clockwork train on a complex layout of track, then moved round the side of the building to look in through the kitchen window. She saw James with his arms round a redheaded woman whose face was invisible because it was pressed into his chest.

Eleanor had knocked on the back door, a hard, firm knock, the newspaper report declared. The woman had opened it and Eleanor had pushed her aside, walked straight past her and shot James four times in the chest, then had turned the gun on the woman. At that moment the door had opened and a small boy appeared. His mother had walked over to him, turned him round and pushed him outside, following him, closing the door behind her.

After a few moments Eleanor had left the house the way she had come, on foot. She had not got very far before the police caught up with her, and the pistol was still in her hand.

She had gone, it seemed, into a state of catatonic shock after that. A clever lawyer had managed to win a verdict of manslaughter and so saved her from hanging, for the death sentence for murder was still in force then. In France it would have been treated with sympathy as a *crime passionel*, but, thought Jennifer, however you dressed it up, it was still murder. Had she intended to kill the woman too?

She'd planned nothing, of course; it was all done in the heat of the moment, and if there had been no gun to hand, she would have used a knife or some other weapon. Blind fury had driven her to what was probably the last passionate act of her life. She had been sentenced to eight years in prison and released after almost six.

One of the papers Jennifer read was a report, dated two years after her own birth, from a private detective who had unearthed the details of this story and discovered that Eleanor, after leaving prison, had reverted to her maiden name. He had obtained the many newspaper reports and articles about the case. Eleanor had arrived in Bournemouth six months after her release and had soon found work as a secretary.

How had her father stumbled on all this? Her mother had concealed her past from him; that was evident when she married in her maiden name. Had she, by some slip, revealed that she was a widow, or had she been traced by a journalist interested in the old scandal? Had James Talbot's mistress, Mary Campbell, sought her out? She might have felt the need for revenge, perhaps saw the chance of blackmail. What had become of her and her family? Her husband must have learned what had happened for it had been a *cause célèbre*. Whatever the reason, Frederick had stayed with the marriage, supported his wife and had loved her in a quiet way. Even as a child, Jennifer had known that there was love between her parents; now, at this distance, she understood that it had been a gentle emotion, at least on her mother's side, but Frederick had never let her know that he had discovered her secret. Jennifer was convinced of that, for otherwise the papers would have been destroyed after his death. Her mother had kept nothing from her past; she would not have retained these documents if she had known of their existence.

Perhaps he had loved her enough to keep her secret.

Now, as Jennifer thought about it again, her mother's eyes opened and she looked at them both.

"Well, Jennifer. Well, Geoffrey," she said, and though her voice was weak, it was distinct. "I'm feeling better today. I'm too tough to be the victim of a hooligan. Or of anyone else," she added.

She was going to recover. She had decided that, watching them plotting together, planning how they would spend their inheritance. Things should not be made easy for them. They must sort out their own problems, not by courtesy of her estate.

26

The bus to Crimpford was half-full. Mavis sat with Jason on her knee, the pushchair folded up and stowed under the stairs. Jason had begun to take notice of what went on around him and he looked about him for a while, amiably enough. When he began to grizzle Mavis pulled a bottle out of the bag she carried and poked the teat between his lips. Made up just before they left home, it was still warm and he sucked for a while, lethargically, then dropped off to sleep again, breathing through his mouth because of his cold. At the moment Mavis was more worried about her own sons than the baby. Now that she thought about it, Kevin's generosity to all of them had begun while Neil was inside; he'd had that room to himself then; there was no one to ask questions if he brought stuff home. Had he been stealing all that time? When Neil came back he would not have been more than superficially curious about Kevin's ways, and would have accepted any tale that Kevin told; so would she and Roseanne; all of them thought that Kevin could do no wrong.

Jason woke up when they got off the bus. By the time she had settled him in the pushchair, strapped in and ready to go, Mavis felt exhausted and she had not decided what to say at the police station. If Neil could be released and Kevin could escape, that would be ideal. She pushed Jason down the street, carving a path between the shoppers ambling past Marks and Spencer's and Boots. Her movements were automatic and she gave no thought to the infant; her mind was on her own two sons whom years before she had pushed about in much the same way, only now there were even more pedestrians, more cars spewing fumes on a level with children's faces.

At the police station she asked to speak to an officer about her son, Neil Smith, and was told to wait. Time passed, and Jason began to grizzle. Mavis pulled out the bottle, now cold, and offered it to him but he turned his head away and set up a loud, unhappy wail. This was too much for the desk sergeant and a woman police officer soon appeared.

"Good morning, Mrs Smith," she said, quite kindly. "Your Neil's got his solicitor with him. You can't see him now."

"I want to help him," Mavis said, forced to raise her voice in order to be heard above Jason's cries.

"I'm afraid you can't," said the police officer.

"You're wrong," said Mavis firmly, her mind made up. "I can."

While Mavis was in Crimpford doing her best to convince the police of Neil's innocence, Kevin was in Portsmouth where, after practising, he had forged Mrs Newton's signature on one of her cheques successfully enough to cash it at a bank in a suburb of the city. The clerk asked for the cheque book, and, anxiously, he handed it over but managed to look nonchalant as she made some small sign at the back of it. He left with the money, a hundred pounds. Then he drove through the town to find another branch of the same bank. This would be a doddle; all he had to do was go from branch to branch and he would net enough to last him for quite a while.

The clerk at the second branch also wanted the cheque book, and Kevin gave it to her calmly. The clerk then asked him to wait and, holding both bank card and cheque book, turned away from the counter.

Kevin had never used a cheque book. In most of his jobs he was paid in cash, and in others, where this was not the practice of his employers, he had used a banker's card to make payments or to withdraw cash from a dispensing machine. He had not understood the significance of the mark in the cheque book: that the second clerk was wondering why E. Newton had already cashed a cheque that day: but he did not wait to find out. One way or another, he was rumbled and he walked quickly from the bank, breaking into a run as he reached the door and thereby alerting both staff and customers to the fact that something was wrong.

Because Mrs Newton's cheque book and her bank card were both missing, the bank had already been notified; Geoffrey had thought of that at once. Kevin had not even reached his car before the bank clerk he had approached and the assistant manager had run into the road to see where he had gone. The clerk saw him and gesticulated, and the assistant manager set off in pursuit—recklessly, he was later told, since the man might have been armed and dangerous but as he said, he felt he had to have a go.

Kevin raced the last few yards to the Moffats' car and jumped in, slamming it into gear, driving off from the place by the double yellow line where he had left it.

"If that had been you or me, we'd have been nabbed for parking there," said the assistant manager to the clerk, as he wrote down the car's number. "They'll get him now," he added, with satisfaction.

They did, though the Moffats' car was not returned to its owners for quite some time.

Kevin roared off down the road, tyres squealing. It was just like someone in a cop film, thought the startled people in the area. Then some of them noticed the assistant bank manager in pursuit and the clerk waving frantically, and realised that this was real. One elderly man in a grey Peugeot followed Kevin, but did not dare to exceed the speed limit in the chase lest, the courts being what they were, he might lose his licence. He mentioned this, later in the day, to a reporter who was interviewing eyewitnesses. It was a nice point: would you be hammered for speeding while pursuing a wrongdoer?

Three police cars eventually converged on Kevin, who leaped out of the Moffats' car and took to his heels, but two fit young police officers ran after him, and one of them caught him, twisting his arm up behind his back, securing him.

He was not armed. Once that was established, the arresting police officers eased off. They did not yet know who they had captured: to them, he was simply a man who had tried some scam at the bank.

Kevin knew they would not take long to realise whose card and cheque book he was using. He did not hesitate at all before saying that he had found them in the room he shared with his brother Neil. Oh yes, well, Neil may have come by them in some illegal way; Kevin knew that, of course, but he wasn't worrying about it. He'd been caught for a minor crime: so what, was his attitude.

The police had plenty to charge Kevin with, for the car, they soon discovered, had been stolen like the card and cheque book. They put him in a cell while they collected up their information.

Kevin knew he might face a three-year sentence, which with remission would reduce to about half that time. But he wouldn't be sent to a young offenders' detention centre like the one where Neil had done his time; he would be in an adult prison and the less time he spent there the better. Neil could take the rap for the big one; if the old biddy died, he'd be famous: lifers acquired a certain prestige inside.

Kevin sat in his cell, waiting to be questioned, determined to protect himself.

Their mum would have something to say about it, though, and who would keep an eye on her and Roseanne?

* * *

Meanwhile, Mavis and Jason were now in an interview room at Crimpford police station. She had been given a cup of tea and a digestive biscuit, and Jason had been removed from his pushchair, his half-empty bottle had been warmed, and a policewoman was successfully placating him. He found her tunic buttons alluring and was uttering little cries of pleasure, trying to grip them with his small scrawny hands.

A detective inspector, no less, had come to talk to Mavis after she had had her say at the desk. She had become noisy in her persistence and had been removed from the public gaze to continue her remarks more privately. With the detective inspector was the man who had searched the house and found Mrs Newton's possessions. Mavis hadn't liked him then, and she liked him no better now, though he had been perfectly civil when he conducted the search. Too cocky by half, he was, she thought. Still, he was investigating a very serious crime.

Mavis did not look at him but addressed her remarks to the inspector, who had a thin, strong face and sparse dark hair. She told him that they had arrested the wrong brother.

"Kevin was out when you came to the house. He shared the bedroom with Neil. When he came home late last night, he went into the bathroom and took up the floor to look for whatever had been hidden there," she said, and added, "You did find something there, didn't you?"

"And if we did?" asked Detective Inspector Wilson. The contents of Mrs Newton's jewel case now reposed in the safe.

"Well, whoever hid it would know where to look for it," said Mavis. "Why would Kevin go there, else?"

"Perhaps they were in it together," suggested Wilson. Why would this woman want to drop one son into it in order to save the other, if she were not telling the truth?

"They don't do things together," said Mavis. "Well, not often. Kevin treats us all, sometimes, as a family, but the boys don't go about together. But they did—" she stopped, remembering.

"They did what?"

"They did a job together for Mrs Newton," she said slowly. "I'd forgotten. They mended her fence when it blew down in a gale a few weeks back. Neil was going to do it and Kevin offered to help."

"So Kevin would have seen the house," said Wilson. "Neil had been working next door for some time, hadn't he? He'd got to know Mrs Newton."

"He didn't tell me that," said Mavis. She must be careful. She did not know what Neil had said and was terrified that out of panic he might have confessed to everything.

"Kevin could have borrowed Neil's van," she said. "Neil wouldn't have been able to say no to him, though it wasn't his to lend."

"Where's Kevin now?" asked Wilson.

"I don't know. He left home last night," said Mavis.

"Has he got a car?"

"Not now. I think it's in dock," said Mavis. "It was ever such a nice one," she added. "A Mercedes."

Wilson would have the car checked out, see if he really had owned it.

"We'll have a little talk with Kevin," he promised her. "We'll soon find him."

"Can we go, then?" Mavis asked.

But first she had to make a proper statement, read it through and sign it. It took ages. Afterwards, though, she and Jason were taken home in a police car. What a pity he was too young to understand that this could be a treat, not a ride to trouble. Mavis hugged him all the way home, wondering how she was going to endure all the misery ahead, but she knew the answer. She had no choice.

Mavis was sitting by the fire when there came a knock at the door.

She thought it might be Neil, already free, and lumbered to her feet.

On the step stood Len, who gently pushed her back into

the hallway and at the same time wrapped his arms round her. Len was always gentle, a big man with huge hands yet with the touch of a feather.

"Poor duck," was all he said, holding her close and stroking her springy dark hair.

"Your van, Len! I'm so sorry!" Mavis began crying, and Len, who had never seen her weep before though she had certainly had cause, was discomfited.

"There, there," he said. "Never mind the van. I expect I'll get it back soon. But I'd never have believed it of your Neil."

"It wasn't him, Len. It was Kevin, and he let Neil take the blame," said Mavis. She sniffed, then detached herself from Len and fished a tissue from her sleeve. Handkerchiefs were only for show, though she'd used one yesterday.

"Kevin!" Len stared at her. "You'd better tell me," he said, and manoeuvred her into the living-room where he put an arm round her and lowered her to the sofa, sitting there beside her. Jason was asleep in one of the armchairs, cushions holding him in place. "Now then," Len urged her.

Mavis related all she knew and voiced fears about Kevin's past generosity.

"Well, he'd lost his job," said Len. "I'd heard that weeks back, from someone at the works. There was talk that he'd been knocking things off, but it doesn't do to believe all you hear." He'd worried about it, but decided not to mention it to Mavis. He drew her close. He was genuinely fond of her and cursed the luck that had made her marry Joe Smith while he was off doing a few years in the army in order to see the world. When he came back after his short contract, intending to settle down, Mavis and several other girls he had known for most of his life had married and some, like her, already had children. He'd looked about and settled for Maureen, who had been a good wife in many ways. She looked after him well and he would never leave her. He'd got it made, really, he thought, with Maureen at home for every day and Mavis for additional comforts.

"He didn't say he'd lost his job," said Mavis. "He told all those tales about promotion and that and I believed him."

"I expect he liked throwing it about," said Len. "Being the provider. He knew you'd had it hard."

"I should have known it was him," said Mavis. "I shouldn't have let them take Neil away." She buried her face against Len's sturdy shoulder and muttered, "I told the police this morning. I told them it was Kevin."

"Well, you couldn't let Neil go down for what he didn't do," said Len. "That was brave of you, Mavis."

"I'm not sure they believed me—I think the inspector did, a bit, at least, but not that cocky sergeant. Kevin wouldn't have left home if he wasn't guilty."

Len agreed with that, but he thought that Kevin, having successfully pulled the wool over his mother's eyes for years, as it now seemed, might be able to string the police along, too. If they caught him.

"It was all too vicious for Neil," said Len, who had been prepared to find his trust in the young man misplaced but only to the extent of petty theft. His earlier violence had been quite out of character and he understood how that had happened.

"You won't want him back," said Mavis.

Len sighed, then hoped she had not noticed.

"I will, as long as he gets off this one," he said.

"Oh Len, thanks," said Mavis. "You are good."

"Well, we've got to stick together, haven't we?" Len told her, stretching out the arm which he had put round her shoulder to glance surreptitiously at his watch. "I've got to go now, Mavis. I'll try to pop in at The Bell this evening."

"I may not be there," Mavis said. "Not unless Roseanne's home. We've lost our sitter for Jason."

27

Jennifer and Geoffrey were back at Yew Cottage. They had consumed fish fingers, baked potatoes and broccoli for their evening meal.

"What dull food Mama eats," Geoffrey had said, taking the fish fingers and frozen broccoli out of the freezer. "Does she ever have anything fresh?"

"Would you bother, just for yourself?" asked Jennifer. "I wouldn't." She laughed, a curious, dry sound. "At least she had the potatoes. And here we are, with no television and no radio, forced to talk to each other."

"What's wrong with that?" asked Geoffrey. He was wondering if he could decently leave in the morning, go back to the office and Lynn. Would Jennifer be all right on her own? Would she stay here and keep tabs on their mother? Surely with this and her own court case pending, no one would expect her at work?

"It's just that we never do," said Jennifer.

"Well, we don't often meet, do we?" said Geoffrey. "But maybe now you'll come up and stay for a bit." As he said the words, Geoffrey hoped that she would refuse. Lynn would not take kindly to a visit from his criminal sister, might forbid the girls her company. "I don't know why you had it in for that girl, Stephanie," he added.

"She stole Daniel from me," said Jennifer.

"She didn't. He went," said Geoffrey.

"He went because Stephanie came along," said Jennifer. "Mother wondered why I hated her and not Daniel," she added. She said this carefully, heavy with her secret knowledge. What would Geoffrey say if she revealed it? But she wouldn't, ever.

"If it was me, I'd walk away from them both," said Geoffrey. "Be narked, if you like. Sad, even. Angry—humiliated—whatever. But I'd rescue what I could of my pride. After all, it is happening to me, in a sense, now Lynn's got this fellow."

"And you don't mind?"

"Not really. She's happier. We go our own ways."

"What if she goes altogether? Will she?"

"She certainly will if we don't get that house she's set her heart on," he said. "I'd mind not seeing the girls, if that happened. In other ways, it might be a relief. I wouldn't have to get along with the friends she chooses for us."

"What about your own friends?"

"I'm like you. I haven't any," he said.

She stared at him, absorbing what he said, realising that the friends she and Daniel saw were his, not hers.

"What's wrong with us?" she said. "Why don't people like us?"

"Is it us? Maybe it's in our genes. After all, Mama doesn't like people much. Not even herself."

"She liked us. And father," said Jennifer.

"In a quiet way. Not to get all steamed up about," said Geoffrey. "Never possessive."

"It was so that she didn't get hurt again," said Jennifer, thinking of James Talbot.

"What do you mean?"

"Oh, nothing. Some old romance she had which went wrong. She said something about it once," said Jennifer.

"I suppose there must have been someone before father,"
he said lightly. "After all, she was nearly thirty when they
got married, wasn't she? And there'd been the war. All that.
Maybe someone she was keen on got killed."

"Maybe."

They were washing up their few things when the doorbell
rang. Detective Inspector Wilson and Detective Sergeant Bennett stood on the step. Wilson held a key in his hand.

"We've already tried it," he said. "It works. Had you
missed a front door key?" He'd turned it in the lock, then
rung the bell, not wanting to alarm the brother and sister by
marching in unannounced.

"Yes," said Jennifer. "The one that was kept outside."

"This key was found in Kevin Smith's pocket when he
was arrested in Portsmouth this morning after trying to use
some of Mrs Newton's cheques and her bank card," said
Wilson. "It seems he was the culprit, not the brother who
worked next door. Neil's only fault was to tell Kevin about
the key which he saw someone remove on Thursday. That
would have been you, Miss Newton, when you came down
from London."

"So you'd got the wrong man?"

"Only for a very short time," Wilson said.

"A day and a night, at least," said Jennifer. "Is he free
now?"

"Reunited with his family," said Bennett. "Quite touching, really. They were pleased to see him."

"I should think so," said Geoffrey.

"The brother had been thieving for some time," said Wilson. "And we think he was involved with a recent raid on a
building society in Crimpford. A car he owned was found
burnt out on some waste ground between Wintlebury and
Crimpford—a Mercedes, an old one. A similar car was used
as a getaway car at the time of the raid, when a woman was
hurt by one of the robbers."

"How do you know the burnt-out car was his?" asked
Geoffrey, who was really interested.

"The engine number was intact, and part of a registration plate," said Wilson. "We might get him to confess to that," he added, and smiled.

Jennifer shivered. She had not liked that smile.

"Sounds a nasty piece of work," said Geoffrey.

"Yes. He'll get put away for a good long time so he won't be troubling anyone else for a while," said Bennett.

Would they say that about her, if she was sentenced to prison on Thursday? Jennifer sat down, suddenly afraid.

"I gather your mother is holding on," said Wilson. "It seems as if she'll pull round. Lucky for Kevin Smith, or he'd be facing a murder charge, though he might get off with manslaughter."

Manslaughter. Murder. The words echoed in Jennifer's head. These were words which had been used about her mother more than forty years ago. They could be used about her, if she carried out what she meant to do to Stephanie. And she could go to prison, like her mother.

She pulled a blind down on that thought, not yet ready to face it.

Mavis had made a good meal for Neil when he came home. There was pork from the day before, warmed up, with chips and peas, followed by cake and ice cream.

"Have you missed me, Jason?" Neil asked the baby, who smiled toothlessly at him as he picked him up and hugged him, hiding his own tear-filled eyes against the slightly damp-smelling little body.

"He has," said Mavis. Who could tell? It might be true.

"Great of Kevin to let me off the hook, wasn't it?" said Neil, who was trying not to be too happy because now he would have the bedroom to himself. "I knew he would. I didn't tell them a thing, not even about him borrowing the van. I knew he'd not let me go down for him."

So he didn't know the truth: that Kevin had been caught because he had used Mrs Newton's cheques and was driving the Moffats' car. Mavis's own trip to the police station had not been needed after all and she would have to live with the knowledge that she had given away her own son. But though Kevin might have admitted taking the car, he could have said that Neil had done the robbery and had sold him the cheque book and bank card. Who would have believed otherwise? She decided wearily that Neil need not find out yet that Kevin hadn't given himself up. By the time he had to know he would be better able to face such knowledge.

"Can you mind Jason tonight, Neil?" she asked. "I'm due at The Bell in half an hour and Roseanne's out with Mike." Mike hadn't yet heard about their misfortunes and Roseanne was going to tell him this evening. Whether he chucked her or not remained to be seen, but she might as well find out one way or the other right away.

"Of course I'll mind him," said Neil. He had a plan for Jason which meant dipping into his car fund. He was going to buy the kid a new pushchair, one with handles that could face either way, so that they could talk when they went out together. Then later, when he was big enough to walk but was slow or got tired, he could face forwards if he wanted to. He wouldn't tell them, though; he'd simply do it and say the old pushchair wasn't safe; it was almost true; it had been bought third or fourth hand at a jumble sale and its joints were weak. "Do you think I should go back to work tomorrow?" he asked his mother.

"Len might be at The Bell tonight," said Mavis. "If he is, I'll ask him."

In the morning Geoffrey announced that he was going home. He would call in at the hospital on the way and he would come back at once if his mother's condition deteriorated.

"I'm going to face up to Lynn," he said. "I decided during the night not to put up with being manipulated any longer." It was now or never: he'd seen that. She must make up her mind whether to stay with him and put up with what he could provide, or to move on.

"It won't work out like that," Jennifer said. "Mother will die and you'll buy the big house."

"I think she's going to recover," said Geoffrey. "There won't be an easy way out for any one of us—not even her. Do you think she likes life? I don't. But she'll struggle on, maybe move again. Now, what about you? I'll come down on Thursday for your hearing. I'll come here on Wednesday night and take you up, in fact," he said. He'd get hold of the solicitor and tell him to keep Daniel away from the court. It would be a good idea if Jennifer never saw him again. Something must be done about the house and the mortgage; a quick loss-cutting sale might be best.

Jennifer was looking amazed.

"Will you really?" she said, and a little colour came into her face. "What about the office?"

"They'll have to get on without me," said Geoffrey. "In fact, I might give in my notice and go and raise sheep in the Orkneys."

Jennifer giggled.

"I'll come too, and weave up the wool," she said, and he laughed.

"We might do worse," he said, more seriously, and dared to ask, "You'll give up your vendetta, won't you? Look at the price you'd have to pay if you did something else and got sent to prison."

"I might be improved," said Jennifer. "It might do me good."

"What an extraordinary thing to say," said Geoffrey.

Jennifer thought of Stephanie's father, the one person who had really tried to console her, as she saw it. What would he do if she turned up again? The knife was still in her bag.

Then there was Mary Campbell. What had happened to her? You'd have thought she'd have wanted revenge but perhaps her mother's prison sentence satisfied that desire. There had been children, too. It might be amusing to trace them, find out where they lived, even meet Mary. If that love affair so long ago had not taken place she and Geoffrey would not have been born, or they would have had a different father, the mysterious James.

Jennifer thought she would like to discover more about him. She might do so when all this was over. She would ask her mother about her grandparents, too: find out what they were like and where they had lived, coax her mother to talk. After all this time she must feel her secret was safe, would suspect nothing more than natural curiosity, which was all that it was.

She remembered the psychiatrist's appointment for the following day and decided that she must keep it if it would help her in court. She could go up to London on the train and return as soon as the session was over.

Geoffrey left the house first, going off to the hospital before heading north, leaving her to follow. Before she did so, Jennifer went to the desk and removed the papers which had told her about the past. She carried them all down the garden to the incinerator, where she burned them. Now her mother could never learn that Frederick Newton had known what she had done.